CRACKER

TO BE A SOMEBODY

CRACKER

TO BE A SOMEBODY

Gareth Roberts

Virgin

First published in Great Britain in 1995 by
Virgin Publishing Ltd
332 Ladbroke Grove
London W10 5AH

ISBN 0 86369 950 2

Typeset by Galleon Typesetting, Ipswich
Printed and bound in Great Britain by
Cox & Wyman Ltd, Reading, Berks

Thanks to Jim Mortimore and all at Virgin for advice and support – and a special thank you to John and Gary, Neil and David, and Gareth and Terry for kindly letting me use their houses at various stages in '94.

ONE

A hole in the ground.

Albie stood apart from the others, face turned away from the coffin as it was lowered. He was still, upright inside his one, well-pressed suit, forcing down his emotions. A chill wind from the white sky, Manchester in March, disturbed strands of dark hair that flapped over his shirt collar. His father in that box, gone at last, and Albie wouldn't show what he felt. Wouldn't share his reaction. It couldn't be shared.

Just stared at nothing, and remembered. Six years back.

Faces. Packed faces, human faces, squeezed against each other. To either side, above and below. An ocean of heads. Elbows jostling. Confusion turning to horror. Breathless, airless. The screams, hollow and drawn-out. Faces pressed against a high wire fence. Criss-crossed, cheeks and mouths turning blue. Bizzies, on horseback, looking on. Watching. Sat there. Not lifting a finger.

The killing ground. Right there, right in front of him and Dad, the proof. You were herded, prodded, worked to death. They needed you to die for them. Packed you in, once a week, penned you in like sheep for your weekly afternoon's entertainment. It was all that was left. Nowhere else to congregate, to unionise.

And if they packed you too tightly, it was your problem.

Spring smells came across the graveyard, the scents of new life. The afternoon sun slipped weakly through the line of trees facing Albie, and the woman who'd been his wife.

1

Jill. Her hand was clasped by his daughter, little Ruth, small enough not to understand.

And seven near strangers. Wartime companions. Dad's fellow fighters, friends from the Legion. Slackening the ropes, their old faces crumpled. They'd given everything, thought Albie, everything for freedom, for the future.

This future. The freedom to queue up outside the post office on a Thursday morning. Freedom to get robbed. Freedom to be ignored, to be swept from the liberal agenda.

The coffin settled. Albie felt Jill's hand on his arm, a gentle touch.

He turned and walked up to the grave. He was holding a couple of things. Important things of Dad's. Symbols. He tossed them in.

It was more than a gesture. This was the only sincere, truthful moment of the whole bleeding ceremony.

A scarf, and a hat. Liverpool Football Club.

This was more than grief. Christ, thought Albie, him and Dad had been grieving for six years. Grieving for ninety-six people, most of whom they hadn't even known. Grief was bad. That was worse. Like a layer of skin was being peeled off. It was more than anger.

The bastards had tried to destroy their city. An entire community.

For Albie, there was nobody who could share this. Not now.

A few minutes passed. Albie continued to stare down at the coffin. Jill, with an awkward nod to him, led Ruth away. The others fell into step along the crunching gravel drive and out of the graveyard, where two black cars waited.

Albie closed his eyes. Ten people. Just ten people. And seven of them for show's sake.

A wrecked country. A ruined system. Propped up by connections of grime. Evil government, useless opposition.

Even the workers themselves compromised, mouthing the tabloid lies.

He muttered his thoughts at the open grave.

He turned and walked to the cars. There was a row of bright white headstones lined against one wall of the cemetery. First World War graves. The war before Dad's. Soldier boys packed together below. Coffins packed tight, boxes jostling for space.

Jill stepped forward. He needed her. Now Dad was gone, could things be different? Could things turn back? Please? But she was about to say goodbye.

'Will you be all right?'

Ruth, hand in her mother's, stared up at him.

'Are you going?' He was surprised. Not so soon, as if she couldn't wait to get away from him.

'Yeah.'

No. Not yet. She had to stay, he couldn't be alone. Not yet. There were things he couldn't do. Couldn't face. 'I was going to ask you to clean out his wardrobe.' Her jaw tightened. 'I can't do it.'

Come back to the house, Jill. Come back to the house with me. You were my wife, for Christ's sake. Come back. I can't be alone, I mustn't be alone.

'OK,' she said, reluctant.

Albie opened the front door. Thirty-seven Oundle Street, terraced, unremarkable. Dark inside all year round, even in summer, when Jill used to knot the curtains up. The sun had never got in here.

She hadn't been back in six years. Albie watched her face as she walked into the front room. Sensed her reaction. All the light and life she'd brought to this house had left with her. A house-sized piece of time had gone back, erased her, and then flowed forward again, accelerating. Decaying. The room reeked of disappointment, lifetimes of making do.

3

Albie's school cups on the mantelpiece (the English prize 1975, the Music prize 1975), scarred mismatched armchairs, the Bakelite clock cracked in three places.

Jill took the old man's clothes from the wardrobe in his room and carried them downstairs. One journey. Albie followed her, carrying the mattress from his father's bed. The bed Dad had died in. It stank of piss.

He watched Jill as she opened up a suitcase and tossed Dad's clothes inside. Three pairs of trousers, all five shirts, a couple of hats. Albie took the last couple of teabags from the packet he kept in a cupboard above the sink. He sipped at his tea, Jill ignored hers. Ruth sat in a chair and stared out into the empty street. Nobody about. Tuesday afternoon, but there was never anybody about. Never any neighbourly chat.

Albie walked to the end of the road with the mattress and laid it gently in a skip. He poured on some fuel. Thought of Dad dying on that mattress, Dad wincing every time he moved. Taking so long to go. Six years.

He threw on a long match and the mattress started to burn steadily. Smoke curled up.

He couldn't talk. Couldn't say, had never said. Even at the very end. Had just sat there, looking down at Dad. Dad, who'd never cheeked his boss, never questioned an order, never taken home more than a hundred quid a week. Couldn't say how he'd felt. Couldn't prove it. Just watched him die.

Jill's voice. 'Taxi's here.' It was the first time they'd communicated verbally since they'd got to the house.

Albie carried the suitcase out for her. The taxi driver opened up the boot and took the case from him. Swung it in and closed the boot. He'd done it without thinking.

Albie stared at him.

'What'll you do with it?' he asked Jill.

'Oxfam,' she said simply.

Don't leave me alone. Please don't leave me alone.

4

What'll I do back in there, alone? In the dark house. I can't be alone.

But he couldn't say. Couldn't tell her.

He kissed her, quickly, on the cheek. Moved to kiss her again – oh, come back, things could be different, you must come back – but she was already getting into the taxi.

Ruth stepped forward, eager to make her farewell. He lifted her and kissed her nose, ruffled her hair.

Albie watched the taxi drive away, back to the flats. Nothing had changed.

His wife and kid, leaving him alone. His Dad, leaving him alone.

Alone in the street.

Albie couldn't sleep. Not alone, in the house. Even the coffin had gone. He spent the rest of the afternoon staring at the ceiling. Tried to watch some telly, but the news depressed him.

He got up to feed the cat. As he opened the tin she pushed her fur-covered skull hard against his leg. She wasn't human. She didn't know much. She wasn't enough of a bastard to hate. Stroking her used to calm Dad down, even when he was in bad pain. Sometimes she'd followed Dad over to the allotment, sat and watched him working.

Now her purr was a gravelly rattle, her eyes thin slits of concentration. It was close, Albie knew. Her belly was huge, she was spending less time out of the house. More kittens on the way.

Her tray needed changing. Albie scraped her shit into the bin and shook out the gravel. The tray was lined with pages from one of last week's *Guardian*s. The only newspaper Albie could stomach to read. Just about gave you the bare facts. Just about fuelled your anger. Got him to sleep of a morning. For however long until Dad called out, needing him.

In a drawer in the front room was a small square of paper. A ticket for the game next Monday night. Albie had bought the thing in a daze. It seemed like fate, Liverpool coming to Old Trafford just after Dad dying. It'd be a test, Albie's first time alone on the stands.

Getting on for nine. Time to go.

Albie took the bus around town, the sky blackening as the journey continued, roundabout to roundabout, the route hugging the outskirts of the city. The men he worked with boarded as the journey continued. A couple nodded at him and joined their mates. He knew what they thought. He could read their minds through their eyes. Obvious. Yeah, acknowledge the thick Scouser. They knew nothing.

Small-minded bastards.

Fitz lifted the receiver of the payphone and punched seven plastic buttons in a familiar sequence. The lights above the bar were dimmed, but he could just perceive the tiny liquid crystal display flashing A. Three rings.

The A stopped flashing and he pushed in a fifty pence coin. This might take a while. He took a drag of high tar.

Judith's voice. Her beautiful voice. 'Hello.' Aha. She'd been expecting him to call. He could tell that. The even greeting she reserved for him. Suppressing her disapproval already, and he hadn't even told the lie yet.

'It's me.'

'Where are you?'

Steady, steady, here it comes. 'I'm having a quick drink.'

'No more bets,' a voice boomed behind him.

Fitz moved to cover the mouthpiece instinctively, but the damage had been done. And now, he thought, the inevitable row. He'd been hoping to postpone it, but of course had also been looking forward to it. He wanted to confirm the response he predicted for her, and use some of the phrases he'd been rehearsing mentally. He might be a bastard, but at least he was an entertaining bastard. And there were things that needed working out.

'You're in a casino,' Judith said. It was a statement, that was all. She sounded neither tired nor angry. Odd.

'An accident,' said Fitz. 'I thought it was a theme park.'

No response to that at all. A three-second silence. That was better, he was familiar with that. A veteran of a strategy. Vintage about 1975.

'Not the pregnant pause,' he said, raising his voice a little. 'Please, God, anything but the pregnant pause.'

'How long will you be?' she asked simply.

'Not long.' Another lie, probably.

'I'll see you later then. Enjoy yourself.'

Fitz frowned. This was all wrong. 'And how was Damascus?'

'Fitz, it's OK.' Another pause. 'Honestly.'

'All right,' he said cautiously. 'Bye.'

'Bye.'

He put down the phone. There was something different going on here. He'd kept his gambling away from her recently, played it down. They hadn't mentioned or discussed it for weeks, except in passing. And now this. The soft approach. Unexpected, but how long would it last? How long until the row?

He'd seen a couple of clients today. Impotence in the form of a cardiganed schoolteacher with stooping shoulders, low self-esteem incarnated in a sweaty library manager with a barking, overcompensating voice. Repressed, both of them, and very, very ordinary. No challenge.

And Fitz needed the challenge. Needed it again. He knew where he could get it, how he could achieve it. Forty-five years of pissing about, and for the first time in his life, he knew.

Until he could start again, until the circumstances were right, this would have to do. He pulled his jacket tight about

7

his bulk and strode smartly to a table, took a wad of notes from his inside pocket and tossed them to the croupier.

The croupier spread the money out, counted it, slid it away. A line of Dickenses pushed down the slot.

Fitz sat. He lit another cigarette. The muscles in his arms and legs tensed. Time to start again.

The croupier slid a pile of chips towards him. He checked his watch. Just after nine. Plenty of time, and a long way to go.

Albie clocked in at ten sharp. He pushed his card into the slot. A bell rang from inside the ancient mechanism screwed to the corridor wall. Good British workmanship. Been there since Armitage & Dean's had opened in 1947. Plenty of promises, then, plenty of optimism. Plenty of other factories.

Now it was one of the few remaining. How had it survived? By cutting corners, not concerning itself with safety, accepting orders from anybloodywhere for anybloodything, sacking its entire workforce and then rehiring them on laughably thin contracts. That was how.

The machines roared. Every night, the same. Seven and a half hours at his place, the end of the middle row. Mask down, gloves on, fire the torch. The country had moved on, it was said. Thrown its workforce on the dole, or into shops, or into crappy part-time jobs. Not here. One of the last of its kind, this place was haunted by something. The spirit of the British manufacturing industries.

Albie found his machine, pulled on his gloves, swung down his mask, fired his torch and started to work. Sweat was building up already.

City lights through the window, wobbling in the heat haze. Out there some people were pushing themselves into boxes or blanketing themselves up in doorways. Other people were drinking or gambling away their minds in legalised, state-approved addiction centres. Others poured out sherries, settled down for *Newsnight* or the late film, blanked out after a day's exhaustion.

And somewhere out there, lies were forming. Great pools of lies, bogs of untruth, slurping together in the sick, smudgy heads of hacks. Chains of words selected to deceive, oozing through modems and onto the presses. From there to the newsstands.

Perpetuating the system. Keeping the workers in line. Giving them their soap news, their gossip, their celebrity pics.

And Dad was lying in a hole in the ground.

And Albie, who knew he'd talked so many irrelevant words in his time, had never said.

He worked on. His muscles twisted with effort.

He worked hard.

It was turning out to be a damn good night. Fitz's mouth was dry. This was an up, a good time. But he couldn't relax. Couldn't dare. He had to keep going, keep pushing.

The adrenalin kept his eyes wide. One of his feet tapped at the leg of his stool. His eyes were levelled at the table. His pile of chips, a rapid agglomeration of yellow plastic, on number twelve.

The wheel span, the ball rattled. He didn't look. Kept his eyes on the twelve. Gold on green baize.

'Twelve,' called the croupier.

The rake extended. Swept up more chips. Pushed them towards Fitz.

Christ, this was better than a good night.

He stretched out his pudgy hands. Felt the moulded plastic, cold against his sweat-slickened fingers. Where next?

Nineteen. Yes, Mark's birthday sometime soon, wasn't it? March the somethingth. He arranged the chips.

Fitz kept his face still. Blanked out. Freed his mind to roam. The moment stretched.

The wheel span, the ball rattled and hopped about the grooves. Tap, tap, bounce, tap. His judgement.

He looked over.

Number nineteen.

That equalled a lot of money. Edging a grand.

So, again.

At tea break, Albie sat alone. He'd never really spoken to any of this lot. He knew what they thought of him. His grimy hands gripped the edge of the table. His hair, bunched up under his cap, was sopping with metal dust, dirt and sweat.

A couple of lads at another table were doing a crossword. 'Ferocious dog,' said the first. 'Ten letters, third one's T.'

The supervisor looked up from his *Evening Post*. 'Rottweiler.'

'Yeah. How'd you spell it?'

The supervisor thought. 'R, O, T, W, E, I, double L, E, R.'

Without turning to face them, Albie said evenly, 'R, O, double T. Two Ts, one L.'

'Are you sure?'

He knew what they thought of him. 'Yeah.'

The crossword continued. 'Cheese made backwards. Four letters.'

He knew how they'd react. What they thought. When they saw him. When they heard his voice. The predictable bastards.

Albie stood abruptly, pushed his chair back, and walked calmly around the table. He looked at the crossword grid. ROTWEILLER.

'Two Ts, one L.'

The lad with the pencil sighed. 'It doesn't make any difference, mate.'

Albie stiffened. 'It's wrong. It's two Ts, one L.'

'It doesn't affect anything.'

10

Albie nodded to the supervisor. 'You're taking his word rather than mine, eh? Why?'

'It makes no difference –'

'Because he's been to university, that's why.'

The lad smiled. 'Oh, piss off.'

Albie looked down at him. That smug smile. Ignorant smile.

He walked out, slamming the door of the tea room behind him.

Minutes later, he was back at his torch. Staring at the brilliant sparks, gobbets of molten iron settling on his overalls.

He couldn't get any of it out of his head. It wasn't going away.

Faces, packed tight. White, working-class faces. Dad, the cat on his lap, watching *Shortland Street*, clawing the arm of the sofa until the stitching split. Jill and Ruth in the taxi, driving away. All the bastards all his life who thought they knew about him. Saw his clothes, heard his accent and filed him away, thought they knew it all. Treated him like scum because they expected him to act like scum.

The supervisor came close to him. 'Are you OK?' he shouted.

Albie pushed up his faceplate. He stared at the supervisor. The supervisor took a step back. Yeah, thought Albie, he was frightened.

'I buried my father today.'

'I'm sorry.'

Albie held his gaze a moment and then returned to work.

The bastard couldn't give a toss, he thought. B/TEC managerial course would have trained him up for all of that. I'm sorry. Pity, sympathy.

Behind his faceplate, Albie was shouting.

At 6.30 a.m. Albie changed, clocked out, got back on the bus. Knackered. He went to sit up top.

There were pink streaks in the sky. Beneath, row after row of slate roofing, block after block of graffiti-smeared flats. Packed in tight.

Albie's thin body was cramped and sore. He ran a hand through his hair. He'd thought that after Dad things might be different, might get easier. But now his anger felt like an open wound. His tiredness couldn't suppress it as usual. It squeezed at his stomach, pulled at the throbbing veins standing out on his temples.

He had to change buses at Purvis Road, the junction of two main roads coming out of the city. There was an Asian shop along by there. Probably open this early. Scott's along by his wasn't open until seven. He had a couple of quid on him. Just enough – yeah, *Guardian* was 45p, cheapest teabags £1.53. He knew the exact price of everything, the sort of knowledge that came with making do.

He'd pop in, get the paper and some teabags. Then go back home. Put on a brew, read a bit. Try and calm down. Get some sleep.

The Asian shop was very clean. Small and well laid-out. Even had a deli counter in the corner. The radio was on, Classic FM. Sibelius. Bit heavy for this early in the day, thought Albie.

'The *Guardian*. Packet of those teabags.'

The Asian shopkeeper, fiftyish, moustached, slid a *Guardian* out from the counter display, took the teabags from the shelf behind him. He rang it up on the till and smiled perfunctorily. 'Two pounds four pence, please.'

Albie picked up his goods and dropped his two pound coins into the shopkeeper's hand. He smiled. 'I'll have to owe you the four pee.'

The shopkeeper shook his head. 'Sorry.'

'It's all right, I'll pass it in tonight on me way to work,' Albie said pleasantly.

The shopkeeper shook his head. 'Sorry.'

12

Yeah, thought Albie, heard my accent, seen my clothes. Written me off. The robbing bastard. 'This comes to one pound ninety-eight in Scott's.'

'Then go to Scott's.'

'He's shut.'

The shopkeeper smiled again. Smugly. 'Exactly.'

The robbing bastard. The robbing bastard. The robbing Paki bastard.

Albie slammed the paper and the teabags down on the counter. His stomach lurched. His aching muscles tensed.

The robbing Paki bastard was smiling. He thought he had power. Thought he was powerful behind that counter. Didn't even belong in this country, and thought he could do what he liked.

Albie shouted through gritted teeth, 'I'll be back with your four pee. Right?'

He slammed out of the shop.

The bus back home. Back to the house. Dark inside, as always. Dark and empty.

The cat had heard his key in the lock, shook herself, and risen unsteadily from her basket. Heavy and slow, her whiskers drooping, she waited for him to complete his task for her. She watched as he took the tin from the cupboard, reached for the can opener.

Albie couldn't let things go. Couldn't let it drop. He couldn't stay here today, alone. He couldn't forget, get on with things, go through the motions. Dad was dead. Jill and Ruth had gone. He had been written off. He couldn't force it down.

It was so much stronger than before.

The robbing Paki bastard.

Albie shook. Why not? Why not think that, say it? Put something in a cage, it'll start to behave like an animal. He'd seen the cages, six years ago, seen the proof. Right in front

13

of him. And to get out of your cage, you had to get wild. Wild and strong. The feeling inside, coating his body in a slurry of hatred, was what he needed now. It would help him.

He let it take him.

Thinking had proved useless. He'd been thinking all these years, thinking, reading, marching, arguing, turning things over in his head. Got him nowhere. Because that was one of their weapons, their strengths. Only they, the bizzies, the politicians, the tabloid scum, only they were allowed the luxury of violence. They never thought. They didn't need to, the violence gave them power.

Albie saw things clearly now. If you didn't think, if you turned off that part of your brain, it was easy. He was going to sort things out. Even things up.

Starting now.

If he was going to be scum, he had to look like scum. Had to look the way he felt. Felt like death. Would look like death.

He left the cat hungry and ran upstairs, three steps at a time. Pulled open a cabinet in the bathroom. There, neatly tidied away, his clippers. He took them out, fitted the trimmer. Grade one. He'd bought them for a short-lived beard some years back. Never thrown them out, known they might be useful one day. There were some clothes he needed, too, things he never wore nowadays. Things he had never put together. A uniform.

His camouflage jacket, his stonewashed jeans, his bright white tee shirt. Boots from his old job at the quarry, dragged from under the bed. Doctor Marten's, fourteen holes. He dressed quickly, and went downstairs.

Albie stood in front of the large mirror in the front room. He saw his face, skin tight over thin lips. His eyes, dark brown, stared at themselves. Burning with anger.

He flicked the shaver on, and raised it. He destroyed his

14

fringe first, then dragged the whirring blades back over his scalp in wide lines. The hum vibrated his skull.

It took him three and a half minutes to reinvent himself.

Fitz swung one wobbling leg out of the taxi, steadied himself, then pulled out the other. Good. So far. Very drunk, very tired, but he could stand up, he was sure. Yes, he could.

Question. Had he enough to pay the fare?

Answer. Oh, yes. Oh yes! Good.

He checked the meter, clicked his tongue suspiciously, and passed a crisp tenner to the driver. 'Did you have that on fast forward?'

He took his change, swung himself the right way about, yes, facing the front door, and readied his key. Stepped forward.

A Fiat Panda very obviously driven by a young person screeched up behind him. The door opened before the vehicle stopped and Mark emerged, yawning, waving a lazy goodbye to his friends. 'And don't call me before two, right?'

The friends waved back and sped off. Fitz waited for his son to notice him. Mark looked at him and frowned. 'And where've you been?'

Fitz grunted, 'Out,' and opened the front door.

'What?'

'Out.'

'What?'

'I wennout and met soanso and stayed at blahdy-blahdy-blah.'

'Eh?'

'Now you know how it feels. OK?'

Judith was awake, auburn hair pressed against the head-board, reading. Fitz entered their room with a glass of

15

whisky in his hand, collected from the kitchen after a lengthy and painful session on the toilet. It's time for the row, he thought. Let's get this done and over, I need to sleep.

'Sorry.' His start.

'It's OK.' Still cool. How long, thought Fitz, how long now? The pillow next to her was exacting a magnetic influence on his head. He wanted to sleep, not shout.

She indicated the glass. 'Whisky?'

He nodded. There were little lines of concern around her eyes, he noticed.

'Are you starting early or finishing late?' she asked.

'I'm trying to avoid a hangover.' He took a sip and looked out of the window.

Judith nodded patiently. 'That's one way, I suppose. Death's another, of course.'

A frosty note struck there, thought Fitz, but still far too controlled. He'd have to intervene, get things rolling.

'This isn't going according to script. You're supposed to bollock me, Judith. And then, when you're halfway through a particularly insulting sentence, I do this . . .'

He brought out a bundle of twenty-pound notes and tossed it on to the bed. Another bundle followed, then another, then another. He slipped off the elastic band on the fifth wad and showered her with it.

She put her book aside and smiled wearily. Her expression confirmed to Fitz that she accorded his winnings about as much value as a box full of Monopoly money. She collected the notes, smoothed them out with her long, feminine fingers, and dropped them in a bedside drawer. Like she was tidying Katie's toys away.

'Thank you,' she said.

'You're welcome.' He finished his whisky in two quick gulps. On top of so many others it tasted like water anyway.

He was doing it to her. Again. She had come back to him,

16

and he was going through the whole routine again. But she knew what to expect. None of this was a surprise, oh no. So. She thought she had some new strategy. Why was she still so damned calm about it? What was her plan?

She threw back the covers on his side of the bed. An invitation. He glimpsed the outline of her silk pyjama-clad thighs. Erotically enticing, oh yes, but not now.

'Please,' she said.

So, this was it. The new tactic. Take things slowly. Treat the addict gently, lull him through love. A sexual apology. A reminder of their unique, long-standing link. She intended to screw him away from gambling.

'I can't,' he told her. He was telling the truth. No lead in the pencil.

Judith's eyebrows creased with hurt. She got out of the bed and left the room. It was, after all, time for the rest of the world to be getting up.

Fitz fell squarely on to the bed, pushing the springs to the limits of their endurance.

Focussed on the pillow, the curtain. Curtain, pillow. Problem, solution. A whisky-lathered chicane in his head. He could see the problem. And the solution. He had to get back there, somehow. Country roads, take him home, to the place where he belonged. Anson Road. Bilborough, Beck. Panhandle. Oh, Panhandle. God. He owed her an explanation.

There'd be time to think things out in more detail tomorrow. Whenever that was. Enough for today.

Albie was back on the bus. Heading back to settle up. He checked his jacket. The nozzle of a spray can poked from an inside pocket. He shifted about on the seat, sorting himself out. He'd got everything.

He knew what he was going to say. His lips formed the words silently. The bus hit a bump in the road and he jerked up and down. This was how it'd go. Listen, you robbing

Paki bastard. Here's your four pee, right? You treated me like scum, I'm acting like scum.

That was it. Get on with things. Don't think. Just get on with it.

A lad across the aisle was looking at him.

Albie forced the anger in. Yeah, good idea, that. Save it, let it build up. In just a few minutes, he was going to get started. Getting even. Yes, yes.

The bus reached the interchange. Albie rang the bell, thanked the driver, and got off.

Walked from the stop, along the road. There. Right. The Asian shop. The Paki shop. The robbing Paki bastard shop. He was back, as promised. Time to start. Time for the scum to rise.

Pushed open the door. Shop same as earlier. Robbing Paki bastard behind the counter. *Guardian* and teabags still on the counter. Hadn't even looked up. Bastard. Bastard.

'Remember me, eh?' Albie shouted.

The Paki bastard looked up. Smug face didn't shift.

'Eh? D'you remember me, you robbin' Paki bastard?'

'No,' the Paki said.

Albie threw two coins over the counter. 'Here's your four pee. Right? Remember me now? Yeah?'

'Yes.' The Paki nodded. He looked confused. Oh, yes, this was a good feeling. Don't think, get on with it. Make your impression.

Albie lurched forward. 'Treat people like scum, they start acting like scum, you know what I mean? Eh? D'you know what I mean, you robbing Paki bastard?'

The Paki was answering, softly. Voice full of intelligence. Thinking voice. 'Please. Don't call me Paki –'

Albie shut it out. Used his own voice to shut it out. Time to make things clear, tell the world. It was now, his time.

'I'm a socialist, me, pal. Trade unionist. Voted Labour all my bleeding life.' His finger stabbed the air over the

18

counter. More. Faster. Louder. Shut it out.

'I've marched for the likes of you, robbing Paki bastards like you, but you just see me in my clobber, don't you, you hear the accent, and you assume things, don't you, you assume the right to treat me like scum. Well, OK, you robbing Paki bastard. You treated me like scum, now I'm acting like scum!'

Shut out the voice. 'Please, don't call me Paki –'

Shut. It. Out. 'Right? Now I'm acting like scum! I'll call you what I like!'

The Paki moved forward, came from behind the counter. Yeah, it was now. Getting close. 'Criticise what I do, not what I am –'

'I haven't come here to listen to you, pal. I earn my poverty, you know what I mean –'

'You think I'm robbing you, fine. Criticise me for that, but don't call me Paki –' Raising his hand, pointing at the door, trying to get Albie out, the bastard.

Albie moved closer. 'I work hard for my pittance, and you think you can rip me off. No. No, you're a robbing Paki bastard. You're not a robbing bastard, you're a robbing Paki bastard!'

'Get out, get out of my –'

Acid in Albie's mouth. Blood roaring in his ears. Heart beating so fast. It was close. Get it all out.

'I call you a robbing bastard, what happens? You get a pat on the back off all the other robbing bastards. You get the Queen's award for fucking industry, 'cause this country's full of robbing bastards. But calling you a robbing Paki bastard, that's going to hurt, isn't it?'

'Out of my –'

'That's a bit of a weapon I've got. That's the only weapon I've got.'

It had to be now. Let go, don't think, let it happen.

'Unless you count this one.'

19

He pulled his jacket open. Dropped his hand to the handle protruding from his inside pocket. Looked with joy at the Paki's wide eyes and gaping mouth.

He pulled out the bayonet and swished it through the air between them. Twice. 'You see this one, do you? You see it?'

Now. For Dad. For the ninety-six. Time to start.

Yes. He lunged.

Straight in, up. Twist. Yes. Yes. Don't think. Feed the anger. Yes. Twist. Yes.

'Get the point, do you? Eh? Do you get the point?'

Yes. Slide it back out. Watch it. Watch the body fall. Watch the body of the robbing Paki bastard fall.

Watch the body of the Asian shopkeeper. Watch him die.

Oh Christ. This was it. Done it now.

Genuine in-your-face yob culture.

Albie watched the man dying on the floor of his shop. That big red wound, satisfying. He wasn't gurgling or anything. Just quiet. Yes, this was it. The first. For the ninety-six, for Dad, for the country, 'cause the time had come.

He wiped the blade clean and stuffed his handkerchief back in his pocket. Returned the bayonet to his jacket. Pulled out the spray can.

Albie took the bus back home. Alone on the top deck, he kept looking down at himself, but there was no blood on him. His white tee shirt gleamed with Persil brightness. The murder weapon was warm against his side. No sign of the change in him.

He had killed an Asian shopkeeper for refusing to allow him fourpence credit. Had lunged, slit and twisted.

No. He had to shut out the thinking voice, but hold the image in his mind, the gaping wound, and bring back the anger, the strength. The necessary violence.

Hot salty tears stung at his eyeballs. He didn't want to cry for himself. This wasn't for him, none of the tears were for him. His actions had been selfless. He was just the instrument. He was doing this for Dad, for the ninety-six. All he had to do was show the murdering bastards. Even things out. It was all he could do, and he was going to do it.

He had to keep himself convinced, shut out the thinking. Force down the tears. He knew a way. He began to chant. The hymn of the final white working-class congregation of the United Kingdom.

'L I V, E R P, double O L, Liverpool FC,
    L I V, E R P, double O L, Liverpool FC . . .'

Willing himself on. Stopping thinking. The chant worked.

He got back home, slid down the stairs, off the bus, key in the lock, into the dark, fed the cat, still keeping up the chant.

He needed a scoreboard. His own league table. One down, fighting back, and he needed to prove it. He needed something to look at, a symbol.

In a cupboard, in the front room. Dad's crib board. He took it out, looked it over. This'd do.

Albie picked up a box of matches from the mantelpiece. He took out one match and struck the pink tip. He blew it out.

The first death. The bayonet, the robbing Paki bastard.

He stuck the dead match in the crib board. That was one back.

Ninety-five to go.

Bilborough was in the bathroom. Eight thirty-five, and his wife Catriona's 'Hello, Jimmy' came through the bathroom door, over the drizzle of the shower. Trouble. Bilborough wasn't expected at Anson Road until 9.30 today. Plenty of late nights and form-filling of late, and not enough time at home.

He turned off the shower, opened the bathroom door. Catriona smiled and passed him the call. 'It's Jimmy.' She deserved more of his attention at the moment.

'I know.'

He listened to Beck's summary of the known circumstances and clenched his teeth. A sensitive situation, a sensitive area. He wanted to get down there, take a look about, and calm things down, quickly, before they could get started up.

Catriona brought Ryan up for a kiss goodbye. The baby's ears stuck out exactly like his father's. In that head, thought Bilborough, a personality is forming. A chance for him and Catriona to give something, to pass on the best parts of themselves. He wanted to be around a lot more, take an equal share.

He collected Jane Penhaligon from her flat. She was waiting at the door of her block, legs crossed, her long reddish brown hair pressed against the wall. She nodded good morning, took the passenger seat, and they swung out of the suburbs and drove towards town.

'Racial motive?' she asked. Straight to the point as usual. She was so much better at this than him. So efficient it hurt.

'Until we know more, no suggestion of that.' He glanced across at her. She'd rushed her hair and make-up.

A cordon had been set up, spanning both ends of Purvis Road. Buses and cars moved by on the busy interchange at the far end, in each window an anxious onlooker. A crowd was gathering. The shop and the area outside had been taped off.

Bilborough looked up. ALI'S GROCERIES. There'd been riots around here, in '88. And '85, and '81. Nothing much in the locality had changed since then. BNP candidate marginally more popular here than in neighbouring areas. Bengali teenager kicked into a coma last year.

He was going to have to be very careful. And, of course,

22

this was going to be a robbery. It had to be.

Jimmy Beck was outside the shop, notebook in hand. With him was a uniformed officer, Skelton, and a witness, a very tall Rastafarian wearing a very tall hat.

'It would have been about five past eight,' the Rasta was saying. Beck was nodding, encouraging him to go on. 'No later, 'cause the eight o'clock news was just starting when I left the house.'

Bilborough strode up. 'DCI Bilborough, DS Penhaligon. Mister . . .?'

'Gregson.'

'Mr Gregson found the body,' said Beck. 'And bumped into a skinhead on the way in,' he added significantly.

Bilborough flashed him a warning look. Keep the voice down. No skinhead, not yet. He addressed Gregson. 'Did he say anything to you?'

Gregson frowned. 'He was dead.'

Bilborough whispered, 'The skinhead.'

Gregson shook his head.

'Would you recognise him again?'

Gregson shrugged. There was a look of casual acceptance in his eyes, Bilborough noted. He wasn't surprised at all. 'He was a skinhead, you know what I mean. They all look alike.'

Skelton, who was black, found this amusing.

Right, thought Bilborough. Try to localise the damage before going any further. 'Have you told anyone else about this?'

'Just the police.'

'I'd like you to keep it that way. Just between you and us. OK?'

Gregson shrugged and nodded. Bilborough nodded back, and made for the door of the shop, Penhaligon following.

Behind him, he heard Beck joke to Gregson, 'Eh. Keep it under your hat?'

23

Gregson didn't laugh.

The pathologist, Jarvis, was already inside, lining up the photographer, tapping his chin and looking from side to side. There were no obvious signs of damage to property. The rows of tinned soups and stuffing mixes and cereal boxes stood undisturbed. Just the body on the floor to show that things had changed. The wide wound, the blackening trail of blood.

Harriman was in. New to Anson Road, twenty-two, looked and acted much younger. Only been with them a month, and already he'd been up before the Chief Super for some stupid mistake. Beck had taken to teasing him. Bilborough found him mildly irritating. At the moment Harriman was thwacking hopelessly with a rolled-up copy of the *Daily Mirror* at a bluebottle that was zizzing about the shop.

'Leave it.'

Harriman looked from him to the newspaper and said nervously, 'It keeps landing on the blood.' His eyes, wide open like Ryan's, kept flicking over and down to the body, the wound.

Bilborough nodded to the door. 'See to the crowd. They're encroaching.'

'I'm OK, boss.' Clearly he wasn't.

'I know you're OK. See to the crowd.'

Harriman nodded, blinked in an ineffectual Stan Laurel way, picked his way around the photographer and Jarvis, and went out, passing Beck on the way in.

'Jimmy. Family?'

Beck pointed past the counter. 'In the back room. I haven't spoken to them. I was waiting for . . .' He nodded to Penhaligon, who was studying the door of the fridge, on which some numbers had been sprayed, in red, in an upward slanting line.

She looked up. Stared at Beck. Then to Bilborough. They were relying on her? 'You want me to see to them?'

24

Yes, they were. Bilborough nodded and moved to let her pass. She stepped over the body without looking down, slipped behind the counter and pushed aside the bead curtain. Bilborough caught a glimpse of bright colours, Asian women's colours, greens and brocade thread.

He interrupted Jarvis, who was earnestly directing his photographer around the body, and pointed to the fridge. 'You've got that number, yeah?' Jarvis nodded briskly.

Bilborough flipped open his notebook and jotted down the number. Red figures on white.

9615489

He took another quick look around the shop. Between the counter and the body, a couple of objects had been knocked to the floor. A copy of today's *Guardian*, and a packet of teabags. He watched as these items were photographed, then stooped to have a better look at the body. Knife wound, but it looked wider, deeper than he'd seen before.

The filth of the day was accumulating, he thought. Tainting him. And not even nine yet.

'What d'you think?' he asked Jarvis.

'I think he's dead,' said Jarvis.

Bilborough stared at him. Second bad joke of the morning.

Time to sort this out. He exchanged a glance with Beck, slipped behind the counter, took a pen from his pocket, and carefully pushed down the till button. The mechanism sprung, the till rang open with a bing. It was full. At least fifty quid in there.

So it wasn't robbery.

He looked up at Beck. 'Nothing to indicate a racist motive. Nothing whatsoever. That's our line. OK?'

Beck nodded and left the shop.

Bilborough closed the till and stepped closer to the bead curtain. He looked through, keeping himself hidden. A small room through there. Sofa and chairs. Three generations of

25

silent grief. The victim's mother-in-law, his wife, their four kids. A daughter, late teens, her face clouded with an infinite disappointment. And again, like the Rasta outside, no surprise.

Penhaligon was sitting opposite, a detective sergeant, intelligent, versatile. Consigned again to a role as bringer of bad news, navigator of turbulent emotional waters. A mobile Kleenex, and she was the sharpest he'd ever worked with.

She sat forward and addressed the teenage girl directly. 'Can you think of anyone who'd want to kill your father?'

The girl replied, 'Several million. All of them white.'

Curtain, pillow. Hammers smashing his eyeballs open like soft-boiled eggs. Drilling. A saw slicing through his skull. Fitz's arms flapped helplessly, a failed attempt to wave the sound away. Half of it was outside coming in, half of it was inside his head already. Oh dearie me.

He hauled himself up, still fully clothed, he noticed. Up from the bed, piece by piece. An enormous mess. Flesh bursting buttons all over the shop. Tingling pains jabbed at his internal organs, deep below his folds of excess tissue.

The hammering, drilling and sawing continued, echoed along the landing, its source the bathroom. This, thought Fitz, has been going on for rather too long.

His head and body aching, he pulled open the door and staggered along the landing.

> 'Rollin', rollin', rollin',
> Though the streams are swollen . . .'

He pushed open the bathroom door. Inside, the workmen. Drilling, hammering and sawing at things he, with only the vaguest knowledge of carpentry or plumbing, was sure they shouldn't.

> 'Keep them dogies rollin', Rawhide!'

The man Fitz had been led to believe was the leader of the
workmen looked up peakily from doing something odd to
the toilet bowl.

> 'Through wind and stormy weather,
> Galloping hell for leather . . .'

'Look, I know it's taken a bit longer –'

Fitz poured a glass of water. 'Four months, three days.'

The gaffer stood. 'OK. That's bad. Accepted. Admitted.
But we've cracked it now. OK? We've found the problem.'

Fitz drank the water, raised an eyebrow.

'We'll have it sorted by tonight. No problem.'

Fitz barged out.

> 'Soon, I'll have my darling by my side,
> Rollin', rollin', rollin' . . .'

The gaffer followed him from the bathroom, shouted after
him as he went downstairs. 'Look, we're not cowboys. We
are not cowboys!'

Judith had kindly laid today's *Racing Post* on top of the
television. Most considerate. He flicked it open, felt for the
remote, switched on the TV.

He'd slip into town, to a turf accountant's. Still rather
pleased about last night. Not thinking, really. Couldn't
remember what Judith had said when he'd got in last night,
this morning, whenever. Plenty of cash, plenty of scope,
things could go many ways today. He struggled to make
sense of the blurring print before him. Couple of Sol-
padeine, a good idea. A ciggie, even better idea. Now.

The TV. It was just gone half twelve. The local news.
Granada logo. Soanso at the scene of the crime. And then
Bilborough.

Bilborough. Outside a shop, a little newsagent's. Flashbulbs popping, microphones arrayed before him. He spoke

27

slowly, headmaster to assembly.

'. . . past, this area has seen racial tension, so I want to make it perfectly clear . . .'

A murder. Bilborough investigating a murder. Obviously a racial motive. Or Bilborough reckoned so, anyway.

'. . . there is nothing to indicate a racial motive for this killing. Nothing whatsoever. Obviously we're anxious to talk to anyone who visited Mr Ali's shop this morning. Whether or not you saw anything . . .'

Not a robbery, then. Must have been early morning, then, or there'd have been more people about, more witnesses, they'd have him by now.

'. . . whether or not you think you can help, it's vital that you come forward so we can eliminate you from our enquiries . . .'

Inside Fitz's head, pushing aside the murk, the pollution, something was forming, unbidden.

A profile.

He had to get back. They needed him. And, God help him, he needed them.

TWO

They'd known he was on his way, thought Bilborough. He ran up, leading the others, warrant card flashed open and then closed in the face of the screaming, scar-cheeked doorman. Then in. In to hell.

There were about forty of them, identical, all blokes, suedeheads, stripped to the waist, sweat-slicked and scrawny, rucking. A DJ's console, four massive speakers, thrumming the floor at full bass, no treble. This wasn't music. It consisted of vocal shrieking in an Eastern European language and blitzing guitars. A repeated chant that the skinheads were taking up. He made out the word 'kill'. There were a few women around the walls, looking on, defensive, noses turning up as they saw the police team enter. A strobe clicked on and off every few seconds.

Bilborough looked into the centre of the ruck. A few pairs of hate-filled eyes stared out at him. The skinheads' grip on each other grew tighter. They danced quicker, shouted louder. They knew, right enough. They were celebrating. He thought back to Ali's daughter. She lived with this every day, faced it on the street. Her father had left the front door of his home wide open every day of the week, knowing that one of this lot could walk in at any time.

Penhaligon was at the console, real anger in her eyes, bellowing up at the DJ, 'Could you turn the music off, please, sir?'

'Can't hear you,' he mouthed. He could.

'Could you turn the music off?'

'Can't hear you,' he repeated. He looked down at her. Shouting, stamping, little girl. Bilborough wanted to break his piggy nose.

Beck to the rescue. He leapt up to the console and swatted the needle from the record. A jagged scratch across the eardrum. The stomping and the chanting continued a few moments. Bilborough saw Penhaligon's eyes turned down, forced to step back while the boys played their games.

Beck grabbed the microphone. 'Sit down, and shut up! The lot of you! You can go back to your aerobics in a moment!'

The anger surged up again. No physicality, no violence, not yet. Lots of abuse. An Oi chant started up. A bloke was pushing his way towards Bilborough, edging his way around the dance floor. In his late forties, well-built tending to fat, incipient paunch. He was waving a mobile phone, shouting. Enjoying this, liked to be a victim. 'I'm getting on to my lawyer, right? Just lay off 'til he gets here, right? I know the score, you know what I mean? I know my rights!'

Bilborough ignored him. Somebody turned on the lights. The skinheads glistened. He waved Skelton towards a line of filing cabinets on the landing, and looked around the place. Copies of Nazi posters, SS insignia, a portrait of the Führer himself. What a pile of hopeless pillocks this lot were. Pillocks that had almost taken over the world.

There was another poster in a corner. He recognised it right away. There was one just the same on the wall of his own office at Anson Road. Three rows of faces. Faces that felt like family. As if someone had pinned up a snap of Catriona and Ryan. Here.

He pointed. 'Whose is this?'

A skinhead slouched across, downing a pint in quick gulps. He stared at Bilborough. No change of expression. Bilborough could just see out on to the landing. Skelton was dumping files into a plastic bag, and not looking at the bastard

30

who was grunting at him, doing a King Kong. Skelton looked angry, but not surprised. He wasn't rising to it.

'Listen,' Bilborough shouted at the drinking skinhead. He ripped the poster from the wall and pointed. 'Parker's black, Ince is black, Schmeichel's a Dane –'

The ape was getting to him. He shouted to Penhaligon – 'Jane, we'll have him!' – and turned back to the poster. 'Kanchelskis is a bloody Ukrainian, and Cantona's French, you stupid, soft sod.'

The grunting continued. Bilborough threw the poster aside, ran to the landing, and jerked the apeman's arm up, pushed him towards the stairs. Skelton didn't react. He dropped the last of the files into the bag and slammed the cabinet shut.

The apeman's greasy hand was clenched in Bilborough's own. More filth he was touching, more shit he was stirring. Long bath tonight.

After lunch, Penhaligon finished her coffee and set off for the incident room. Her level of irritation had increased in sudden leaps all day. The early morning call. The shop, Beck waiting, openly waiting for her to materialise, the spirit of Florence Nightingale. The fascist pub, the skinheads' desire to violate. Bilborough rushing about, not listening, not asking for her opinion, only throwing her an occasional look. Keeping her happy, ticking over.

He smiled at her again as she walked into the incident room and leant against a table. Every time she looked at him a remote part of her brain suggested something, and her conscious mind told it to keep quiet. It would be good to sleep with him, she knew. She could do a lot worse.

She had done a lot worse. Almost. She saw an airport lounge, an empty checker-patterned seat, a plastic-boxed chicken curry and apple crumble sitting unclaimed on the steward's trolley.

Bilborough spoke, addressing his team. Beck was absent, Jane noticed. Popped out a couple of minutes ago. 'Right. We've got names and addresses for sixty-eight Fascist party members.' He waved a grey folder, lists of neatly typed information visible. 'We're checking them out for previous –'

Time to remind him that she existed, an underused resource. 'Forty-nine with previous. Forty-four of them violent.' She'd run them through the computer over lunch, Biro in one hand, M&S sandwich in the other.

Bilborough sighed. 'OK, those forty-four are top of our list.'

Another irritation. Eyes at nine o'clock, wide adolescent eyes. Harriman, paying more attention to her thighs than to Bilborough. Little prat. She turned to him, hitched up her skirt, gave him a look that told him just how she felt today.

He blushed like a thirteen-year-old and his eyes rolled around the room like scattered marbles.

Bilborough continued. He hadn't slowed down since the raid on the pub. The look on his face when he saw the poster. A picture of boyish indignation.

'Plain clothes, unmarked cars. We don't want it known that we're looking for skinheads. A non-racial motive, that's still the official line. We'll go in early morning. Any self-respecting skinhead's going to be in bed with his dick in his hand. If he's up and about, the chances are that he was up and about when Ali was murdered. So get the alibi, and check it out.'

Harriman still had his head down. He was staring at something on his lap. Bilborough leaned over him. 'Am I boring you?'

Harriman looked dazed. 'What? No, boss.' This is a school, thought Jane. A classroom. And today we're doing how to catch the murdering racist bastard.

Beck entered, grim-faced, his regrown moustache looking more than ever like a drooping rodent on his upper lip.

Bilborough took the folded evening paper from him without taking his eyes off Harriman, like it was a relay baton. 'Then listen!'

He flopped the first edition open. His jaw quivered, his big ears twitched back a couple of centimetres. His eyes found hers. 'Jane!' he barked and strode from the room.

She took the paper from him. *Manchester Evening Post.* CITY MURDER. SKINHEAD SOUGHT. Well, that put the tin lid on it. Beneath, Ali's smiling face. Some family occasion, baubles, little stars, behind his head. A smaller photograph, a woman's face. By CLARE MOODY. She looked like a Page Three girl.

Albie had slept for a couple of hours. He'd had the usual dreams. Woke up with sore temples and a head full of yelling blue faces. The ninety-six. Yelling for revenge.

He went to Scott's. Got a *Guardian* and some teabags. £1.98. He was just paying when a motorcyclist came in, nodded to the shopkeeper, and slammed down a pile of *Evening Post*s on the counter.

There was a thin sheet of paper on top of the pile of *Post*s. Through it, Albie saw the word MURDER in big black letters. Something he had done was in the papers, for the first time since 1976, the *Liverpool Echo*, the Music prize. He made an impact. He was important. His actions were going to be investigated, analysed. His killing of the robbing Paki bastard was going to have people shaking their heads and sighing all over the country. There'd be some racist scum who'd be cheering him on, and all.

The shopkeeper stared at him. 'All right, mate?'

Albie jumped. He was still standing in front of the counter. His eyes flicked down to the floor, the correspondent squares of lino. Saw Ali falling back again. And he'd done it.

'Yeah. And a . . .' He waved a couple of fingers at the pile of papers. 'Is it all right, er, I'd like an *Evening Post*, please.'

The shopkeeper cut the string on the bundle and handed him one. Albie paid for it, tucked it under his arm against his packet of teabags, and left Scott's. He really wanted to look at the *Post*, and read all about it. See the evidence of his worthless, white working-class life connecting up to the media. The paper burnt against his armpit, like the comic he'd run back from school with as a kid. And just like the comic, he was going to walk quickly back home, breath quickening, spread it out on the table and read it through, page by page, interesting bits first. The Spider, Kelly's Eye, Dr Sin. His murder of the robbing Paki bastard.

If Anson Road was a schoolroom, thought Penhaligon, their visit to the offices of the *Manchester Evening Post* was its trip to a city farm. Gofers scampered between desks, telephones were answered by the anxious claws of rats in hats. In her pen sat Clare Moody, a swine, flanks poured into a Donna Karan two-piece, tapping swill into her PC. For her the 90s, the big façade of confused concern, hadn't happened yet. Wouldn't happen. She was just waiting, confidently, for Portilloism. Any day now. Beneath Moody's purple-blue eyelids, Jane could see a shining faith in absolutely nothing. She'd peeked at Moody's biog while they waited in reception. Colchester County High School, London College of Printing, the *Sun*, a fortune, an enormous lawsuit. She'd pushed a soap star too far, lost the sympathy of the seven-figure setting jury, and thus her editor. She'd gone freelance, technically she still was, but her legs were pretty far under the table here at the *Post*.

Bilborough waved her front page at her. 'A Pakistani's killed in a racially sensitive area. And you print this?'

Moody didn't flinch, kept her eyes on her screen. 'It's the truth.'

'Oh. And that makes everything OK?'

She double-clicked her mouse, sent the update over to her sub. 'Yes.'

Bilborough snorted. 'You got sacked by the *Sun* for writing lies. You actually got sacked by the *Sun* for writing lies. That'll get you in the *Guinness Book of Records*. So don't give me any crap about the truth.'

Moody seemed completely unmoved. Without looking up, she asked, 'Will that be all?'

'No. Who gave you the information about the suspect?'

Now she smiled. Thought she had a weapon. She turned to face him. 'I can't tell you that.'

'Don't hide behind journalistic integrity, you've got none,' Bilborough said. Somebody at another table looked over and laughed, gave Moody a quick thumbs-up. Something to laugh about in the pub later for them, thought Jane. Coppers who got upset about things. 'Who gave you this information?'

'I can't tell you.'

Bilborough caught her eye. It was time to ask the big question. They'd checked with the Rasta, Gregson. He'd stayed quiet. 'Was it one of my officers? If you don't answer, I'll arrest you. Was it one of my officers?'

Moody smiled, so pleased with herself and her sad, childish, hurtful world. 'Yes.'

'Which one?'

She smiled again. 'I'm not telling you.'

Albie laid the paper out on the table, and read. CITY MURDER. SKINHEAD SOUGHT by Clare Moody.

The tearful family of Mr Shahid Ali, 51, were today attempting to pick up the pieces of their shattered lives after he was murdered in his own grocery shop early this morning. Although the police are keen to play down the possibility of a racist motive in an area notorious for race violence, an eyewitness reported seeing a skinhead leaving Mr Ali's shop just before his body was discovered. No money was taken from the till, and it seems likely that the killer was motivated by race hatred. It's believed that Asian community leaders are trying to calm the situation and stop revenge attacks.

Albie slammed his hand down, hard, on the table. More assumptions. A skinhead, a white man, so he must be a racist murderer. Well, wrong, Clare Moody. Albie had rocked against racism at Sefton Park in '79. He had an Artists Against frigging Apartheid record somewhere upstairs. He was no racist. He was proving a point, and they couldn't see, because they were a part of it. They couldn't see what he was proving, they assumed things. He'd made it to the paper, and they said he was a racist. He laughed a bit about that.

There was more.

Mr Ali was a respected member of the local Asian community. His wife Rejia was too upset to talk to us, but neighbour Pat Long, 46, commented, 'We're all very shocked. Mr Ali had moved in over ten years ago and was always there with a smile for his customers.'

The lies. They'd made that up, trying to get people to feel sorry for the robbing bastard. Clare Moody had made it up. He looked at her face in the little box beneath the headline. She was making her name out of things like this. Making her name out of him, feeding off him. That photo, she'd had it taken specially, it wasn't a photo booth job. Her hair and make-up were perfect. She'd glossed herself up so that when she broke the news, titillated you with her version of the facts, after you'd read about the murders and the accidents and seen the bodies, you'd want to screw her. She was a whore, Clare Moody.

Clare Moody.

Albie sat up in his chair, took his eyes away from the paper, looked into the empty street, looked down at the picture again. He recognised the face. And the name, now he thought about it. About three years ago, some actress had cleaned Clare Moody out. A fortune. Got her sacked. It was on the telly, on the news, he remembered. He remembered because he remembered everything about the *Sun*.

Clare Moody. The *Sun*.

Uncle Rupert's empire. GOTCHA! News International. IF KINNOCK WINS, WILL THE LAST PERSON IN BRITAIN TURN THE LIGHTS OUT? Shite Incorporated. April 19th 1989, THE TRUTH. Bollocks Unlimited.

Clare Moody had written, for all he knew was still writing, for the *Sun*. And today she was writing about him, about what he'd done. Lying about him.

It was going to be her. She was going to be next.

Judith had called a meeting of her outreach workers at the Salford Project. She watched them as they trailed in to the central lounge and helped themselves efficiently to coffee and biscuits. She liked these people, all of them. Her daily contact with them reinforced her beliefs, propped her up. Working at human problems, working out the best way to help, was what inspired them, and she understood that. She was driven by concern. Other people's worries were like rocket fuel to her, a part of her, pushing her. She'd never seriously questioned her capacity to forgive and understand. Her career was an extension of her personality and it suited her. She'd found a small place where tolerance and patience were rewarded and not abused.

Her team stared up at her. The rows of kind eyes were creased by worry, the reason she'd called the meeting.

They weren't working well recently, with talks of cutbacks and loss of funding floating. There was evidence of weariness and resignation. Judith had recognised the signs and decided to do something about it, nip it in the bud. A large dose of confident-sounding reassurance, mother-knows-best. She leant against a table and raised a finger to gain their attention.

'Your job is to care for people who are terminally ill and their families. My job is to secure the funding that allows you to do it. Now, if you start to worry about the funding, you cease to do the job you're paid to –'

Fitz. In the corridor outside, his wide black outline unmistakable through the frosted glass window. Judith tried to ignore him. The other side of compassion. Forgive people their faults, and you offer yourself up to be trapped with them, forever, whatever.

'You cease to do the job that you're paid to do. And if you cease to do the job you're paid to do, why should anyone agree to renew the funding?' She added emphatically, 'The funding. It will be there.'

Fitz ambled into the lounge. He was tattered and unshaven, and was pulling a cute face. She wanted desperately to strike him. How dare he just stagger in here!

He waggled a hand about. 'Have you got a minute?'

'I'm busy.' She returned her attention to her team. 'If I have to walk the streets of Manchester with a begging bowl, I'll do it, the funding will be there.'

They were still looking up at her but not listening. Her fascinating husband had diverted their attention. 'Please,' he said, immersed deeply in his own childlike world. This sort of thing wasn't, thought Judith, endearing any longer.

She reached into her handbag, pulled out what he wanted and brandished it. Her team froze with embarrassment. She enjoyed the moment of hurt that flashed across Fitz's face before he regained control.

Still holding up the money, she asked her team, 'Any questions?'

Fitz, stony-faced, turned to them and put on his lecturer's voice. He was about to say something smug and clever, she could see it forming on his lips. 'How to handle an addict, chapter three, verse twelve: public humiliation.'

'Any questions?' Judith repeated. He came forward, took the money. She looked away from him.

When she looked around the room he had gone. She smiled at the shuffling, embarrassed project workers, and retreated to her office. She had a long list of calls to make and plenty of anger to work off. People with real problems, problems they hadn't invited upon themselves, needed her help.

Albie sat before his father's crib board again. His head was filled with the picture of Clare Moody, fixing the image of her. He needed to ensure he'd recognise her face.

He counted the matches as he slotted them, slowly, one at a time, into the board. Each match, a life. A life for a life. When he reached ninety-six, he stopped.

Moody second. It was three o'clock. Plenty of time. He'd get the bus into town, have a look about the *Evening Post* building. There'd be a corner somewhere, a place where no-one passed. A place for them to conduct their business.

Christ, he wanted her to know. He was going to tell her, remind her of what she'd taken part in. Before the blade. Yes. This was going to be better than Ali. This was really going to mean something. There'd be no doubt about it this time, no misunderstanding. He was really going to get his message across through the medium of Clare Moody.

The 3.45 at Haydock Park. Going, even. Two hundred on Stark Sonata. Twelve to one. Reasonable start.

Fitz stood among the punters. His brain was still somersaulting inside his head, but he gave no outward sign of that, or of his feelings as the bloody animal cantered around the first bend. His shoulders shifted and a signal raced to his vocal cords before he could stop it. A small grunt up at the screen.

Stark Sonata dropped back. The thing was strolling along, Badminton-style. Its blue-green livery was swept from the camera view as the winner and its company raced to the finish.

The fellow next to him was jerking the whole top half of his body up and down, as if he was riding a horse. Well, at least somebody was happy.

Fitz unclenched his fist and tore his betting slip.

Then he took another from the dispenser.

An Asian shopkeeper. Not a robbery. Racial motive. Early morning. Exactly when, exactly where? He needed to know more before he could pin down his thoughts.

Were they going to call him? Of course, if they hadn't caught the bastard by tonight. Even though he'd called Bilborough everything he had, walked out, left Panhandle standing at the airport, and snuck back home to Judith.

Perhaps they wouldn't. He'd have to approach them. Would he? Oh, of course. Pride, he had none. Not that kind of useless, self-important compensatory pride, anyway. No point in that. Particularly not if you were desperate.

Four o'clock, Goodwood. Going, good to firm. Four hundred, then. On Well-Thumbed Machine. Fourteen to one.

The incident room at Anson Road was getting active. Photographs of Ali and his shop were going up. Skelton was at the blackboard, chalking up details of recent racial attacks in large white letters.

Penhaligon sat at her desk. She punched a sequence of keys on her computer console, and a long list scrolled up. The names and addresses of fascist organisations, their members, their sympathisers. She ordered the machine to print the document. Continuous stationery emerged jerkily from the printer. She watched the information as it appeared.

In the car, on the way back from seeing Moody, Bilborough had asked her calmly and casually if she'd been the source of the leak. As if it was a matter of no importance. Just checking. She understood why. He just had to sort it out, treat everybody the same. Procedure. But it had, illogically, added to her irritation. She replayed the scene a few times in her head, satisfied herself that he was right. Of course, he was only doing his job, and doing it properly. She'd have done the same. But it had pissed her off, that tiny hint of distrust. The conflict between personal and professional relations. Procedure could be a bugger. You just had to forget about things like that afterwards, remember why you were doing the job, and get on with it.

She looked up from the print-out at the sound of raised voices. Beck was in Bilborough's office, shouting. Every word was audible.

'I can't believe you're talking to me like this. Asking me that. I just can't believe it!'

Penhaligon looked away from the office door. Beck was a fool. He should know to treat it casually, not display his irritation. His pride wouldn't let him.

Bilborough's voice now, rising reluctantly. 'Just answer the bloody question, Jimmy, will you? Did you talk to that bloody woman? Yes or no. Did you –'

'I won't answer the bloody question. For Christ's sake, what do you think I am? I've been doing this job for fifteen years –'

Exactly, so think, and shut up, while you've still some dignity left. It doesn't matter. It's bloody obvious what the boss is doing, narrowing the field, because it's bloody obvious who talked to Moody. Don't make an issue of it, don't make things difficult. Because out there some bastard, probably someone on the list spewing from the computer, is wiping his knife and laughing.

'Jimmy, I haven't got time to massage your ego. OK? Did you talk to that bloody woman?'

Penhaligon urged. Just answer and get out, Beck. You're making yourself look a prat, and I can't think that of you, we're supposed to be a team, I have to work with you.

'That shows you haven't got any faith in me whatsoever. For God's sake, fifteen years –'

Bilborough bawled over him, 'Somebody did. Somebody talked to her. Now was it you?'

'No!'

'Thank you!'

But Beck couldn't leave it there. He had to get back in. 'It crossed your mind, though, didn't it? That's the point. It crossed your mind that it might have been me.'

'A process of elimination, Jimmy. You are eliminated.' Bilborough paused. 'Send Harriman in.'

At last.

Beck went on. 'How do you think that makes me feel?'

'I've got the picture, Jimmy. Right? You're feeling a bit aggrieved. Fine. Noted. OK? Now send Harriman in.'

'You're treating me like some bloody prick fresh out of training, still wet behind the bloody ears –'

'Send Harriman in!'

Beck bashed open the door and stormed into the incident room. His face was flushed. Penhaligon kept her head down. She didn't want to look at him or think about him for a while, until she'd sorted out her own feelings. In the silence that followed his emergence, she heard him light a cigarette and call to Harriman, 'You're wanted.'

Harriman walked slowly into Bilborough's office. Penhaligon watched him go. There was a red patch burning across the back of his neck.

More silence, more pretending that nothing had happened. Beck stood up and pulled on his coat. 'I'm going for a drink,' he mumbled, and left the room.

Bilborough had no time to collect his thoughts before Harriman poked his head around the door, guilt written all over his teenager's face. Jimmy Beck and his idiot grievance would have to wait, there was a more important area of weakness in his operation.

He held up the paper. 'Is this down to you?'

'Yeah,' said Harriman. The lad was plucking awkwardly at his shirt.

Bilborough was taken aback by Harriman's honesty, but only for a moment. He pointed to the door. 'Shut it.'

Harriman closed the door and turned back to face him. Bilborough could tell he was expecting the sack. The stupid little prick. Ten GCSEs, three A levels, and none of the sense he'd been born with.

'Why?'

Harriman swallowed. 'I don't know.'

'Did she pay you? If you took money for this, you're finished.'

'No, boss. She didn't pay me.' Said with the same stupid honesty as the initial confession. And, thought Bilborough, that was only to be expected. Harriman and greed weren't concepts that went together. It was going to be something a lot simpler than that.

'She's a nice bit of stuff,' he suggested.

'It wasn't that.' Harriman looked down. 'You sent me out of the shop.' He paused, confused and embarrassed. 'I don't know, boss, I just wanted to prove I was involved.

That made sense. Bilborough nodded. 'I see. Knowledge is power, eh? Show people you're in the know, you get a bit of respect. Yeah?'

'Yeah.'

Bilborough thought back to Clare Moody's satisfied smile. 'No. She just thinks you're a bloody clown.'

'I know.' Harriman swallowed again. 'What'll you do?'

Bilborough let him stew for a full five seconds. The lad was scared shitless, he wouldn't forget this in a hurry. And if tonight there were upturned cars, petrol fires and race murders all along Purvis Road, well, he wouldn't forget that either. Enough warning had been given.

'Nothing,' said Bilborough. 'Get out.'

A bad afternoon. A very bad afternoon for Fitz. There was only one way he knew to make it good. To turn things back the way they'd been last night. He'd managed miracles before.

He tried to push Judith's accusing face from his mind. Christ, she hadn't even looked at him, had just passed over the money like a machine. A cashpoint on legs, was that what she had become?

Now, there were two alternatives. He'd win, and feel good, and get drunk, and get home late, and she'd blank him out again. Or he'd lose, he'd get drunk, go home when his cash ran out, and she'd blank him out again. If that was the response she had decided on, fine. So it didn't matter which way things went. Still, better to win, though.

Three thousand pounds. To win. Shepherd's Hey.

He took the slip, hot in his shaking hand, to the counter. There was a new girl in here. Not attractive, and she made it worse by chewing gum. The jaw rolled, the eyes stared straight ahead. Fitz wondered if there was much going on in there. His life, the decisions and thoughts tumbling about inside him, seemed massively complicated to him. At this moment Shepherd's Hey, Judith, the embarrassed workers at the Salford Project, Shahid Ali, Bilborough, Panhandle, and a TV programme he'd seen last week were all sloshing about up in his head. Was there a similar set of processes passing through her mind? Or had she settled for a slow spin?

She called over to the manager, 'Three grand, Shepherd's Hey.' The manager nodded, reached for a telephone.

Fitz passed his money over the counter. The chewing girl treated the wads of notes with apparent disinterest. Was the swift-dissipating tang of Juicy Fruit the only sensation left for her to appreciate? She started counting. Fitz caught the briefest flicker.

'You stopped masticating for a wee moment then, didn't you?'

She frowned. 'Y'wha'?'

'There's something macho about it, a bet like that, don't you think?' Fitz said happily. 'Like slapping a certain part of your anatomy on the counter and saying, "Look how big it is, everybody, look how big." '

'Y'wha'?'

Fitz took his place before the TV screen. His fellow punters parted to let him pass. There was none of the good humour he might have expected. Ah, that was because they were afraid he was going to win, despite the odds.

Time passed quickly. Half past four. The stalls opened. Out they come. There it goes, Shepherd's Hey. Three thousand pounds riding on its back. His judgement.

The horse fell.

People were leaving the *Evening Post* offices. Well-dressed, chatty, empty heads. Albie stood behind a pillar in the courtyard outside. He wore a woollen hat. To cover the skinhead, now they'd be looking for him. The spray can and bayonet were tucked into the inside pockets of his jacket.

He was finding it easier this time. He didn't have to work so hard to bring out the hate. The *Sun*. It was enough. An entire community, a city. Its industries smashed, its working men thrown out of work, told they were lazy and should get on their bikes. Its councillors outlawed for doing their job, trying to provide. Young men forced to become training scheme slaves, or starve. And this lot, string-pulling journalists, the hardest decision they'd ever made was which university place to take up. They were the unofficial propaganda department of the Conservative Party, spreading shit to keep the bastards in power.

She appeared. Clare Moody, a pig in a woman's body. Her fat curls bobbed as she walked across the courtyard. She was smiling. Christ, thought Albie, she counts this as a good day's work. A headline. A thousand words of twisted crap. And he was seven and a half hours at Armitage & Dean's, five nights a week, and his Dad to dress and take to the lav every day, on a hundred and sixty quid a week before deductions.

He followed her. She was heading for the multi-storey. There was nobody else about. Excellent. All he needed was a moment alone with her. To tell her, and do it. No, it wasn't a racist skinhead that killed Shahid Ali. You were wrong. It was me.

She entered the car park. He waited a moment, followed her. Still nobody about, great.

The lift doors were closing. She must be in there. He couldn't let her go. He ran forward, jammed his hand in the door. The mechanism sensed the intrusion, opened the doors again. Albie got in the lift.

'What floor?'

It was her, up close. Over made-up little cow, little pig. Looking so, so pleased with herself. She was in love with hate, she loved telling lies, she worked for the *Sun*, she'd told lies about him, about his Dad, said they'd pissed on the dead.

'What floor?'

'Top.'

She'd looked at him, and smiled. She was smiling to

herself about him. Had written him off already. Seen the clobber, heard the accent, written him off. She was still smiling. Was he that amusing, eh? Was he that fucking funny?

But he couldn't do it here. Not in here. The lift could stop, the doors might open, there'd be too many people about. He was going to kill her, but it couldn't be in here.

Or why not? Why not do it right here, right now? Why not?

Albie reached down for the bayonet.

The lift stopped. The doors opened. About twelve people walked in. Albie stepped back instinctively. They pushed into him, talking loudly. Not looking at him. The doors closed.

Where was she? Where was Moody? Albie pulled himself up in his DMs, agitated. He couldn't see through the gabbing crowd to the far wall, where she'd been standing. The lift started to go up. He looked again, ducking his head to peer under someone's arm. No sign. Where was she? He had to finish this, now, he'd planned it that way. He couldn't wait, she wouldn't make him wait. He'd waited long enough.

The lift stopped again, a couple of levels up, and the doors opened. People got out. There were so many he couldn't be sure if Moody was among them. More people were getting in. He hadn't looked at the indicator when he'd got in, to see where she was getting off. He hadn't thought, the sight and nearness of her had overwhelmed him. She might be getting off on this floor. She might have got out before!

He pushed his way out, his bony elbows jabbing into the suited sides of the office workers.

No sign of her out here. She wasn't part of the bunch walking away. He ran down the concrete stairwell to the level below, vaulted the steps two at a time. He couldn't lose her.

He pushed the door of the lower level open and ran

47

through. It was half empty, just a few cars, and no sign of Moody. Where was the lying cow? He'd brought the hate out, he'd been so close, he had to use it. She couldn't escape him. He wanted to get her today, with the body of Ali and the newsprint of her headline still warm. He wanted to move fast.

A car pulled out on the far side of this level. A Ford Escort.

Moody was inside, her smug, smirking face visible for a second as she turned the corner and drove right past him. As if she knew, thought Albie, as if she knew who he was and what he wanted and found it amusing.

Albie knew something that'd wipe the smile from her face.

He watched the car drive away. Tried to calm himself. His legs felt weak and his breath roared in his ears. She wasn't going to get away. He was going to deal with her. He was going to shut her up. Not today, not here. There'd been too many people about, anyway.

And he owed it to the ninety-six, to Dad, not to foul things up.

Tomorrow, then, Clare Moody. Tomorrow the blade will stop your lies.

Fitz hurried along a street he didn't recognise, cursing Shepherd's Hey, its rider, its owner and its trainer. The fact that the beast hadn't even seen fit to get twenty yards around the course increased his umbrage. A big swaggering brashness was building up in his chest. He identified it instantly as one of his most standard reactions, as yet unsupported by drink. Unreasoning flippancy. Don't think, cover the hurt by opening your gob and letting it flap. Let it, and the Glenfiddich, lead you where it will. Part of this reaction was, of course, a small voice that urged distantly for him to stop, take stock, react sensibly. It never triumphed.

48

Fitz's unthinking haste was increased by his full bladder, and his dick, which felt like it was going to burst at any moment. He had no wish to slosh round for the rest of the day in wet trousers. There was a pub on the street corner ahead. Good. He remembered unfortunate occasions, not long ago, before the change in the licensing laws. Entire chains of dry cleaners must have been bankrupted since then.

He burst into the pub, which he didn't recognise. It looked the sort of place that might get a bit rough later on, but it was only about six, and there were just a few old fellows, some lads and their girlfriends. The barman looked up as he entered. Fitz used a series of hand-signals to indicate his intentions, mouthed his promise to return and buy a drink and hopped off to the gents, desperate for release.

There were three urinals. Those at either end were occupied by tall, muscular, crop-haired gentlemen engaged in a muttered conversation. Fitz had no wish to disturb them, and tried the cubicle door. It was occupied.

He said loudly, 'In this kind of situation, the heart sort of sinks a bit, doesn't it?'

The skinheads stopped muttering and looked over their shoulders at him. Their gazes were accusatory. Shut up, you fat, drunken old twat, Fitz could tell they were thinking. They were wrong, of course. Oh yes. He was a fat, drunken old twat with a PhD in Psychology, and that made all the difference.

'Nothing,' he said sweetly.

He stood between them, flopped himself out, and tried to begin. Unbelievable. For the last half hour, the waterworks had been screaming, and now the tap had dried. He'd have to loosen his mind, lessen the tension. Shepherd's bleeding Hey.

'About half seven this morning, they reckon,' said the skinhead to his left. Fitz glanced quickly down at him with the corner of his eye, noting his technique. Interesting. 'He just walked in, and done him. Good style.'

'What, a skin?' asked his companion. Fitz sneaked a glimpse to the right. Hmm. A marked difference between the two neo-Fascist pals.

'Yeah,' said the first skinhead. 'Think I'll lie low for a bit, you know what I mean? Those Pakis are gonna go apeshit. Anyone with a skin'll do –' He broke off and stared straight at Fitz. Fitz realised he must have been grinning foolishly and looking between the two of them. Flippancy leading him on.

'Have you got a problem, mate?' barked the first skinhead.

Fitz shrugged. His mouth raced on, leaving his mind far behind, not twenty yards from the starting post before it fell. 'Bashful bladder,' he explained. 'I'm telling it – do something. These two are going to think I'm some kind of pervert, please do something. But no luck as yet.'

The skinheads looked across him at each other. They weren't amused.

Fitz rattled on, not caring. 'I can't help noticing,' he told the skinhead to his left, 'that you're a straight down into the channel man. You clearly relish that gratifying gurgle when a good healthy stream hits the main flow. But you,' he turned to the other, 'now, you're more of a Luke Skywalker type, aren't you? It's some kind of laser beam and you can etch lovely patterns into the urinal. A sort of piss artist, really, aren't you?'

'Will I butt him or will you?' the first skinhead asked his mate.

Fitz ignored the warning. 'Personally, I'm the type who can't resist a quick glance.' He glanced quickly at their penises. He didn't give a damn what they did to him. This was another sensation, after all. More danger, leading him on. Who cared. 'Lots of people find it annoying, I'm sure.'

The first skinhead shook and zipped himself away. 'Are you trying to get your nose broken, pal?'

Fitz felt a wave of anger rushing to his head. He looked into the skinhead's eyes. Six hundred and fifty thousand years of human evolution, and this is the end result. A person who didn't think twice about not thinking.

He just walked in, and done him. Good style.

'Yes, do you know anyone who could do it, pal?' he shouted back.

They hadn't broken anything to prove their point. Fitz let the cold tap run and rested his forehead on the cold white edge of the basin. That butt hadn't done much to improve his headache. He watched spots of blood plip from his nose on to the tiles below, and inhaled instinctively in an effort to clear his head. His lungs drew deeply on the odour of blocked cisterns, shit-smeared paper towels, fermenting piss.

He still didn't let himself think. That would be too painful. Christ, he couldn't think of Judith, of coming home to her tonight like this.

Time for a look. He raised his head to face the mirror. Oh, a lovely bruise, and lots of blood. What a super mess he was getting himself into. There were no towels left, of course. He cupped some of the running water and splashed himself with it gently. The wound didn't look too bad, anyway.

But there was something else. A thick black border around his vision. Oh good, he thought, my life is being repackaged in wide screen. This is the kind of thing you either worry about and run screaming to the hospital – too embarrassing – or you have a couple of drinks, a long sleep, and wait for it to go away. He'd follow the latter course. Take the risk.

He cleaned himself up as best he could and slipped back into the bar. The skinheads had cleared off. The barman offered no comment on his injury, and provided a neat double as requested. Somebody had put a couple of quid in the CD jukebox. The volume was up way too loud, particularly considering there was hardly anyone in the place. 'We want the same thing, we dream the same dream.' The inspirational philosophy of Belinda Carlisle, which Fitz appreciated. It aided him in his efforts to stop thinking. For the moment, this place would suit him fine. He was just going to sit here and do nothing. There wasn't a part of him that didn't ache.

The black borders were encroaching.

He ordered another drink. There was a television set suspended above the ragged snooker table on the other side of the pub. Local news again, the Granada logo. The jukebox blotted out the sound.

The shopfront of Ali's groceries. A reporter, mouthing silently to camera. Bilborough again, the same shots from the morning. No racial motive.

A skinhead, about half seven this morning. Just walked in and done him. Good style.

No. Too easy. Too bloody easy. Half seven in the morning. Just walked in. Strange. All kinds of strangenesses going on there. Not as straightforward as they – Bilborough, the news media, the Cro-Magnon lavatory-dwelling butt beasts – obviously thought.

I'm intelligent, thought Fitz. In fact, better than that, I'm a genius. At this, at their job. Even when I've been butted, even after six standard measures of Jack Daniels, I can see what they can't. And I'm sat in this dive, a fat drunken old twat with a bloody nose, getting the nerve up to go stagger home and shit on the woman that loved me enough to take me back.

Beck had spent half an hour in the pub, cooling off. He tried to empty his mind, think rationally, but the anger kept coming back. All right, so Bilborough had followed procedure, he'd had to check everybody out. But, and there was no doubt about this, there were some things that shouldn't have to be questioned. They'd worked together fifteen years, there were surely things to be taken for granted. What it came down to, what this incident had showed, was that Bilborough didn't trust him. Thought he was a prat. Tolerated him.

Beck slipped back into the incident room quietly. A number had been given out through the TV and press, and the phones were ringing. Penhaligon seemed to be co-ordinating the phoneline. Reports were being dumped on her desk by Harriman, Skelton, and others. Beck returned to his chair, picked up his pen and a pad, and took a call. He'd get himself back into the heart of things, try to forget, prove himself.

The call came from a woman with a long and unpronounceable Asian name that he asked her to spell out letter by letter. She'd been into Ali's shop very early that morning, about half six. Had she seen anybody else? No. Why was she up and about so early? She always was. Her phone number? She provided it. Fine.

He took his report to Penhaligon and laid it down on top of the others piling up on her desk. She was on the phone, her long stockinged legs folding and unfolding. Beck waited for her to react to his presence. He smiled pleasantly.

Penhaligon glanced at the report and frowned. She covered the mouthpiece of the phone, and hissed at him impatiently. 'What did she buy?'

Beck was startled. 'What?'

She looked at him as if he was a moron. Beck suppressed an urge to slap her. Had Bilborough asked her the big question, he wondered. Had it crossed his mind that she might have spoken to Moody? Or had they both thought it might have been him?

Bilborough emerged from his office. Penhaligon beckoned him over, asked her caller to hold on a moment. So cool, thought Beck. She has to make some kind of scene, swing the spotlight on her own super efficiency.

'We've got the till roll,' she said to Bilborough. 'We ask people what they bought, what it cost, then we tick it off against the till roll. If there's anything unticked, we know whoever bought it hasn't come forward.'

Bilborough nodded.

Beck scowled. 'Why didn't you say that earlier?'

She took her eyes away from him. 'I thought it was obvious.' She refolded her legs, went back to her call.

Beck returned to his desk. The phone rang again. He answered.

'Right, got that, everyone?' Bilborough called out. 'Find out what they bought, and what it cost. OK?'

There was a general mumble of understanding.

Bilborough moved back towards his office. He leaned over to address Beck as if nothing had happened that afternoon. 'Jarvis'll have had the post mortem done by tonight, we'll go over later, OK, Jimmy?' There was a plea in his expression. Come on, Jimmy, pal, I'll forget today if you will, give us a smile and we'll not mention it again.

Beck wasn't going to give him the satisfaction. He nodded briefly and reached for his pen.

Albie was back at work. He hadn't missed a night for years. On his contract he couldn't afford sickies. He'd got back home from town, had another couple of hours' sleep, then put on his hat and set off for the bus as usual. He had to keep things looking ordinary. And he liked the routine. Now Dad was gone, there was no reason left for him to work nights, but he'd got used to it. Besides, the way things were going, he was going to be busy during the day from now on.

On the bus over he'd heard a couple of the other men

talking about Ali and the murder. They didn't have an opinion about it. Mostly they just repeated the crap they'd read in the paper. That was how it worked. People were trained like parrots to repeat all the lies. Albie had listened to them, and laughed to himself. They were going to get confused over the next few days, when he'd explained himself better.

There was a copy of the *Post* lying next to his machine. Somebody from the day shift had left it behind. They liked to mark out their territory. Often they'd leave things behind just so they could accuse the night workers of tampering with their stuff. That everyday pettiness seemed a long way back to Albie now. He'd ascended the social scale. By foul means, yes, but they were the only means he had available.

He pushed up his mask and picked up the paper in a gloved hand. Moody stared out at him. If he'd got it right she'd be dead now, and the papers tomorrow morning would have had something new to say about him. A fresh angle. She'd cheated him today, got away, but there was no way she was going to get away from him. She was worse than Ali ever could have been. She was scum.

Predictable, that was her. He knew how she'd react to anything. He had to get her away from the building, somewhere they could be alone. Getting her there would be easy, all he had to do was to bait the trap and he had her. Easy.

Slowly, carefully, he tore her picture from the paper. He was going to do her a favour. He was going to make that face famous.

Penhaligon got a lift from one of the uniforms back to her flat. Bilborough had suggested she get some sleep, but she'd insisted on coming back for the post mortem. She needed just a couple of hours for a break, to wind down. And Beck was looking at her in a way she didn't like, as if she was responsible for his stupidity.

She waved her lift goodbye, took out her keys, and approached the door to her block. A cup of tea, a bath, some sleep. Forget about Ali, and Beck, and Bilborough for a while. Let them worry.

Footsteps, on the tarmac behind her. Quick and dainty. In the glass of her door she saw a huge figure looming out of the darkness behind her.

She turned. 'Oh no,' she said. Standing before her, his gargoyle's face twitching in a manner she could not believe she had once found attractive, was Fitz. Blood was dripping from his nose and he reeked of alcohol and smoke. He was the last person on Earth she wanted to see.

He leaned close to her before she could react. 'I'm not wearing any underwear,' he said.

Did he really expect her to fall into his arms at this point? To giggle girlishly, ruffle his hair, and take him by his nicotine-stained hand up to her bedroom for a wild night of mad, passionate lovemaking?

She opened her door and nipped through. He tried to say something, began some sort of explanation. God, the embarrassment of him! Her neighbours were going to love this. Sod them. And there was a practical matter that needed to be sorted out.

She whirled round and shouted, 'You owe me nine hundred and seventy-two pounds, for the flight, and the hotel.'

'You'll have to join the queue.' He smiled. Fat, ugly stinking man. A wreck. And she had almost let herself become his mistress.

'I'll understand if it's in cash,' Penhaligon went on. 'We wouldn't want the wife to find out, would we?'

That hurt him, and oh yes, it felt good. 'Slight whiff of bitchiness there, Panhandle.'

'What happened to your nose?' she asked with a total lack of concern. 'The missus hit you with her handbag?'

He grunted. 'A skinhead gave me a piece of his mind.'

Even better. Well done to that man. A civilian citation to him. Penhaligon smiled broadly and closed the door on him. That was it, then. All done and dusted. He was out of her life. Forever. Nine hundred and seventy-two pounds was a small price to pay.

He kept ringing the bell. Like a kid, drawing attention to himself, too pissed to care. Christ, this was so adolescent! She was halfway up the stairs to her flat, fully intending to ignore him. He'd go away eventually. There were more important things for her to be doing. That bath she'd promised herself.

The bell kept ringing. Again and again and again. She stared at the peephole in the door of her flat. There was a tiny reflection of herself in there. She looked very angry. There was disturbed movement and grumbling voices from the floors above and below.

Again, the bell.

Right. This was it. She was going to finish it. A kick in the balls if necessary.

She pounded down the stairs, wrenched open the door. Kept her eyes down, kept her hand on the door. 'Fitz, piss off,' she said. 'Piss off now.'

He gestured behind her, the stairs. 'Can I come in?'

She met his gaze. 'I'd let Oliver Reed in before you, Fitz.' She made to close the door again. 'Now, piss off and don't come back.'

He stretched out an arm to the door, stopped her from closing it. 'What are you going to do, Panhandle? Call the police?'

'Goodbye, Fitz.' She pushed the door.

He pushed back. 'You need a profile.'

She stopped a moment. That was it, then. The reason he's suddenly appeared. Not the wife throwing him out, not a confused reaction to the injury he'd suffered. Not even the drink. He wanted to come back to them, get himself involved, didn't want to be left out in the cold with only his self-loathing for company. Git. Well, no way.

'If we need a profile, we'll get one. Psychologists are ten a penny.' His pudgy grip tightened on the door and his eyes flashed dangerously. 'Let go, please.'

'No.' The pretence disappeared. The drunkenness, the flippancy, dissolved instantly. Look at me, his face was saying. Forget what happened between us, but remember the results I got. Don't view me as a person, then. Think of me as a resource. A utility. The best you'll get. 'You know what he'll say, your ten-a-penny psychologist?'

'Let go of the door.' She spat out the words.

'Possibly. He'll also say the killer's white, unskilled, unemployed, a fascist, a football supporter, and he lives local.' He was almost shouting now, his whisky breath wafting over her.

'Please let go.' She pushed again.

'If he says that, Panhandle –'

She slammed the door shut in his face.

'– you'll know he's a prick!'

Fitz lurched off unevenly into the darkness. Lit another cigarette. In the dim light of cracked streetlamps, his shambling figure and bloody face caused a stir with passers-by. An elderly couple in matching Fair Isle sweaters cast him a glance of curious disapproval. Patronising self-satisfied bastards. He crooked his shoulder, closed one eye, and snarled. 'Yes, I must find new flesh for my master, new flesh . . .'

He found a public toilet, muttered, 'Excuse me, gentle-men,' to the men engaged in a sexual act against one wall, and cleaned himself up again. The blood looked worse than it was.

Panhandle. He'd hurt her so much. The look on her face. She really hated him. Did she? No, of course not. He'd seen that look before. On the faces of everybody he'd known for more than a couple of weeks. She'd get over it. Of course.

He dabbed away the last specks of blood and went out. 'Keep it up, lads,' he told the men.

Those black borders were coming down again. Slowly closing. And something deep inside his head, far behind his eyes, tingled, a Brillo pad scraping against his brain. Ignore it, add it to a half-forgotten file of interesting symptoms of overindulgence.

Couldn't afford a taxi, took a bus. He squeezed himself onto a double seat, rested his hands on his thighs, rested his head on the thrumming glass. It started to rain. The lights of the city became the lights of the suburbs. There was a terrible smell. It was him.

He got home. It was after ten. He walked along the pleasant, tree-lined streets, coughing and moving his head slowly from side to side. He was starting to get ever so slightly worried about those black borders on his vision. Tiny flashes of light glittered like silverfish around them. That was kidneys, wasn't it? And there was a noise, a very fast, very loud, electronic kind of row.

It was coming from his house, which appeared to have been converted into a discotheque. The curtains of the living room had been taken down. The building teemed with teenagers, oozing from the door. The volume was incredible, or so it seemed to him. There was dancing, laughing, drinking. Fitz had been looking forward to a good night's sleep, post-row anyway. He was not prepared for this. Nobody had told him about it. Had they?

He nodded to the youngsters grouped outside the door. They nodded back. Their faces were full of something that looked to Fitz like a kind of amused sympathy. Look at Mark's fat, drunken old twat of a father, what a laugh, eh. Well don't laugh too soon, he thought, it's all ahead of you. Your ambitions are going to be shat upon, my young friends, so smile while you can. You are going to be levelled down.

He pushed into the packed hall. 'Excuse me, excuse me, I just live here.' A cloud of cannabis fumes tickled his nostrils. Ah, now there was a more sensible drug. Far too sensible for him, of course. A timid weed. Not enough wrecking capacity there to be Fitzworthy. He looked around at the kids. A lot of the boys had long hair pushed back into pony-tails, goatee beards, check shirts. They looked like retarded farm labourers. God, fashion was a stupid thing. Something he couldn't relate to personally, anyway. He headed for the kitchen.

Judith had cordoned herself in with Katie. His daughter was sat on a worktop, picking at the enormous spread Judith had laid out. Quiches, salads, dips. Very impressive. The kiddies were going to treat it like a trough.

'Hiya,' Katie greeted him, her mouth full of doughnut.

Fitz belched, 'Hi.'

Judith turned to face him, a very large flan, the centrepiece of her display, in her oven-gloved hands. For a moment he really thought she was going to lob it at him. His face, the blood, the stench of him, must be telling her so much.

'We're going out, Dad,' said Katie.

Judith put the flan down, took off her oven gloves. She had the look, the look Panhandle had given him not an hour before. 'Wait in the car, Katie.'

Katie went out.

Still the look. He didn't want to speak. Strangely he didn't want to eat. The buffet, what he could see of it over the black borders, repelled him. His stomach was churning.

Judith spoke. 'You lost it all?'

Fitz clapped his hands together. 'The row. At last, the row. We could always skip it if you like. Just don't speak to me for a week, you know.'

'Did you lose it all?' A little louder. A good sign. She'd given up on the cool approach.

'Ah. Short. The first tentative step up the emotional ladder –'

'Did you lose it –'

'Yeah.'

Judith's face hardened. The look increased. Fitz was sick of it, sick of what it represented. His worthlessness. His inability to surface, to get himself sorted out. He let his mouth run ahead of him again, gave voice to the first reaction. 'You've perfected that look, you know. Utter contempt. You've got it off to a tee.'

'I've had plenty of practice.' She remained still. God, she was so reasonable. She hadn't changed. It was him, he'd messed everything up. But he couldn't say that. And his vision was blurring.

So instead, 'Gamblers top themselves to avoid that look. Do you know that? A man's a few quid down. So he goes for the housekeeping. He's going to have to go home, tell the wife, and get that look. No thank you. So he tries to win it back, loses even more, tries to get that back, loses the lot. And now the look's going to be even more contemptuous. He tries to kill himself. Fails. He decides to kill her, hit her over the head with a hammer, drown her in the bath. Anything so long as he doesn't have to see that look in her eye.'

Judith didn't flinch. His best shot, and he was boring her.

The door burst open. A girl wandered in, squeaked, said sorry, wandered out.

'I can't help noticing,' said Fitz, 'that there are one or two strangers in the house.'

'It's Mark's birthday,' Judith said.

Bad one. Yes, it was about now, March the somethingth. Bugger it. 'I'm sorry.' But no, don't let up, don't climb down, don't let it be used against you. 'Two or three rungs up now, aren't we? I predict a torrent of abuse fairly soon. And then we'll be there. At the top.'

Judith shrugged. 'I could give you some money to give to him.'

He raised an eyebrow. 'Was that a little twist of the knife, dear?'

Her nostrils flared. 'No. It would be nice for Mark, that's all. It would be nice for him to get money from his father on his birthday, that's all.' She leaned close. Her eyes thinned to slits. She whispered, 'You selfish, arrogant sod.'

That was new. A most unexpected tactic. A direct hit. How to react?

He put a hand on her shoulder. 'You're not in the mood for a quick shag, then?'

She ignored him, pulled away. Fitz realised. They had lost it. Whatever the argument, however big the scene, in the past, there'd always been a window somewhere, an escape route. The possibility that any moment they'd catch each other's eyes in a certain way, smile, burst out laughing. It had been going the last few years. Now it was gone. Sealed up. No escape.

What did that mean?

He leant on the table, tried to focus. His legs were actually shaking. 'You hate me winning anyway,' he pointed out. 'So cheer up. I lost.'

She started to stack cutlery in the dishwasher. 'That odd win, once in a blue moon, it justifies day after day of this. That is why I hate you winning. I want you to lose and lose and lose. I want you to think there's not a hope in hell of winning again.' She looked up at him. 'Then even you might think of stopping, Fitz.'

His hearing was imitating his vision. Several times during that little tirade she'd faded out completely, swallowed up by the bass beat shaking the house. That itch behind his eyes was getting worse. Now she'd stopped, well short of what he'd anticipated. He could tell she expected a reply.

'Oh, is that it? The top of the emotional ladder? Anticlimactic, I'd say. Ten years ago you'd have thrown something at least.'

She took off her apron and washed her hands. 'I'm tired, Fitz. Bored, even.'

Bored. This was it, then.

'We're going to Jo's. You're not invited.' She pushed past him without looking, opened the kitchen door, shouted, 'Food's ready!' and was gone.

The kitchen was invaded. Eager teenagers, moving fast. Youth, speed, efficiency, enthusiasm. The prime of life. A streak of envy flashed through Fitz's dulled senses. Somebody else, he thought vaguely, might be able to look at all this, sigh, and recall fond memories of their own youth. He couldn't. He didn't have any. Never young, one of those old children. Mental age had leapt from thirteen to twenty-nine in a day. Everything before twenty, and a good deal after it, tinged with pain, suffering, rage, frustration. And the one person he'd found that could ease that pain had just told him that he bored her.

An automatic reaction. He elbowed some of the kids out of the way, reached up to a cupboard. Something made him switch on the portable telly. His hand groped about inside the cupboard. Where was the bloody thing? He needed it.

'Police are appealing for calm tonight after a series of violent reprisals following the murder earlier today of local shopkeeper Shahid Ali.'

Fitz looked down at the telly. Now a line of white oval shapes was moving from side to side across his eyes. Between the black borders he saw a familiar face. Bloody Bilborough again. New pictures, he was walking fast down a street, trying to avoid questions from journalists.

'I can only repeat what I said this morning. There's absolutely no evidence of a racial motive for the killing of Mr Ali . . .'

Fitz's hand located the bottle at last. He shouldered his

way out of the kitchen. He needed his bed, sleep, a drink, sort things out, write off today. Blot it out. Start again tomorrow.

But he couldn't. Things were different now. Panhandle had slammed the door on him. Judith said that he bored her. The two escape routes he'd been holding out for had sealed. He had fucked things up massively. Still. He'd stop thinking about it, that was his prerogative. A rest. He needed to lie down.

Somebody turned up the volume on the stereo. It rattled Fitz's aching body as he tottered up the stairs. Fresh young faces stared at him. They might as well have been another species. This is what getting old is like, thought Fitz. You don't notice it, you feel pretty much the same inside as you always did, but you don't understand new things. Your body winds down, you die, some other sod comes along. He knew this was all self-pitying bollocks. But a bit of self-pitying bollocks now and again was good for the soul. A healthy dose of melancholy, a good medicine. It had picked him up before.

The moaning bastard from next door was in the house. Actually inside, following him up the stairs. In his Debenhams pyjamas and matching dressing gown and moccasins. 'Would you keep the noise down, please? If it's not too much to ask. Are you listening to me? Can I ask you to show a bit of consideration, a bit of common decency, and keep the noise down? Please don't ignore me, I know you can hear me . . .'

He was a good reminder. Fitz might be a wreck but he knew he was alive. Moaning bastard, the chewing-gum girl at the bookie's, those kids on the front step. They were going to get through life OK. They weren't complex enough to end up like him.

Fitz came to his bedroom door. He steadied himself against it, pushed it open. Oh Christ. The party had spread, infesting every room. There were a couple in there with their hands down each other's fronts. Up against the wall. They didn't even look up. And they were in his bloody bedroom. He thought of ordering them out, clapping his hands together, there's a time and a place, et cetera, but he hadn't the energy. He just needed to rest. The whisky bottle was shaking in his right hand.

Bathroom. He opened the door. In his head, something was thudding. Those black lines. The oval shapes. The glistening silver threads. That scraping pain across the back of his eyeballs.

A face he recognized. Four months, three days. The gaffer and his team of cowboys. Rawhide. In the bathroom, still, now, hammering, sawing, knocking clouds of plaster from the walls.

'Didn't work,' said the gaffer. 'It might be the piping into the bath, we reckon –'

Tell them to piss off. No. Piss off. Panhandle. Was she here? No. Judith? Gone. These kids, who were they? He didn't know any kids. Toilet. Try the toilet. A girl was there, about seventeen, head of the queue, about to go in. Gorgeous. A bum to die for. 'Sorry, dear.' He pushed her aside.

He was in. Alone. The toilet. He turned to sit. The mirror. Him, covered in blood. No. He tried to raise a hand. It wobbled crazily. He looked down into the bowl. His face again, a reflection in the bogwater. He unscrewed the bottle, brought it to his lips, sat.

That noise, that music, getting louder and louder.

Whisky on his lips, running over his tongue. He dropped the bottle. He couldn't pick it up. More pain, not in his head. His chest. Shit, he couldn't breathe. Something, a long blade, jabbing into his left side. The black borders closing up, joining, meeting in the middle.

Fitz fell off the toilet. He knew he was dying.

THREE

Shahid Ali looked good on the table. His face was calm, his eyes closed. On a table in the corner was a plastic bag, returned from Forensic, into which his neatly folded clothes had been bundled. His shoes lay on top. To Penhaligon it looked like he might sit up any second, have a glance at the results of his post mortem, pop on his clothes and go home. In her experience, nobody looked dignified in death, but he came close. The wound in his side was massive.

Jarvis joined her, Beck and Bilborough in the lab. Penhaligon thought of him as a weasel. His head came up to her shoulder, his face was lined, he had a long pointed nose. An aura of quiet enthusiasm surrounded him when he worked. A firm Lloyd Webber fan, he whistled showtunes to keep up his spirits. One of the qualities that she guessed must have drawn him to his vocation was a delight in adversity. The smile he pulled whenever he had to break bad news.

He gave her a grin and a wave, nodded to the men. Nodded to Shahid Ali. His little joke. 'Lots of trouble around Purvis Road tonight, I hear?'

Bilborough sighed. 'Not too bad. Could be worse. How about him?' He pointed to the body.

Jarvis put his hands together and his smile grew wider. 'Good news and bad news, I'm afraid. The bad – it's a single knife wound, all right. Difficult to make a murder charge stick.'

'And the good?'

'He's twisted it round a bit,' Jarvis said enthusiastically, miming the action.

Penhaligon looked away. Even Beck looked a bit sick at that one.

Quite carried away, Jarvis went on. 'You see, he's gone through the stomach wall, through the aorta,' he spread his arms wide, 'massive haemorrhage, and then he's chipped a bone in the vertebra.' He wagged a knowing finger. 'I warn you now, the defence will say the damage was done when the victim fell.' His eyes cast about the room, looking behind them as if somebody was missing. Somebody to share his bonhomie. Like attracts like. Insensitive cynic seeks similar. 'Where's Fitz?'

Bilborough wasn't going to answer that. 'What are we looking for?'

'A long, narrow blade.' Jarvis's eyes flicked down to the cleaned wound. He hesitated, then said, 'For what it's worth, I saw a wound exactly like this a few years ago. I recognised it straight away. Fellow stabbed his wife. She'd been off with his best mate, you see –'

'Yes?' Bilborough prompted.

Jarvis nodded again. 'British Army bayonet. Got it down from the loft, waited for her to come back home, and that was it.' He counted on his fingers. 'Would have been Sheffield Crown Court, about May '78 time?' His eyes shone. He was glad to be of service, could recall exact details of his every court appearance in the last twenty years.

Back to Purvis Road, then. Now they knew what they were after. Bilborough got Beck to call for more officers and equipment. A good gesture, to display his trust.

As they walked out to the car, Jane took a look at Bilborough. He'd maintained a professional distance from both her and Beck this evening. He looked tired, and more than that, he looked angry. She'd seen frustration flash in his eyes at Jarvis, at the body of Ali. But he wasn't pissed off with the killer any more than usual. He wanted to get back home, to Catriona and the baby. The job was in his way, again. Deep in her mind, so far back it didn't even really register with her consciousness, there was an urge simply to hold him.

'This is going to be tricky,' Beck observed as they made their way across town. He wanted to remind them he was there. Tired as she was, Penhaligon wasn't finding him particularly irritating. Compared to Fitz he was an angel.

Bilborough tapped his hand against the steering wheel. A siren sounded behind them. He swung onto the kerb to let the ambulance flash by.

Judith had just said goodnight to Jo and her husband when the phone rang. It couldn't be him, he wouldn't dare. No more talking, rowing, apologising. She just wanted to sleep.

For her. It was him, no-one else would have the bloody nerve. She smiled, took the receiver from Jo. Jo looked slightly worried.

Mark was on the line. There was something wrong. There was no music behind his voice, just a sort of startled murmuring from his friends. 'Mum, Dad's ill. He's really ill.'

'What? have you called an ambulance? What's wrong with him?'

'He's just collapsed. He was locked in the toilet. He says he can't breathe. I had to kick the door down.'

'I'm coming over.'

She collected Katie and rushed out to the car. He wasn't going to die. He couldn't. That would be his final revenge. The ultimate victory. She told him he was boring, he keeled over, she's racked with guilt for the rest of her life. The bugger. She wasn't going to let him get away with it. She was going to kick his coffin all the way to the cemetery.

Katie was sobbing as they pulled into the drive. The ambulance had arrived. Mark and his nonplussed friends, some of whom had already begun to walk away, were standing silently as two ambulancemen manoeuvred a heavy stretcher-load slowly down the porch stairs. No. The bastard. He had done it. He'd died to spite her.

A huge hot ball of tears exploded in her chest. The guilt surged up.

She wrenched open the door, ran forward through the rain. Mark was shouting something. She didn't hear, couldn't make sense of it. She had to know.

There was an oxygen mask clamped to Fitz's mouth. His eyes were open. He saw her. He pulled a face, lifted the mask.

'Heart attack, dear,' he said.

He was babbling under the mask all the way to the hospital. Judith just had time to pass Katie over to Mark and they were off. She gripped his hand tightly. He didn't object.

Surely now he was going to see. This made a difference. A warning to both of them. He couldn't ignore it this time.

They reached the hospital. He was loaded on to a trolley, pushed down a corridor. Doors whished open automatically to admit them deeper into the complex. The rain was pounding now, hissing at the windows. The mask was pulled off. As they sped smoothly along the corridors she leaned closer to make out what he was saying.

Gibberish. He had to keep his mind active. This had always been his way of doing it. She remembered nights, long ago, listening to him rattle on in his sleep. She'd thought that Scottish stream of consciousness the most beautiful sound in the world, a clear brook whispering through a sward.

'Now. Energy. Nuclear, bad idea. Total safety – crap, no machine is safe, Thatcher was a scientist, she should have known that. Windmills, solar batteries? Bollocks. Scandinavian mobile home seventies balsa wood bollocks.'

There was a rumble of thunder, a crack of lightning. 'Ah. Lightning? Could be it. Where does the lightning go when it's not flashing? There's a question waiting to be asked. There could be a never-ending source of energy out there, but we don't go looking 'cause lightning is the flash. Suppose it isn't? Suppose it's out there all the time and the flash just makes it apparent . . .'

A doctor was waiting in a large white room fragrant with antiseptic and filled with pieces of gleaming aluminium surgical equipment. A door led off to a theatre, Rupert the Bear and the Flintstones visible through the panels of glass. Judith watched helplessly as Fitz was stripped and dressed in the biggest gown the hospital could provide, his flabby teddy-bear body flopping all over the place, every blemish on the wide surfaces of skin exposed to harsh white light. He was full of venomous substances. She reminded herself she had done everything she could, right from the start.

More gibberish. She took his hand and he didn't even acknowledge her, kept looking straight up. 'Something that annoyed me as a child. Herbert Lom, that show, *The Human Jungle*. He's got a patient, right, a woman, say, and she's an absolute nutcase. He delves into her background. She set fire to the hamsters in school. Accidentally knocked over a bunsen burner. He tells her this. Cue the music, credits roll, end of programme. I used to go bloody berserk –'

The doctor swabbed his arm, the nurse pushed hard on the rolls of flab on his forearm, prepared a syringe to take a blood sample. He didn't wait to be asked, made fists.

'I used to go bloody berserk. You've told us what's wrong, Doctor Korda, that's all. Now where's the bloody cure, eh?'

Judith moved away as the doctor logged the sample and waved over his team of nurses and their ECG machine.

Fitz's gown was untied and the nurse attached electrodes. Now Fitz looked like Gulliver in Lilliput. She realised suddenly that he was going to live.

'You're his wife?' asked the doctor, picking up a clipboard. 'Can I ask you a few questions?'

She nodded. Her emotional level was slowly stabilising. Thoughts started to sequence themselves in rational order again. 'How much does your husband drink, Mrs Fitzgerald?'

Fitz shouted over, 'Six or seven a week.' Damn him. Virtually on his death bed, and he was still trying to humiliate her.

'Pints?' asked the doctor, a little surprised at the patient's sudden degree of awareness.

'Bottles,' said Fitz with relish.

Judith glanced at the machine. It started to beep and flash. Steadily.

'Bottles of beer?'

'Bottles of whisky.'

The doctor nodded. His eyelids fluttered. 'And you smoke?'

'Fifty or sixty.'

'Please say a week.'

'A day,' said Judith.

She watched as Fitz rolled himself over to face them, flab flopping over, trailing wires. There was nothing wrong with him. Had he done this deliberately? Put her through it on purpose? Was he capable of going that far?

'Give it to me straight, Doc,' he said in an American accent. To her own astonishment and alarm, Judith found herself smiling. 'I've always wanted to read *War and Peace*. Is it any use me starting it?'

The doctor put his clipboard down on top of the ECG machine. 'There's nothing wrong with you. Nothing physical. But I'd like you to see a psychologist.'

● ● ●

It was raining heavily. Beck was kitted out in full protective gear, gloves, the lot. There'd be used syringes about, almost definite. He was crouched down in one of the alleys running off the back of Purvis Road, emptying the bins. He kept losing his balance and slipping into the muck. His elbows were covered in grease from a three-day-old cod supper. The stink, the rain. The people round here were poor, oppressed. Supposedly. God forbid they should get their arses in gear and do something for themselves. Oh no, nobody was going to suggest that.

Skelton was doing the gutter across the way. His arm was down the drain. He kept his face still. You had to admire him. He was keeping his mind on the job, he really wanted to get the man.

There was an Oi chant coming from over the houses. Not enough skinheads lived round here to make that kind of row. They were being imported, doing some sightseeing. In the middle of the night, in this rain. There was dedication.

A pair of fluffy slippers appeared before Beck. He looked up. A huge woman stood there, arms folded across her dressing gown. And this was her shit he was rifling through. Her Tampax he was treading in. Daft cow. What did she want?

She pointed behind her. 'There's four more bags back in the yard. And you missed me last week.'

He gave her a look of contempt.

'You missed me, I said. And you can take that look off your face, son. If you don't want to do the job, pack it in, and –'

'I'm a copper!' he shouted. Oh, to grab her and stick her head in the bin. Rub her face in the slime.

'Pack it in and give somebody else a chance. There's three million on the dole, son, who'd be glad of the work –'

'I'm not your bloody binman, I'm a copper!'

● ● ●

73

Fitz took a bath at the hospital while Judith waited in outpatients. He stared up at the ceramic tiles, checked for black borders, oval shapes, silverfish. Nothing. In the bright light his view of the world seemed suddenly super-real, the edges of the tiles defined sharply, the tulips on the poster by the door impossibly colourful, the squeaky vinyl lav seat extra comfy. There must have been many people took their last bath in here. A last chance to clean their armpits and goolies and spare the undertaker his discomfort. A last chance to wonder at the beauty of nature, airbrushed budding crocuses. The NHS probably had a big stockroom full of those posters somewhere. Maybe Virginia Bottomley chose them personally.

He must have been sick. He couldn't remember it, couldn't remember anything between falling off the bog and seeing Judith running up outside the house. And my, hadn't she looked put out. But vomit had been the answer, spewing to his rescue as it had done many times before. His head and his nose still hurt a bit, but it was the kind of faraway pain, a background babble he'd got used to over the past few years.

And it had done the trick. Judith was back. When he'd swung himself up from the trolley she'd actually hugged him. Excellent. Result achieved. Shame he'd had to puke his guts out and nearly frighten himself to death, but she was back. Tonight was going to mark a new phase in their relationship. All the wonderful rows to come about the incident. All that guilt, on both sides. Fuel for years in that.

There was some kind of hold-up on the way back. The storm had eased off, but the rain continued, rattling on the roof of the taxi. Judith hadn't spoken to him properly on the journey. Interesting. Cooling down already.

Fitz angled his head, trying to make out what was causing the obstruction. There was light up ahead. Blue lamps flashing. A crowd, a big crowd, had gathered. The taxi crawled on.

This must be Purvis Road. There were families, Asian and Chinese. Parents, grandparents, kids, grouped under the dripping awnings of their shops. Huge dogs at their feet, panting, their eyes wide and alert. Alsatians, Rottweilers, unmuzzled.

He heard the Oi chant. 'Oh, the stupid bastards. Shit for brains.'

Judith nodded, making the connection. 'Oh. That man who was killed today.'

The taxi lurched on again, getting closer to the chant. Fitz felt his hand close comfortingly around Judith's knee. He looked across the road, to the taped-off front of Ali's shop. The skinheads stood outside, only about six of them, they'd been trained up on how to make the maximum row. Police cars all around. The van in front of them had been stopped and a young-looking copper was tapping on the driver's window.

Bilborough and Beck were standing right in front of the skinheads. Fitz sat upright. A shiver ran through him, top to toe. He belonged out there, and they hadn't called him.

'I'm not going to tell you again,' Bilborough was shouting, his finger raised, pointing past the skinheads. Something boyish about that face, thought Fitz. The ears added to that. 'Just turn around and walk!'

'We've done nothing!' the lead skinhead shouted back.

'You're being provocative. An Asian shopkeeper has been murdered and feelings are running high, and if you don't clear off, I'm taking you in.'

'We've done nothing. It's still a free country, isn't it? We're entitled to walk along the bloody road, aren't we?'

Fitz watched as Bilborough, exasperated, shifted his head. Looked along the road, along the line of stationary vehicles. The cab shifted forward slightly, right into a wide beam of light cast by one of the big police arc lamps.

Fitz caught Bilborough's eye. Saw inside Bilborough's head in the second it took him to run through the possibilities, reassure himself that no, Fitz hadn't turned up uninvited with the intention of barging over, or having a go, or trying to take over.

Then wondering whether it would be such a bad idea. Then deciding that yes, it would. There were psychologists ten a penny.

Fitz considered giving him a cheery wave and a smile. He was about to when Bilborough turned away. Without even acknowledging him.

The skinheads chanted on. As the taxi moved along, the van in front finally waved through, he heard Beck give them ten seconds to shut up. He smiled. Countdowns, hide and seek, ultimatums, and threats. There was a personality type it was even easier to read. A walking textbook of neuroses. Different beliefs to the skinheads, same reaction.

The young copper, rain-soaked in his yellow jacket, appeared at the driver's door. To Fitz he looked about thirteen. 'Sorry to keep you waiting, sir.'

There was a tap on the window next to Fitz and the passenger door opened. Bloody hell. Panhandle. He almost smiled. But he was with Judith, and Panhandle was pissed off with him. She wouldn't say anything, would she? No. There was one advantage of being an embarrassing fat old fool. Women aren't going to fight over you or cause a fuss about you, it'd make them look silly.

She hadn't looked up yet. Ha ha. Surprise coming. 'Sorry to keep you waiting. Could –'

He smiled and waved. Only me, only little me.

She recovered. 'Could you tell me what you're doing in this area, please?' And there was a hidden agenda in that question.

I've come to take charge of this investigation, lady, Fitz

76

desperately wanted to say. But Judith was present. And there was an opportunity to do a bit of self-righteous blameshifting, couldn't resist that. 'I've been at the hospital.'

Judith smiled at Penhaligon. 'We've met.'

'Yes.' She turned back to Fitz. 'Nothing trivial, I hope.' She slammed the door.

Judith shot Fitz a questioning look. She was wondering, he realised, how much of a scene he must have caused to get himself that hated. And smiling. She was actually smiling.

Bilborough summoned Penhaligon to his car, a quick nod of the head, an exchange with Beck. She sat in the passenger seat, the soaking back of her jacket clammy and sticking to the leather. Her back ached. She needed another bath. In the mirror she saw her hair stuck down, plastered in spikes on her forehead. She knew what Bilborough was going to ask.

'So. Nothing in the bins or gutters. Except needles, used condoms and half a gallon of puke. That and a dead dog.' He smiled. Paused. 'You think a profile would help?'

She'd been preparing for this. For months. 'No.'

'No?'

'No.'

'I do.'

Penhaligon nodded. He must have seen the taxi, she thought. An unexpected complication, throwing her strategy off keel. She'd confront it, direct. 'From Fitz?'

'Is that a problem?'

'No.'

A lie. She had to keep her feelings out of this, on the surface. And she knew Bilborough had feelings about Fitz that were probably not much different. That last argument, about Cassidy. Fitz's biggest problem, she decided. He attacked, he pushed for the truth, diagnosed for everyone whether he'd been asked or not, but didn't stay around to pick up the pieces. That was boring, and there were a load more people waiting to be insulted. Christ knew how his clients stood for it. Or his wife.

'He's not the only psychologist in the world,' Bilborough was saying. 'He just thinks he is.'

Excellent. She hadn't even had to suggest it. 'Well, I've done a bit of research,' she said. 'There's a guy at the university. Nolan.'

The relief on Bilborough's face was a picture. He nodded. 'Right. Wake him up.'

Penhaligon flicked to the back of her notebook. She'd had the number ready for months. Checked Nolan out the day she got back from Kos.

The house was empty and dark. The party was over, thought Fitz. He'd ended it. As if forgetting Mark's birthday wasn't enough. He ought to feel guilty. He was too tired.

Only alcohol could cure the tiredness.

Mark was waiting for them in the hall. 'When are you going to get your head straight, eh? Eh?'

Guilt, guilt. Drink, drink.

Mark went. Fitz looked down at his shoes. He wished his emotions would follow his instructions. Another pang of guilt. Katie. He hadn't even considered her. Getting butted by skinheads, throwing away three grand, rattling along on a hospital trolley spouting crap to piss everybody off. How old was she now? Eleven? A difficult age. Like seven, and ten, and thirteen, and forty-five, and every other stupid number.

He crept into her room. She was awake and she'd been crying. She saw him and rolled over, turning her head to the wall. Guilt. But Fitz knew her mind better than he knew any other. She had all the adolescent stuff to come, the self-pitying bollocks, the revelation of any sex neuroses, all ahead of her. She was untouched by it. A child's mind, complex, full of secrets and worries, and her father wasn't helping with behaviour like tonight's. He had to be straight with her, absolutely direct. She deserved that.

'I'm sorry I frightened you.'

No response. He came closer, sat on the end of the bed. Direct. Get right to the nub. She's eleven, right?

'When I was your age, I'd get depressed and I'd think, I didn't ask to be born. But because I've been born, I'm going to have to die and I don't think that's fair. Is that what you think sometimes? Hmmm?'

She nodded almost imperceptibly.

'When I die, Katie, I want Mark to carry the coffin. On his own.'

It worked. She started to giggle. In another five minutes she was sleeping. Well done, Dr Fitzgerald. You cynical, manipulative swine. When those adolescent traumas begin all of that's going to come right back at you.

Having sorted the guilt, he got the drink. He stood in the living room, surrounded by balloons and wrapping paper. Segments of quiche had been ground into the carpet, marks left by cigarettes stubbed out on the wall. The storm surged back. He looked out of the window, let the alcohol take him, and forgot his personal share of humanity's woes. That lightning. Power sources. Nuclear. No machine can be safe. He'd lay odds on an accident. Or perhaps nuclear terrorism. Yes, more likely. The human race was going to go down. He saw it. Out there, in his head.

'The doctor wrote you a prescription.' Judith entered, picking up paper plates.

He took another sip of the whisky. All medicine should taste like that. 'I keep seeing this image. A symbol of the future. Post-nuclear catastrophe. All life obliterated. There's a mattress in a pool at the bottom of a block of flats. Storm after storm. The water lifts the mattress. Drops it. Lifts it. Drops it. Until one day the mattress crawls out of the pool. And that's the start of the next evolutionary cycle. A stinking, sodden mattress.'

'Please stop drinking.'

He ignored her. 'Millions of years pass. It learns to reproduce. Adapts. Wanders across continents. Diverges. Differences evolve between the different groups. Wars begin. Duvets against sleeping bags. Then a futon gets clever and invents the atom bomb.'

'You drink because you are anxious and depressed,' she said. 'You get a hangover. That makes you even more anxious, even more depressed. So you drink even more.'

Correct, in every detail. That didn't mean he had to take any notice. He knew it all already. She couldn't give him any answers. He already knew the answer, had seen it tonight, yards away, in Purvis Road.

'That can't be the answer, Fitz.'

'Scunthorpe,' he said.

'Sorry?'

'Even Scunthorpe can be the answer. Question: name a town due west of Grimsby. Answer: Scunthorpe.'

She faced him. 'You don't want me to help you?'

'No. In my old street, women used to run up and down every time a man was sick or dying or dead. I'd watch them all clucking, relishing every minute. It did the man no bloody good whatsoever, but it made those women feel a lot better.'

'Bullshit,' said Judith. 'You don't want anyone to help you because only ordinary people need help. And you think you're special, unique.'

Damn. That hurt. Because it was the truth. He was special, unique. He had talents. A way about him. He couldn't be compared to any other person.

Self-importance, self-pity. Empathy. His enemies, his fuel. It's bloody hard to handle other people when you're a genius, he thought.

Then again, perhaps everybody thinks that.

● ● ●

Morning. The night shift at Armitage & Dean's clocked off, emerged into the light. The sky was white. The rain had stopped and there were puddles everywhere.

Albie sat in his usual seat on the top deck of the bus. He felt strange. Like he was being transformed. Only twenty-four hours ago he'd sat here. Same seat. Same bus, he recognised the graffiti on the back of the seat in front. RIGHTS FOR WHITES.

The Purvis Road interchange came up. He was back. Murderer always returns to the scene of the crime. There were bizzies all around. Stopping the cars in front, questioning people.

Damn. They were going to come up here.

He put his hand to his head, pulled the woollen hat down a bit lower. He was still in his work gear. Didn't look any different from usual. But his heart beat faster. No. He wasn't going to give himself away. Had to stay calm, keep it down. The anger.

The bus stopped, the engine stuttering to a halt. Albie heard the hiss as the doors opened. Then, coming up the stairs, the voice of a bizzie. Albie saw him in the mirror. Plain clothes, must be CID. Short fellow, balding, moustache. Irishman. Reckoned himself.

'Right, lads. I promise we won't keep you any longer than necessary but it's vital that we have a quick word with everyone on board. It's about a murder just across the road about this time yesterday morning. Can you all just stay in your seats until we've got round to you, OK?'

Albie thought fast. He couldn't let them speak to him. They had no evidence, no case against him. But the anger. He wanted to tell them, leap up, shout to the world what he'd done and why. Smash that Paddy's face in, wipe that important look off his face. To stop himself, he had to get off the bus.

The mirror on the stairs. It showed the door of the bus,

open, unobstructed. The copper must have gone up to the back seats.

Albie had to do it now. Had to move, or it was over. Over for the sake of one robbing Paki? No. There had to be more, he still had sorting to do.

He stood. Down the stairs. Off the bus. Into the street. Unchallenged. Yes, yes.

''Scuse me, sir.'

Albie turned. A copper, talking to three other blokes from the bus. He looked about fourteen.

'I've just seen your mate,' said Albie helpfully, pointing over his shoulder to the bus.

He walked away without looking back.

Bilborough had got about three hours' sleep. Showered, crept in to the bedroom, kissed Ryan on the forehead, set the alarm, climbed in next to Catriona. Fell asleep.

He was up and dressed before his wife and child had woken.

Today, he thought, I want to get this skinhead, whatever. I want to be back home tonight at a reasonable hour, not stood in Purvis Road again trying to keep the peace. They needed more of an idea about the bloke.

Nolan was waiting with Penhaligon at the shop. Nothing had been touched. Ali's daughter, Razia, had been staying with her family in a friend's home. She'd opened the place up for them, and slipped behind the counter. Bilborough couldn't bear to look at her eyes. They accused everyone.

Penhaligon was standing very upright. Trying not to look tired. Her eyes were fixed on Nolan. Willing him to be of use, to wipe their doubts away. To be better than Fitz, to make them wonder why they had ever been impressed by that seedy individual. Bilborough could tell at a glance her wish wasn't going to be fulfilled. Subconsciously, he realised that he must have been expecting another Fitz, and there was no way those methods were going to be duplicated. Nolan was older, a real academic, right down to the leather elbows on his tweed jacket. He spoke like a scientist from the Open University. Bilborough imagined him twenty years ago. His beard would have been massive, a big knot in the wide purple tie below.

He blinked owlishly around at the shelves of magazines, noted the number sprayed on the fridge, nodded and tugged his chin.

After they had been introduced, Bilborough asked, 'Have you got anything for us, sir?'

Nolan viewed him pettishly. 'Psychological profiling isn't a science, you know.' His vowels were clipped. He'd never gambled and he drank two gin and tonics a week at most, Bilborough reckoned.

'I'm aware of that, sir. I'd just like to know if you've reached any conclusions.'

Nolan nodded. 'Nothing stolen, so I'd say yes, you're right to consider a racist motive.' His nod became more enthusiastic. He wanted them to know he really knew what he was talking about. 'It's a classic disorganised murder. The pattern always makes itself clear.'

Penhaligon asked, 'So what do you reckon we're looking for?'

Nolan smiled at her. 'I'd say he's white, unskilled, unemployed, possibly a member of a far right extremist group –'

Penhaligon interrupted him. 'A football supporter, and he lives local.'

Nolan looked at her curiously. 'Yes.'

The cat woke Albie. She leapt on to his bed and scratched at his shirt until he stirred. Her eyes were huge and yellow, she was swaying from side to side. She looked different. A line of foam had dried over her mouth and nose. Heck. She'd had the kittens and he'd slept right through it. It was nearly five. Gone feeding time.

She led him down the stairs, one of her back legs buckling each step she took. She must have climbed up like that, hobbled up. For the sake of her young.

In the kitchen she went straight to her basket. The kittens were tiny, fluff-covered balls, eyes glued together. Pearl-white fangs were visible through their sighing mouths. Albie had planned to have the cat doctored. Him and Dad couldn't afford to keep kittens, even for a short while until they found homes. He'd planned to drown them. One look at them and he knew he'd never do it.

He knelt down and looked closer. 'Mum's going to need feeding, isn't she?' he whispered to the kittens. 'She's going to need a rest.' He felt daft, talking like that. But nature could get him like that. Without humans on it the planet would be a great place.

He fed the cat and turned on the radio. Always listened to the news, liked to keep himself informed. There was some load of crap about protesters and a motorway. Then they started talking about him, what he had done.

'Manchester police have now called in a psychologist to help them in the hunt for the murderer of shopkeeper Shahid Ali yesterday. Earlier today he spoke to Jill Duggan . . .'

A psychologist. Albie laughed. He was keeping people busy. Making them earn their pennies for once.

'Professor Nolan, can you give us a clearer idea of your co-operation with the police?'

'Well, psychological profiling isn't an exact science, it would be wrong for the police to think it is. And they don't of course.' Albie smiled. The bloke sounded a right prat. Was he the best the police could do? Had they put him on the radio to try and scare him?

'All we can say,' the psychologist continued, 'is that probably he's white, unskilled, unemployed –'

The smile dropped from Albie's face. The bastard. The patronising bastard.

'– possibly a member of a far right extremist group.'

Albie poured the cat's milk. The liquid slopped around the saucer as his hand shook. This was worse than Moody. This bloke was worse because the bugger wasn't even thinking about it, wasn't actively trying to destroy people, keep them down, slur them. He was just trotting it out, repeating the lies. In his ivory tower, at the unibloodyversity. He was probably paid ten quid a frigging hour to come up with this sort of tenuous crap.

'The bayonet's interesting, of course. It suggests he might be ex-army, a survivalist, in which case he'd keep himself fit. Sport, then, football, especially –'

The rest was lost to Albie. He screwed up his face, kicked the fridge, swore loudly. Football supporter equals white equals Nazi equals dolescrounger equals lazy drop-out murdering scum. That's what they expected, what Professor Nolan of Salford University expected.

If he expected it, that's what he was going to get.

Back to the newsroom. 'There were angry scenes at Westminster today as local MPs rallied against a report based on DTI figures that, said one MP, seems to brand northerners as workshy scroungers –'

Albie switched it off, put his coat and hat on, went out. Down the empty street, to the phone box. Directory enquiries. Salford University Psychology Department. He rang the number, the blood roaring in his ears. He kicked the side of the box. Had to keep his voice calm. Nice accent. Lovely southern accent.

The department secretary. Department of bullshit. Excuse me, I've lost my timetable. Just moved house, don't know where I've put it. Don't want to miss my lecture with Dr Nolan. Hold on, love, she'd have a look. Here we are, dear. Tomorrow, ten o'clock, the main lecture theatre, the Kenneth McKay building. Super, lovely, thank you.

Thank you for your information.

Nolan's description fitted neatly over the names of thirty-five of the forty-two fascists on Penhaligon's priority list. Of those, twenty-two had solid alibis. Most of them still lived with their parents. Out of the others, six weren't even skinheads. Another three were women. None of the rest lived anywhere near Purvis Road.

It was all too easy, she thought. If she'd given it the thought she would have come up with the same profile as Nolan. She'd chosen him, he'd failed her.

Which meant that Fitz was right.

She put that thought right to the back of her head.

The day passed uneventfully. No more leads, no breakthroughs. Bilborough had given Beck another mission to try and patch things up, sent him round to talk to the big four suspects. Nothing came of it. Skelton and Harriman spent most of the day answering calls and staring at that number, 9615489, putting it through every test they could think of.

Back to the flat, then. Penhaligon was leaving the car park when a monster appeared from behind a pillar. A crumpled bloated monster in a crumpled raincoat. She put her foot on the brake. The monster threw itself in front of the car.

She wound the window down. 'Piss off, Fitz.'

'The professor's a prick, Panhandle,' he shouted.

'It takes one to know one.' She revved the engine.

He confronted her, thrusting his huge face into hers. 'You'd be better off getting one of the Nolan sisters to do you a profile.'

'I said piss off.'

'The killer's not on the dole,' he said urgently. 'You're not up and about at half seven if you're unemployed –'

He was right. The truth shone out of him, light escaping from a black hole. It was so unfair. 'Come near me again and I'll arrest you.' She closed the window.

'I don't think he lives local. There's plenty of housing around there, yeah, but –'

She drove away, swinging out of the car park at sixty. No, she thought. He wasn't coming back. He might be a genius, he was also a git. She was going to shut him from her mind.

Fitz had decided to take the direct approach. Panhandle was taking longer than he'd expected to crack, but all the signs were there. He knew her, she knew him. Nolan was going to get them nowhere, they'd realise that soon enough. Fitz had met the guy a few times. A fine academic, perhaps, but no imagination. Could only see what was there in front of him, couldn't work backwards, start from what was missing. He probably wrote brilliant essays, had a lovely speaking voice. It wasn't enough. And he had a bloody ugly wife.

He wasn't giving up on today yet. He'd woken at four to an empty house, heard Nolan on the news and come rushing right down. Bilborough next? Walk in through the front door, spell out the situation? No, better to press on the weak link, sneak in the tradesman's entrance, creep up the back passage.

Beck. The pub.

Fitz walked up to the bar, surveyed the rows of upturned bottles. He looked about casually as he waited to be served. No sign of Beck. Standing next to him at the bar was a young chap. Didn't look old enough to get served. Of course. Last night, the taxi. Excellent prospects here.

'You're one of Big Chief Bilborough's Indians, yeah?' Fitz asked politely.

The lad turned to look at him, startled. 'No.'

The barmaid approached. 'Pint of bitter.' Keeping off the shorts for a while. He asked the lad, 'And you?'

'No,' said the lad. Fitz smiled. He'd heard the accent, seen the suit. He was really very young. A very young policeman. What does a very young policeman, right at the bottom of the heap, want to do?

'Would you like to impress your boss?' he asked.

'No.'

Fitz was getting angry. He shouldn't have been reduced to this. He had to get in now, quick, to make his point. 'There are questions so obvious nobody bothers to ask them. Why did the apple fall? Newton worked backwards. It fell because something pulled it down.'

He leaned closer. 'If a killer's on the dole, what's he doing up and about at half past seven?'

The kid's eyeballs rolled.

Fitz paid for his drink, sat down, gulped it down in three, and walked out. Operation Trojan Horse. Mission accomplished.

Penhaligon was back at the incident room for nine. Bilborough wanted to get an overview, which was fair enough. A brainstorming session. She watched him as he came out of his office, passing his signed football from hand to hand. Football supporter, Nolan's profile had said. Bilborough didn't like that, she could tell. Again, too obvious, the sort of assumption made by somebody who'd never been to a game in their life, who'd never felt that bond and known it was a good thing.

His eye had been caught by the board on which Skelton had been trying another code grid on the number. I F A E D H I. Skelton shrugged. ' "If" made sense.' Hopeless.

'Did you see the daughter?' Bilborough asked Skelton. Razia had made it known that she considered Nolan and their investigation a waste of time.

Skelton nodded. 'I went over tonight, yeah. I saw an old Asian geezer, well respected. He's having a word, going to tell her to leave it to us.'

'Right.' He turned to Beck. 'A British Army bayonet?'

Beck shook his head. 'Ex-army shops, done them all. Nothing worth following up.'

Penhaligon noticed Harriman, who was squirming in his seat as if he had piles. He kept licking his lips. He looked for all the world as if he was going to put his hand up. Something about this made her tense.

She became aware that Bilborough was staring at her, asking for her contribution. 'Survivalist magazines,' she said. 'He might subscribe. I thought if I ring round –'

Harriman interrupted her. 'I think the professor's a prick, boss. If the killer's on the dole, what's he doing up at half past seven?'

Penhaligon froze. Oh God.

'And yeah, he might live local,' said Harriman, his delivery speeding up as if he expected to be silenced at any moment, 'there's a lot of houses around there. But it's a busy crossroads. He could've been on his way to work, changing buses, anything.'

Impeccable logic far beyond the grasp of Harriman.

'This prof, he's heard the word skinhead and he's jumped to conclusions. We all have.'

Bilborough was nodding. It looked like his estimation of Harriman was rising. Out of the mouths of babes and sucklings, et cetera. It fell to her to bring him back to earth.

'And how was Fitz?' she asked Harriman.

'Come again?'

'I said, how was Fitz?'

Harriman looked around at them, confused. Bilborough and Beck both looked at the floor.

'Who's Fitz?' asked Harriman.

After work, Albie got himself ready. Got the bayonet and the spray can, fed the cat, checked on the kittens, put his gear on, popped the hat on his head, took the bus to the university.

He'd always hated students. They were given a privilege and treated it like a holiday, didn't care about learning, just needed to fill up three years pissing about. He followed them into the lecture hall, sat at the back. He listened to their voices, a reedy babble of middle-class southern accents. Thought it was cool to be in Manchester, didn't they. No bleeding talent or creativity in their own poxy backyard so they came and leeched off it up here.

Nolan got started right on time. Yes, very efficient, thought Albie. Beard clipped just right, hanky creased and folded in his top pocket, all his notes and slides arranged just so. The lights went off. Nolan's subject: 'The disorganised killing, which I know has been in the news just lately.' Polite laughter. Ha ha, sir's been on the radio.

Nolan had a collection of slides of murder scenes. All neatly catalogued, Albie was sure. Sick man. He clicked the wheel along, giving a commentary. The students were trying to write down every word he said. Spoonfed, they could never think for themselves.

'The disorganised killer doesn't choose his victims, doesn't hide the body and usually walks to the scene or takes public transport. Much more environmentally friendly than his organised counterpart.'

More laughter. But you're wrong, pal. Way off. I chose Ali. I wanted the body to be seen for a reason. Put that through your computer, feed it some reality.

Another slide. A doomed, ugly face. Mug shot. Staring eyes. 'He'll probably be unattractive, often with low self-esteem. Sexually impotent, so he invariably lives alone.'

Wrong again, Professor. I was married, I've got a kid. I had the choice of women 'cause I wasn't thick, I listened, I cared. Until bastards like you took that away from me, until you showed me that was pointless.

'In many cases he'll have had a harsh childhood, an alcoholic or violent father.'

No. No. My father fought for your sort. Fought for this shitheap, fought for your right to stand up there and talk bollocks. No.

'He'll often take something from the scene. As a souvenir. But it's likely to be a part of the body rather than a stick of rock.' Nolan clicked to his next slide. A woman's body, thrown back, her belly slashed open, her skirt ripped up and over her legs. Albie couldn't look. Nolan, the sick man. He got his kicks out of this, probably wanked himself silly over it.

'If there's sexual abuse of the victim, it will take place after death. Nearly all of these killers have themselves been victims of child abuse, usually at the hands of their violent or drunken fathers.'

Albie forced down the anger. Not yet, he told himself. Save it, save it.

He slipped out of the lecture hall. Nobody saw him. Right. Outside, in the empty lobby, there was a floorplan of the building. Staff offices, downstairs. Right.

The place was almost empty. Albie locked himself in the toilet downstairs. He sat on the bog, put his head in his hands. Disorganised killer. He'd seen organised killing with his own eyes, an organised massacre. And those responsible for it? They'd retire on a huge pension, drink themselves to death on it, get knighted. And nobody called them what they were, nobody could see it.

He was going to make it clear.

He waited until he heard movement, the students leaving the lecture hall and coming downstairs. He slipped out of the toilet, followed the long white empty corridor to Nolan's office, right at the end. Perfect.

There was music coming from the office. Albie walked in, found the stacked CD player, turned up the volume.

Nolan was using a photocopier on the other side of the room, holding up the lid to turn pages of a book. Humming along to the music. He sensed Albie's presence, whirled round.

He blinked. 'Who are you?'

Albie gestured to his gear. 'What do I look like?'

Nolan was still unsure of him. He sighed. Thought this was a student prank. Kidnapped again for Rag Week, eh, Prof? Wrong, Prof. 'What do you want?'

'What do I look like?' Albie raised his voice. 'Come on, there's only the two of us. What do I look like? What do I sound like? *Sun* reader, fascist, football supporter, hooligan, yeah?'

Nolan put down his copies. 'Would you please tell me what you're doing in this office?'

Albie nodded to the stereo. 'This is Beethoven, right? Sonata number fourteen in C sharp minor, otherwise known as the Moonlight Sonata, yeah?'

'Yes.' Impatient. A bit confused, surprised. Not such a thick scally after all.

It's time.

Albie pulled out the bayonet. Yes! That look on Nolan's face was sweet. It felt like the best moment in Albie's life. Finally getting something done. Sorting things.

'This was my father's. He fought for this country. Africa, Egypt, France, Italy. He died a week ago, and there was only ten people at his funeral.'

Nolan was still, his mouth hung open. Yes!

'D'you know why there was only ten people at his funeral? 'Cause he was only a white working-class man so he didn't matter. He didn't bleeding matter!'

Nolan's eyes were fixed on the bayonet. 'I'm sorry,' he said.

'You're *sorry*?' Albie screeched.

'Yes,' said Nolan.

'You're sorry . . .' Albie shook his head. 'I was gonna kill a *Sun* reporter. I *am* gonna kill a *Sun* reporter. But meanwhile you'll do.'

Easier this time. The blade just slid in, hot knife through butter. Beautiful. Easy.

Nolan fell on to the photocopier. His face was pressed against the copying glass, blood flowing from his mouth. The weight of his body slumped against the copying controls. The green light flashed again. Sheets of paper shot into the copy tray.

PAPER JAM. The message came up on the inbuilt screen. PLEASE CLOSE COPIER LID.

Albie cleaned his blade, sprayed the number. Then he took a souvenir, and walked out of the building.

Albie tacked up his souvenirs to the living room wall. The picture of Ali from the front of the paper. One of the photocopies, Nolan's squashed dead face, the blood trickle smeared across the glass.

No going back.

He went to the crib board. Lit the second match in the line of ninety-six.

He blew it out.

FOUR

The builders put down their tools and stared as Fitz entered the bathroom, pulled down his fly and started to urinate, whistling 'Ramblin' Rose' all the while.

'It's all right, mate, we'll wait outside,' said the gaffer.

'Oh, no, no,' said Fitz. 'Think of yourselves as part of the furniture. I do. You've spent more time in this house in the last four months than my own son, after all. Why be shy?'

'Look, we're on the home strait, we've almost –'

'As I say, if me or my wife or any of my family fancy the occasional dump, I wouldn't want you to feel embarrassed.' He shook, tidied himself away, and looked at his watch. 'Heavens, is that the time?'

Local news time. Time to catch up on the latest stages of the investigation. They'd be having a great time, questioning all the wrong people and asking them all the wrong questions. The Keystone Kops and their new colleague the nutty professor.

'Police have named the victim as Professor William Nolan, a criminal psychologist at Salford University,' the television reported.

Well, goodness me.

'Professor Nolan had in fact been working with police investigating the murder of Shahid Ali, a local shopkeeper.'

Hadn't he just. Fitz smiled. Somebody had a grudge. Somebody didn't want to be written off as an unskilled, unemployed football hooligan with far right sympathies. He'd gone for Nolan. It made sense. It made perfect sense with Fitz's theories. Now Panhandle would realise.

Another face on the screen. A woman in her early fifties. Her face was cracked with pain and grief. Fitz recognised her. Nolan's wife.

'My husband lived for two things.' Her voice was breaking. Flashbulbs popped in her face. The camera zoomed right in, yes, extract maximum impact, capture that pain, give it to us. 'He lived for his work and his family.' The picture wobbled slightly as the camera operator stumbled and tried to get even closer. 'He wouldn't harm a fly.' She was crying now. 'I'd like to meet whoever killed my husband and ask them,' tears running down, capture them on tape, 'why?'

Back to the studio. Newscaster, serious face, tactfully raised eyebrow. 'The widow of Professor Nolan.'

Fitz felt the guilt. He'd heard of the death of another human being. And he'd loved it, just for a moment. Relished the destruction of a life, a murder, because it made things easier for him, was probably going to get him closer to gaining a bit of self-actualisation.

Fitz stood. It was time to forget the personality, cast aside the self, as far as he could. He was a resource, and one that was needed desperately, because as sure as eggs is eggs that feller was going to kill again.

Bilborough watched Jarvis and his chum having a good fuss over Nolan's body. 'Yes, very similar wound, bayonet again!' Jarvis cried over to Bilborough, thumb up. 'It's definitely "him".'

'I'd gathered that.' Bilborough turned to the display board of the office. 9615489 had been sprayed red, in an upward-slanting line, over a timetable and some pinned-up seminar notes. Essay titles. 'The disorganised killer's attempts to justify his killing conceal a frustrated desire for self-expression. Discuss.'

Penhaligon sat in Nolan's chair, looking out into the

quadrangle. Bilborough stared over her shoulder. The students were a damn sight better behaved than the residents of Purvis Road, and had scuttled back to their halls of residence as soon as the police turned up. The air was thick with fear. Music carried across from the jukebox in the students' union bar. Somebody had been unable to resist. Talking Heads, 'Psycho Killer'.

Bilborough spoke softly. 'Jane, I know it was you who involved him, but –'

Her head whipped up. 'I wasn't thinking about that at all.'

A ridiculous picture entered Bilborough's mind. Fitz, setting it all up, sending some skinhead to kill Ali, then Nolan. Certainly things couldn't have worked out better for Fitz. They were going to have to call him.

The phone rang. Harriman answered, passed the line to Bilborough. 'Chief Super wants a word, boss.'

Bilborough took the phone. He didn't need this. He wanted to put the phone down, put the whole thing down, let Penhaligon and Fitz and Beck get on with it. Just get in the car and get home. He fought that down. In a few days they'd have the bastard and that'd be it. Then there'd be time to think. 'Yes, sir.'

'What now?' Two flat syllables. Not enough the usual pretence of good humour. This isn't going to look very good for any of us.

Bilborough was aware of the sudden hush in the room. He watched as Jarvis picked up one of the photocopies with a plastic-gloved hand and shook his head from side to side like a bemused pixie. 'We'll get all the evidence we can and we'll assess it, sir.'

'You haven't got a clue.'

'I didn't say that, sir.' Bilborough's eyes flicked over to the display board, caught the number again. 'We're going to gather all the information and reassess the situation.'

'A university. A university is an intimidating place. It's full of people. But he attended a bloody lecture, walked right through the place, and killed a white academic. Do you still think he's just a yob?'

'No, we don't, sir.'

'So your line of enquiry's been totally wrong?'

'It looks that way, sir.'

A long pause. For a moment Bilborough thought the Chief was going to hang up. 'I'll see you later.' End of call.

Bilborough turned to Penhaligon. Her eyes widened. She could tell what was coming. But there were going to be no arguments. There was a job to do, they were paid to do it, end of debate. That was what he was trying to convince himself, anyway, but there was a sick taste in his mouth as he told her, 'Get Fitz. I'll see him in the nick,' and left the silent room.

Her footsteps echoed behind him as he marched down the corridor, shoulders down. 'I'm sorry, sir, I can't do that.'

He didn't look round. 'Get Fitz. It's an order, Jane.'

'I don't care.'

Bilborough turned. That was what she'd been thinking about just now. Not Nolan, stabbed and lying half-in half-out of a photocopier. Fitz. It hadn't even been her Fitz had insulted directly. He'd been the one to suffer that, and if he was prepared to forget it, why couldn't she?

Unless there was something else going on.

'I'm disobeying you,' she said. A casual pronouncement. She'd rehearsed that.

He opened the nearest door, grabbed her by the shoulder, and guided her in. A small lecture room, chairs stacked neatly. A poster of Anthony Hopkins as Hannibal Lecter by the window.

'Right. Tell me everything.'

'It's a private matter,' she said coolly.

'It's not private any more.'

He'd never seen her behave like this. She looked at the ceiling. Behind the truculence there was a glimpse of something else, the response she was trying to conceal. It wasn't anger.

'It won't go any further. Did he try something on?'

That affected her. She laughed and played with her hair, gritted her teeth. That was it, thought Bilborough. The woman was deeply embarrassed. She had reason to be if she'd had some sort of fling with Fitz. The bloke was hardly Richard Gere.

'I didn't go on holiday with Peter,' she said. 'I didn't go on holiday with anyone, in fact. I know what I said. "Me and Peter did this, me and Peter did that." I spent the entire holiday on my own. Apart from two nights with a Greek waiter.' She smiled. 'I liked his kebabs.'

'What's it got to do with Fitz?'

'Fitz was supposed to meet me at the airport. He didn't show up.'

Bilborough kept his face still. His mind ticked over, matching all her reactions over the past few days to this information. She'd had Nolan ready and waiting in the wings, just waiting for him to give her the word. One of her talents, to anticipate.

She only looked at him.

Harriman burst in. 'There's a bloke on the phone, boss. Keeps asking to speak to you.'

Bilborough waved him away. 'Right. I won't be a second.'

Harriman's bright eyes shone. His beaky nose twitched. Seeking new gossip, wanting to be in on things. Bilborough waved him away again. 'Off you pop, OK? Don't go blabbing to any journalists.'

The remark took the glint from Harriman's eyes. He went.

Bilborough turned back to Penhaligon. Why was she so worried about this business with Fitz? 'Well. Is that it?'

'Yes.' But there was plenty more, he knew. Much unspoken denigration, chinks in her self-image.

'You feel humiliated? It would be embarrassing to have to ask for his help?'

'Yes.'

He nodded. 'Fair enough. But what's your embarrassment compared to the grief that two families are feeling?' And, he reflected, that embarrassment stopped me calling Fitz in first of all. It led to Nolan's death and she doesn't care about that, has to keep herself intact at all costs.

'That's not fair,' she said. 'It is not fair. If you feel so strongly about it, sir, why don't you ask him?'

Bilborough shrugged. 'If I ask, he'll refuse.'

She shook her head.

He altered his tone without thinking, converted his request, professional to personal. We're really in trouble, Jane. The Chief Super is on my back. I've got Catriona, Ryan, to think about. 'Please.'

Her face screwed up. It had to be done.

They left the room. Harriman was outside. He took a short breath and the words flowed. 'Sir, I made a mistake. I've had my bollocking and it won't happen again, I promise you, so can I ask you to forget about it now, sir?'

Penhaligon walked away.

Bilborough blinked. 'OK.'

'Thanks, boss.' Harriman pointed down the corridor. 'That bloke's still on the phone, sir. He says you know him. Fitzgerald.'

Fitz sat in Bilborough's office, fag in mouth, cup of tea in hand, attempting to keep his face as still as possible. Faces in the incident room, peering in. No point in crowing, he'd decided, could be counter-productive. He'd try the genuine approach, which'd be difficult, he didn't have much experience.

Panhandle was first in. Her eyes flicked over his head and for a moment he thought she wasn't even going to register his presence. Then she pulled a file from her desk and handed it to him as if it was a ticking bomb.

Photographs of Shahid Ali's body, his shop. Fitz took in every detail. That number, 9615489. 'I think I owe you an explanation,' he said quietly.

'Think again.'

Very direct. Not like Judith. Panhandle was already up the emotional ladder, at the summit.

'An apology, then.'

'You owe me nothing.'

He itched to make a joke. Play it genuine, he reminded himself. Tell the truth for once, this is important. 'My life's a bit of a mess at the moment.'

'I had a wonderful time, Fitz,' she said brightly. 'I met a waiter with a nice little bum and a fetish for yoghurt. You've nothing whatsoever to apologise for.'

He doubted that. She wasn't that cool. 'Tell me about Nolan. The same?'

'Pretty much. Some of the students saw the killer at Nolan's lecture this morning. Wearing a woolly hat. Beck's putting the photofit together with them now. We'll have it for the evening news. Nolan was killed in his office, the killer just walked in and stabbed him.'

Fitz tapped his chin. 'He left the number again?'

'Yes.'

'Right. Anything else?'

'Nolan's body. He pushed it into the photocopier. Made copies of the face.'

'How many?'

'About ten.'

'He'll have taken one of those,' Fitz said, nodding.

101

'Wouldn't have been able to resist it. He'll have it pinned up on his wall.'

Bilborough entered, walking very fast. He nodded to Fitz without meeting his gaze and started to go through his desk. A reaction Fitz might have expected. Confront a difficult situation, any kind of irregularity, and just soldier on, keep working, don't stop to consider.

'Jane'll take you down to the university,' he said. 'We've got the whole of the psychology department cordoned off so you can have a good look round.'

Fitz forgot the genuine approach. It was time to expose a bit of truth. He'd forgotten how much Bilborough's methods irritated him. 'Busy?' he asked.

Bilborough started sifting through files, still not looking up. 'Very. Is there anything else you need?'

Fitz sat forward. 'There's a man called Cassidy doing life for a crime he didn't commit.'

'I'm not getting into it, Fitz. Is there anything else you need?'

'Oh, yes, keep busy. It stops you thinking. Stops your conscience pricking, eh?'

Bilborough straightened and raised his eyes. He looked tired. 'My conscience is fine. I'm getting a slight pain in the arse but that's all.' He gestured to the door. 'I did my job, Fitz. The job I'm paid to do. Now, is there anything else you need?'

Fitz's temper pushed him on. He'd decided that he wasn't going to do this, and here he was, doing it, trying to get himself kicked out again before he'd even got halfway through the door. 'You did your job?'

'That's what I said, Fitz.'

Fitz sniffed. 'What's that smell? Ah yes, gas ovens, six million corpses, people doing their jobs.' He stood. 'There is something else I need. A promise. We are going to seek truth. We are going to see justice done. Good old-fashioned

British justice, where a man's innocent until proven Irish, all right? Justice, not a bloody result on your record.'

'I'm going to do my job, all right,' said Bilborough. 'And my job is to gather evidence and hand it over. So that's what I'm going to do.'

'Tell me something,' said Fitz. 'Do you sleep at nights?'

'Like a log.'

'You can close the door on the world, can't you? Just you, the wife, and the baby. The sewers are overflowing –'

Bilborough's eyes flashed and he strutted forward. Raised a finger. That'd got him. 'You leave my family out of this!'

'The sewers are overflowing, there's filth bubbling up your path, but you've got sandbags out and all's right with the world. Everything clean and dry inside –'

Bilborough pushed his face in close. 'Stop it there, OK? Just stop it there.'

Fitz stopped. Gone too far? No. He'd needed to get that aired, express it. Better out than in. He calmed himself.

'Will you give us a minute, Jane?' asked Bilborough. She'd been observing the little row, Fitz realised, without giving any sort of reaction. She nodded and made for the door.

'What did he do, by the way?' Fitz asked her.

'I'm sorry?'

'Your waiter friend. With his yoghurt.'

No reaction. She left the room.

Fitz turned back to Bilborough, spread his arms wide and smiled. Bilborough had come even closer. Keeping his voice low, he snarled. 'Right, Fitz. My turn in the pulpit now. You leave her alone.'

So Panhandle had talked. Most unexpected. Although what concern it was of Bilborough's he couldn't fathom. Unless, of course, there was some sort of repressed rumbling of the gonads between them.

'It's nothing to do with you,' he told Bilborough.

'Listen, you brought my wife and child into this so shut up and listen. If you hurt that woman again, Fitz –'

So she had blabbed. But only under orders, he would have guessed. There'd probably been a touching little stolen moment when all was confessed. It was nice to have it confirmed that he *had* hurt her, anyway.

'Yeah, she'd told me everything, but it won't go any further. If you hurt that woman again, you'll be walking round on crutches.'

Fitz decided to smile and brazen it out. He wasn't going to respond in kind to any display of male aggression for a while, at least until his nose stopped feeling sore.

'OK,' he said mildly. 'I can take a hint.'

Albie still wasn't able to sleep. There was too much going round in his head, so he took himself over to the allotment and had a look around. The first time he'd been back since Dad had died. The first time he'd been back after killing Ali and Nolan.

He had a look at the houses over the road. The allotment was at the bottom of a small valley, and the houses opposite were stacked in rising lines, leading to the city. He'd looked over there so many times, and stood here with Dad before he'd got too sick to come. All of the houses were the same. It was only him that had changed.

Keeping busy was a good idea. Might even tire himself out a bit. He found a seedling tray in the allotment shed and started laying out the contents, carefully scooping each small plant out and positioning it along the line, just so. Everything he did now felt different, much more significant. He wasn't just a bloke in his dad's allotment, there was a lot more to him now. He'd proved it.

He finished his task and shook out the compost left in the tray. Something caught his eye. A simple design, white letters on red. The tray was lined with a copy of the *Sun*.

Four million homes took that in every day. He was just one man. But he could make a difference.

Ali, Nolan. And Moody. She'd got away from him. He hadn't thought about her for a few hours, was going to save her for tomorrow. But if he couldn't sleep, and there was a job to be done, why not?

And somebody that predictable, that pathetic, was going to be easy to get alone.

He got his stuff and walked towards home, stopping at the first phone box on the way. He'd decided where and how he was going to kill her. But what would really get her going, what would get those journalistic juices flowing?

He got through to the office. Was she in? Yes.

'Clare Moody.' That voice, so full of herself, so proud of her lies.

He had to make sure, feed the anger. 'Do you still work for the *Sun*?'

'Who's speaking?'

'I can't tell you that.'

She could sense something, those instincts were sharp. 'I work for them now and again, yeah. I'm a freelance.'

'Could you sell them a story?'

'That depends what it is.'

Albie gripped the phone tight, whispered, 'A Labour MP. He's into little boys.'

'Can you prove it?'

'I've got pictures.'

It was working. Her voice raised in pitch, a piglet's squeal. 'Can we meet?'

'Half four this afternoon. Mill Road car park. Top floor. Stay in your car.'

He went to put the phone down. 'Wait,' he heard her say. 'How will I know you?'

Albie smiled. 'I'll know you.'

Easy. He was going to do another one, two in a day.

Moody might even make it to the late edition of tonight's evening papers.

Fitz had decided to start at the shop, where the killer had started. Penhaligon, still tight-lipped, had driven him over without once looking at him. She'd declined his offer of a mint.

'They're a minty bit stronger,' he'd said. 'I won't buy the others. Where there should be a mint there's just a hole. And they expect us to applaud the fact.'

A couple of minutes had passed, Penhaligon's eyes fixed on the road ahead, Fitz looking about, shuffling in the passenger seat, his huge legs crammed right up against the dashboard. 'Is there any way of moving this chair back?' he asked, straining to reach underneath for a lever.

No response. 'In any case, I'm a cruncher,' he'd gone on.

'I know. You crunch your sherbet lemons. Instant gratification.'

Telling. She noticed those minor details about him, remembered them and importantly drew conclusions. Now, you only do that about the eight most important people in your life, Fitz knew. First-year textbook stuff.

Ali's daughter Razia was waiting for them at Purvis Road. Fitz noted the abundance of police cars and uniforms in the area.

Razia led them through into the back room. The afternoon sun peeked through closed curtains, the room was spotless. A purple rug, bookcases. Ali's wife was sitting on the sofa facing Fitz and Penhaligon. She nodded to them and smiled her plea. Just to find the killer, so we can have peace.

Razia was keeping a lot down, Fitz could tell. There was a lot of certainty about her expression, which was a bad sign for the investigation. He needed her to be honest, not to victimise herself and obscure the issue. That was a racist thought, he reminded himself. White honesty, police honesty, meant Bilborough handing over his files like a good boy, Cassidy serving life.

He devised a tactic. Razia needed to know him better, see how he thought. Appreciate his value as a resource, the best way she'd find of getting her revenge.

'We've been attacked dozens of times by skinheads and you've never lifted a finger,' she was saying to Penhaligon. 'Once our people attack them you swamp the area with police.'

'It's for your own protection,' Penhaligon said levelly.

'I don't believe you.'

Fitz was watching her mother's eyes, flicking back nervously to her daughter. She shook her head, a very small gesture, the sort of thing that made him despair for humanity's cruelty and admire its capacity for forgiveness. The woman muttered to her daughter in their own language. Gentle words.

'Your mother wants you to help us,' said Penhaligon. Fitz was glad of that heavy-handedness, he'd come over better for that.

'Do you speak Urdu?' Razia's eyelids flicked impatiently. 'Actually, she wants me to throw you out.'

'You're lying,' said Fitz.

Razia ran a hand through her hair. Fitz tried to trace that resentment. It had been heightened by the murder of her father, but it wasn't a new feeling. Yes, there was the oppression, the racism, the abuse, but there was something else in the way she was reacting. A kind of disappointment. She'd been there and back.

'I'd like you to leave, please,' she said.

Fitz kept his voice calm. 'I understand why you're lying. I understand your anger and your grief.'

'I'd like you to go, please.'

'I'll let you into a secret, shall I?' He pointed to himself. 'Me, I'm a racist.'

Razia didn't flinch. She really thought she had the measure of him.

Fitz turned to Penhaligon. 'And what about you, Pan-handle? Are you a racist?'

'No.'

'Oh really?' Fitz leaned closer. He took no pleasure in disquieting her, he found, rather surprising himself. 'Your history's white, your language is white, your culture's white, your job's white, but you're impervious to all that. All those influences, Panhandle, and they've had no effect on you whatsoever. Is that what you're saying?'

'Yes,' she replied, more patiently than if they'd been alone.

'You're lying.' He turned to Razia, who was standing now, glaring down at him. 'All whites are inherently racist, yes?'

She nodded. 'Am I supposed to find you impressive?'

Razia was already a better psychologist than Nolan had been, thought Fitz. 'You're supposed to say you'll help us to catch the man who killed your father.'

'*We'll* catch him. We'll get justice for my father.' She pointed to the door. 'Leave.'

There was nothing left to use but the truth. 'Have you had many white boyfriends, Razia?'

She snarled, leapt for the phone.

'They'd all of them be white at first, wouldn't they? Teenage rebellion and all that. They'd be sharp, political.' He got up, moved to stand beside her.

Razia picked up the phone, turned to Penhaligon. 'This is harassment. I'm phoning one of our own people, a lawyer. She'll be here in five minutes.' She began to dial.

Fitz tried to ignore the look that Penhaligon gave him as she walked past him and called, 'We're going.'

He carried on. 'Young socialists. Right on. The sad thing is, you'd be wanting to talk about Ryan Giggs, *Reservoir*

Dogs, Blur. They'd be wanting you to talk about "the black experience", wanting you to share it with them because that's switched on, that's trendy.'

It was working. She stopped dialling, turned to face him. She looked almost amused. Still a breakthrough.

'And it gets boring, doesn't it, Razia? And you start to think, he's with me 'cause I'm black, the racist bastard, he's with me for street cred. Pakistani boys in future.'

She put down the phone. 'You're nowhere near as good as you think you are. Police psychologist, are you?'

'I do work for the police, yes.' He glanced at Penhaligon. 'Occasionally, if they'll have me.'

Razia nodded. 'A maverick, a loner, they rely on you for a sideways approach to their problems, but resent your independence?'

'You could be right.'

She nodded to her mother, walked into the shop, beckoned them in. 'Or perhaps you make an impressive show. Make it look as if you're wonderful. I suppose the police may be stupid enough to be impressed by it. I'm not.'

'There's more to me than that.' Fitz replied.

'There's more to me than my white ex-boyfriends. So what have you got to offer?'

Fitz shrugged. 'Watch me.' He pointed to the number sprayed on the fridge door. 'That mean anything to you?'

Razia rolled her eyes. 'No.'

He spotted something interesting on one of the shelves. Nothing to do with the murder, but it brought back memories. A white plastic bottle with a cockroach printed on the side. 'Don't kill the cockroaches, Dad.' He'd been a strange lad, if Mark or Katie had kept on like that he'd have been worried.

Another look around. This skinhead character. Work backwards. The killer didn't like Nolan's profile, he really resented it, being written off as a thick skiving hooligan.

Hooligans do certain things, according to people like Nolan. The received wisdom, a skinhead enters a shop, kills the Asian shopkeeper. Skinheads drink lager, cause riots, are unemployed, identify themselves with the far right, and if they read a paper it's likely going to be the *Sun*.

Fitz had brought the photographs of the murder scene with him. He flicked them open, careful to keep them away from Razia. There, under Ali's head. A packet of cheap teabags, a copy of the *Guardian*.

Skinheads don't read the *Guardian*. It's the one thing you are not going to find them reading. Unskilled, unemployed football hooligans with fascist sympathies and the *Guardian* are two concepts that don't connect, it's absurd.

But the bloke that killed Nolan killed him precisely because Nolan had called him an unskilled, unemployed football hooligan. Had jumped to conclusions, written him off.

'What would it cost,' he asked Razia, 'the *Guardian* and a packet of this tea?' He took a box from the shelf behind the counter.

'Two pounds four pence,' she replied instantly.

Penhaligon was ahead of him. 'It's on the till roll, yes, but whoever bought them hasn't come forward.' She looked uncertainly at Razia before continuing, 'Earlier that morning Mr Ali was seen arguing with a man over the price of those items.'

Fitz waved an arm impatiently. 'A man, a man, what sort of man?'

'I'd have to check. But not a skinhead.'

'And he hasn't come forward?'

'No.' She was getting pissed off now. Never mind, he was getting to the truth now. He could scent it.

'Did the till balance?' he asked Razia.

'Yes, eventually. There was four pence on the floor, behind the counter. Where you're standing.' She was responding now, excellent.

Fitz considered. Two pounds and four pence. An argument between Ali and this mysterious man over the price of two pounds and four pence for the *Guardian* and a packet of teabags. He asked Razia, 'What sort of man was your father?'

That was a bad question. He'd been too hasty. 'I mean, was he an exact man?'

She replied firmly, but she was calmer now, on equal ground with him. 'You mean, please keep to the point. You haven't got the time or the patience to hear the good things about him, just the stuff that's relevant to his death.'

'You're right. I did mean that, and I'm sorry.'

Razia's head snapped up. 'You're sorry? That makes all the difference. My father's been killed, the man who brought me up, he's just been taken away, and you're *sorry*?'

She controlled herself with difficulty. 'My father was very exact. The till was always spot on. White people are thieves.'

Fitz blinked.

'They say they gave you a tenner when it was only a fiver. You've got to know exactly what you should have in the till.'

Bilborough took the photofit from Beck and flicked the folder open. The face could have belonged to an imp, an evil pixie. Small pointed ears, a frown, a face full of hate. Looked to be in his late twenties or early thirties. Beck leaned forward and slapped a plastic sheet over the face. A woolly hat appeared on the shaven head. It seemed to Bilborough that there was something important about that face. Nolan had been wrong, he didn't look like just a yob. The hate in that face, there was something else mixed up with it. Disappointment.

'It'll be up at the university by tonight, I can get it down Purvis Road tomorrow morning. And I've sent it over to the

111

telly,' said Beck. 'They say they want an interview as well.'

Bilborough nodded. 'I'll do it. Get Skelton to ring them, fix it up for about half four, OK?' He picked up the football from his desk, tossed it from hand to hand. He wanted this thing finished. Next Monday night, United at home to Liverpool. He had a ticket, he wanted it over by then.

Beck was hovering. 'Yes, Jimmy?'

'Getting Fitz in. You think that's a good idea?' There was no open aggression in the question. There'd been no open emotion in their dealings since the row.

Bilborough wanted to keep it that way. 'I had to do it, Jimmy. He might turn something up. Might. I don't think he's as brilliant as he thinks he is.' He might have added that he was already regretting the decision, that Fitz had already wound him up badly, within a minute of his return to Anson Road.

The door of the office burst open and Fitz burst in. His hands were tapping at his sides, he was taking deep drags on one of his cigarettes. He looked alive. He really got off on this, thought Bilborough. Reckoning himself, insulting people and their families, poking his nose in. Penhaligon trailed behind him. She kept her head down.

'You've got something for us?' Bilborough asked.

'Yes.' Fitz gestured with his cigarette, punching the air with tiny movements. 'On the floor behind Ali, the *Guardian* and a packet of teabags. Somebody bought them and walked out without them. An argument, a trauma.'

Bilborough felt his heart plummet. 'What?'

'An argument over the cost of the *Guardian* and a packet of teabags,' Fitz repeated.

'Bollocks,' said Beck.

Fitz opened up the folder of photographs, tapped the space behind Ali's head with a thick nicotine-yellow finger. 'Whoever bought the *Guardian* hasn't come forward. Why not?'

'That row was witnessed,' said Bilborough, not bothering to conceal his disappointment. 'He was an ordinary bloke, ordinary clothes, ordinary haircut. It's got nothing to do with the killing.'

'A load of bollocks,' said Beck.

Bilborough's irritation grew stronger. 'Jimmy, will you shut up.' Don't make it any worse. I'm responsible for encouraging this pillock, building him up in my mind. I don't need to be told.

'It's a load of bollocks,' Beck repeated.

'The bloke comes back with his four pence, throws it down, throws it over the counter.' Fitz jabbed his finger at Bilborough. 'Why didn't Ali pick it up? Because he was dead.'

Bilborough glanced at Penhaligon. She was staring right ahead, not looking at Fitz, not looking at him, not looking at anybody.

'He probably had a bad back,' he told Fitz. 'Fitz, we've got a description of the killer. He's a skinhead, for God's sake, a bloody skinhead. Not a bloody *Guardian* reader.'

Fitz looked almost manic, his eyes popping and rolling. 'There's a row. This *Guardian* reader, he goes home, broods a bit, shaves his head, comes right back, throws the fourpence at him, then stabs him. Right?'

'Bollocks,' said Beck.

'You need a Thesaurus,' Fitz told him. He wiped his sweating brow, looked expectantly at Bilborough. A middle-aged alcoholic wreck with a weight problem and an ego that needed bringing down.

'Are you on drugs?'

Fitz stubbed out his cigarette and immediately lit another. He was ignoring them, just kept talking. 'Yes, he could live local. But I think he was going to or coming from work. Purvis Road's a busy interchange, he was probably changing buses. If he was on his way to work you're looking for a small employer, no canteen, which is why he needed the tea.

If he was coming from work, you're talking shifts, that means a large employer. Also, if he was coming from work, then he lives alone.'

Bilborough looked at him blankly. He couldn't believe he was paying to hear this.

'The teabags again, I mean,' said Fitz. 'And if he lives alone he's separated from his family. Why? Because a single bloke with no responsibilities isn't going to be working a nightshift, eh?'

Bilborough had heard enough. He realised he was still holding the football. He put it down. 'It's guesswork, Fitz. I'm not prepared to spend time and money on guesswork.'

Fitz's eyebrows shot up. He pulled the cigarette from his mouth. 'You're throwing me out?'

'If I need you, I'll send for you,' Bilborough said patiently. 'If you think of anything, give us a ring. Meantime, goodbye.'

Fitz turned red. 'He went home, shaved his head, went back and killed him!'

'Goodbye, Fitz.'

Penhaligon wasn't showing any reaction. Beck was rearing up, fists clenching. Fitz made for the door, swearing under his breath.

'Fifty quid says I'm right. I'll give you odds, you windy bastard. Two to one. A ton to fifty, I'm right!'

He was gone.

Bilborough turned to the others. 'Jimmy, get that interview set up and see those pictures go up. Jane, I want you to go through that list again.'

'Start again?'

'Yes, start again. Find out where they were this morning, between 8.30 and 12.'

Externalise your feelings, Fitz told himself. Find a melancholy place that suits the way you feel, wait, let yourself burn out. They were going to call him back in soon enough. Over another dead body. Somebody was going to get killed, the skinhead *Guardian* reader with his trusty British Army bayonet was going to target another enemy. His opponents were just no match. Beck, the runt, Fitz would have bloodied his nose, risen to that, all right.

He counted his change. A couple of quid and some coppers jangling in the furry lining of his wallet, amongst the betting slips and receipts. He was walking somewhere, to the melancholy place his feet were dragging. Ah yes, aggression, despair, ennui. The wonderful pub at the end of the world, the home of the head-butt.

The place was worse than he remembered it. It proclaimed its greyness from every surface. Time had slowed right down here, frozen in the smudged ashtrays and bent-legged stools, the torn coasters. The jukebox was silent and Fitz's eyes were drawn to the television set. Richard had just rung the bell for the Countdown conundrum. Nariyreit.

'Itinerary,' Fitz boomed to get the barman's attention. His voice shook dust from the pumps.

'Yeah?' asked the barman.

Fitz played with the coins in his hand. 'What's a large scotch?'

'It's a well-known alcoholic drink.'

'Don't give up your day job.'

'One pound twenty,' said the barman. His face looked as if it was about to slide off his head.

'That's very reasonable,' Fitz remarked.

The barman reached for a dirty glass. 'That's because it's happy hour.'

The cerise Ford Escort arrived on the top floor of the Mill Road car park at exactly five. As Albie had planned, the place was empty. It was near Jill's place, near the flats. All the offices and factories round there had closed up years ago.

There were just two other cars parked on the top floor.

Albie hid behind a pillar. Two in a day. This was going to work. They were going to have a nice ride out to the suburbs, a little tour of all the pretty houses. More *Daily Mail* than *Sun*, really. And nobody about. A good place to be alone. To talk. Albie was going to make it even clearer this time.

He'd seen a headline on the way over, somebody reading the *Post* on the bus. PROFESSOR KILLED − SECOND SKINHEAD MURDER. He was going to change that headline, make it mean something.

She sat upright in the car, completely still. It was parked right in a corner, enabling her to see anybody that approached. Cautious, she was expecting the worst. She hadn't told anyone about this, was desperate for the sleaze, an addict, sick. Nothing she wrote or said meant anything to her, Albie knew. She'd probably already forgotten Shahid Ali. People meant nothing to her, she just wanted to make her name.

Albie walked out to the car. She noticed him, wound down her window ever so slightly.

'Clare Moody?'

'Yes.'

There was so much conceit in that voice. Like the Paki, 'Go to Scott's,' like the Professor, 'What are you doing in this office?' So full of themselves until that moment, the sweet moment. Albie was starting to love that, the revelation of the blade.

He tried one of the back doors. It was locked. 'Open the door.'

'The pictures first.'

Albie looked about. 'Not here.'

'Show me the pictures. For all I know, you could be some kind of axe murderer.' She said it sarcastically. She'd already written him off. Not impressive enough to be an axe murderer, she was thinking. Real dregs.

Albie shrugged. 'Forget it.'

He walked away, not really concerned. That look in her eyes, the way she'd been sat there, she wasn't going to drive away.

'OK,' she called.

Yes, it was time. The hate was flowing through him as he walked back, careful not to give any outward sign. The back door was open. He got in behind her, closed the door. The upholstery was new, very comfortable. Her thick blonde curls were right in front of him, her perfume strong in the air. She was wearing too much make-up, he thought.

His hand felt for the haft of the blade.

'Where to?' asked Moody.

It had to be now. Yes, this time it was even easier. This time there was direct involvement. This time he was really going to get it sorted.

Albie sprang. He grabbed her hair, pulled her head back. The blade went to her throat, the full white hogsflesh. He sensed the terror rushing through her body.

It was good.

She moaned, took a sharp breath. He could see her eyes reflected in the mirror. Beautiful, she wasn't smiling now. He had respect.

'Don't scream!' he shouted. 'Right? Don't even think about screaming. Right?'

He gripped her hair tighter, pulled her head back again to make his point.

'I won't,' she squealed.

'You scream and that's it, right, you're brown bread. Right? You scream –'

'I won't scream, I won't scream, I won't scream –'

'Scream and you're dead –'

'I won't, I won't –'

'Have you got that? Eh? You understand what I'm saying?' He brought the knife closer to her throat.

117

'Yes.'

There was movement, outside. Without moving his head, Albie looked. One of the other cars, somebody was getting into it. A bloke, whistling to himself, putting his briefcase in the back.

Albie pressed the tip of the knife to Moody's throat. It was up to him, he had the power. The power and the right to slash a throat open. 'You feel that?'

'Yes.'

'I know what you're thinking,' he whispered in her ear. To himself his voice sounded strong, confident. For the first time. Thirty-two years of pissing about and he was finally making some headway, doing something worthwhile.

The bloke outside was getting into his car.

'You're thinking of sounding the horn.'

'I'm not, I'm not.'

'You sound that horn and you're dead. You're dead, he's dead, don't even think about it.'

'I'm not.'

The other car drove away.

'What do you want?' she asked him.

Give her the truth, thought Albie. Be direct, be honest.

'I'm going to kill you.'

She made a noise, a sort of sigh Albie had never heard anywhere else. He smelt her fear. Her world had altered, she'd lost control, he had taken control from her. He was in charge.

'What'll the headlines say?'

'I don't know.'

'Come on, you're a reporter.'

'It won't make the headlines. I'm not that important.' So she was still thinking straight. Albie liked that. A challenge, somebody to talk to. He was going to make her break before he killed her. She still sounded defiant, even now there were traces showing. That made it more equal. It also made him

118

more angry. She knew how much of a cow she was and she loved herself for it.

'It'll make the headlines in the *Sun* 'cause you work for the bloody thing.'

'I'm a freelance.'

'You told me you still work for them.'

'I work for every paper.'

He let his fingers press against her scalp, kept the knife right up to her throat. 'What'll it say, then? Front page of the *Sun* newspaper?'

'Moody murdered.'

'Oh, that's arrogant, Moody. That implies they all know who you are and they don't.'

'*Sun* girl murdered.'

Albie turned the knife slowly. 'Butchered.'

'Yeah,' she said.

'Slaughtered. *Sun* girl slaughtered. That's got a nice ring to it, hasn't it?'

'Yes.'

'Start the car,' Albie ordered.

He felt her shake. That really got to her. She tried to turn, to catch his eyes. Trying to establish a rapport, trying to let him know she was a human being. It wouldn't work.

'I can give you money,' she said.

He might have expected that. That's how she saw the world, you could change anyone, stop the rotation of the earth itself if you had the cash. Wrong. 'Start the car.'

'I can go to cash machines. I could get you a thousand pounds.'

Patronising bitch, as if she expected him to be impressed by the figure. 'I don't want your bloody money. Start the car.'

'You want me?' she asked, her eyes wide.

Albie was disgusted. 'What?'

'I'll get in the back, do anything you want. I mean it.'

119

She was filth. Stinking filth. Albie, who had marched for a woman's right to choose, shouted, 'What do you think I am, you dirty bitch? Start the car!'

'Anything, anything at all –'

He pulled her hair. Hard. 'Start the car!'

Her hand reached for the ignition key. 'Where do you want to go?'

'Just drive, Moody. I'll tell you where.'

They left the car park. He directed her, sliding the tip of the blade down to her stomach. There were loads of people outside, it was the rush hour. Nobody looked in, everyone was minding their own business. They reached some lights leading out of the city. Another car pulled up right beside them. Albie saw Moody's head turn ever so slightly towards the driver.

'Eyes on the road!' he shouted.

A couple of minutes passed. The crowds they left behind, moving out into wider roads, industrial estates, brickyards, gasometers. A grey sky. They were getting faster. Albie looked at the neck he was going to slit. He saw faces, packed faces, faces pressed against the fences, the police just sauntering about, clueless, watching it all. Him and Dad and everyone, shouting, pleading. Do something, help them, we're watching them die. We've got to help them, our brothers, sisters, fathers and mothers. Our family.

His breathing quickened. 'Let's have the radio on.'

Local news, right on time. 'Manchester police are continuing their investigations into the murder this morning of Salford University professor William Nolan. They have refused to confirm any link with the killing of shopkeeper Shahid –'

'No, let's not have this,' said Albie. 'News is a bit depressing, isn't it.'

'What would you like on?'

'Don't try the rapport crap, Moody, you're not a human

being, I've worked that out.' He whispered into her neck, 'Classic FM.'

She pressed the button. Albie hated Classic FM. Chunked and segued, all the stuff he'd loved. Impatience music, all those middle-class crawlers who'd rushed out for the Gorecki CD, the segregation of genre. Change something full of meaning, suck out the value.

Beautiful. The Berlin Philharmonic Orchestra. Typical choice. 'Turn it up.' She did. There were speakers in the back, Albie realised. His legs were tapping up and down. He was going to do it very soon. But first she had to know.

The music was loud. The engine was loud. The anger was loud in his head.

'They used that in *The Omen*. They used it in the Old Spice adverts, you know, the surfer. But it's "O Fortuna" from Carl Orff's *Carmina Burana*. Does that surprise you, eh? Does it surprise you that I know that?'

'Yes.'

The factories, the boarded-up shops, whipping by. The movement reaching its climax, crashing up.

'It surprises you?'

'Yes!'

Getting angry again, showing it, very bad idea Moody, though it doesn't make any difference. Not for you, certain to die very soon.

'Because I'm a white, working-class male. I'm a football supporter. Therefore I'm an animal. Right? Therefore I piss on the dead at Hillsborough!' He had to shout now, over the music, over the engine. 'Right? I piss on the dead at Hillsborough! Moody!'

She knew now, he could see it in the way she shifted slightly, moved her hand to get a better grip on the wheel. Guilt, not likely. She just hated being found out, made to pay.

'Were you there?'

'*Yes!*'

'We only printed what we were told.'

'You believed it!'

She was trying to move her head, to turn to face him. Genuinely attempting to communicate with him. She had guts, but she hadn't used them for anything, had just gone along with it, taken the easy ride. 'We believed what the police told us, yes.'

It was going through Albie's mind again. Watching his family die, watching Jill and Ruth die. Watching Dad die.

Faster, faster.

'The police killed ninety-six people, I can understand them telling a pack of lies. But your lot, your lot believed it, you soaked it all up. You believed that people would piss on the dead, piss on the dead, piss on their families –'

'We believed what the police told –'

It was now. 'I'll tell you why you believed it, Moody. I'll tell you why. We were animals to you. You expected us to act like animals. Well, now you're getting what you expect.'

He trailed the tip of the blade across her side.

'You, the bizzies, that patronising bloody professor, the Paki in that shop.' That got her, yes, that's right, that's me. 'You expect me to look like this, to act like this. OK. Fine. I've got rid of my hair. I've got rid of every scruple I've ever had. I killed that Paki, I killed that patronising bloody professor, that patronising bastard, and now it's your turn! Right? This is it!'

Faster, faster. The anger, for the ninety-six, for their families, for Dad.

'This is what you expect, this is what you get! It's what you deserve, Moody!'

It was now. He readied the bayonet. Didn't think about the blood. This was going to feel the best, it was going to be beautiful to feel her die.

'This is what the country expects, it's what the country *deserves* –'

Albie flew over the seat, she screamed, she'd slammed on the brakes. Bitch, no. His nose hit the glass, he didn't let go of the bayonet, pain and confusion, skidding, turning. A brick wall, high. Almost right into it. Round again, the car stopped. He couldn't move, he couldn't think.

'That was "O Fortuna" from *Carmina Burana* by Carl Orff, performed by the Berlin Philharmonic Orchestra under the direction of –'

She couldn't get away from him, not again, she wasn't smart enough. He'd find her, they'd never stop him, he'd slice Moody.

He couldn't move, his nose was right up against the windscreen, he couldn't think, and there were horns sounding outside, and Moody was getting out.

'Will you help me, please? Please, will you help me?'

He'd kill her, he'd slit her throat, he'd see her dead. Out on the tarmac. The back of his head was burning. One of his arms was useless, just hanging, but it'd be all right. Moody, on the other side of the car, standing still, just calling for help. A bloke, and another bloke, getting out of their cars.

'Please, will you help me?'

She saw him. Her face was scrunching up, not scared. Angry.

'You bastard.'

Albie looked about. There was an alley. Those men were staring at him, looking down at the bayonet. He realised they were frightened of him.

'You bastard. You bastard! You bastard!'

Back out, get away. Albie ran up the alley, Moody shouting after him.

She had to die, she had to die.

FIVE

Judith got back to the house after a good day, expecting it all to be ruined. Her pep-talk had gone some way to reinspiring her staff. She wondered how much of their belief in her methods came from her reaction to Fitz stumbling in and to her brushing away their concern when she'd explained about the trip to the hospital.

Katie was sitting on the porch. All the signs of ruination were present. Judith had the idea of grabbing Katie and heading straight for Jo's. There was no point in that. Katie was confused enough already, all the changes of address. They were going to have to stay, a few years. When Katie was old enough, they'd leave again. Judith shocked herself with the logic behind that thought.

'He's on the floor again,' Katie said, her eleven-year-old brow furrowed. She looked like her father when she frowned, her father after an all-day binge.

Fitz was in the front room, propped up against the coffee table, whisky glass and cigarette to hand. His head was turning from side to side like a malfunctioning robot's.

She knelt. Her impatience was growing. 'There's nothing wrong with you, Fitz.'

He moved away from her. 'A philosophical question. If you don't see a cockroach, does it exist?'

No point in making a display of concern. Fitz only needed a sounding board, somebody, anybody, to listen. In fact the listening itself wasn't that important, he needed only a token presence. Judith caught a glimpse of Katie standing in the doorway, staring down at her drunken father with confusion and a kind of pity. She remembered Mark at the same age, staring that same way. 'Go upstairs.' Katie obeyed.

Fitz hadn't noticed Katie. 'If my mother put down powder at night, the cockroaches'd be there in the morning. On their backs, their legs jabbing away. I used to beg her not to put it down. Let them live, Mum, let them multiply. Just so long as I don't have to actually see them.'

Judith took the glass from him. Time for action. 'Scunthorpe is not the answer.'

She chucked the whisky down the sink and took down one of his bottles from its hiding place. He followed her into the kitchen just as she unscrewed the cap and upended the bottle. The contents glugged down the plughole.

'We're going for a walk. Right now. Me and you.'

He put a hand on her shoulder. His breath stank. 'What are you doing?'

'I am throwing it all away. Your cache.'

'My what?' He followed her into the hall. They'd reached the point where the only way she could attract his attention was to destroy the means of his destruction. She'd been tempted before. What annoyed her most was that he'd hidden it so badly. It didn't matter to him if she saw, like it was a game.

'Listen, I don't need to hide booze away. That bottle in the kitchen, Mark must have put it there. Mark or one of his mates. He's just had a party, for God's sake.'

Blaming his own son. The desperation, the sadness. He had no shame. 'I don't believe you.'

'I don't hide my booze away. I'm not an adolescent.'

Up the stairs. In Mark's wardrobe, hidden under sweaters he'd grown out of. Two sherry bottles. She brandished them. 'All the evidence points to the contrary.'

She made for the bathroom.

The gaffer gave her one of his knowledgeable nods. 'I think we've sussed it –'

Standing over the toilet she unscrewed the caps.

'I don't drink sherry, Judith, I wouldn't drink it if you paid me!'

He was right, but she was past caring. It all had to go. No alcohol in the house, she wanted it clear. She poured the bottles into the pan.

'You drink like a fish, you smoke like a chimney, and if you carry on, Fitz, you are going to die!'

The gaffer shouted, 'Don't flush it!'

Judith had already pulled the chain.

'Oh dear,' said the gaffer, shaking his head. 'Oh dear. Oh dear.'

Fitz shoved his face into the gaffer's ear. *'What?'*

The gaffer pointed. 'We cracked the u-bend.'

Judith backed away from the toilet. Water and sherry were flooding the floor.

The kitchen ceiling was dripping sherry. Judith ordered Katie and Mark back to their rooms and arranged a collection of pots and pans to catch the drips. Fitz watched her, shouting insults at the builders all the while.

'We're going out,' Judith told him, shaking droplets of sherry from her hair.

'What, now?'

'Yes, now.'

'But –' Fitz gestured to the kitchen. 'We have a structural problem.'

She threw him his coat.

They walked to the park. It was gone six, there were few other people about. Judith kept her eyes on the pathway, the dead leaves turning to sludge.

'It's not just an ordinary drunken, nothing-else-to-do, pity-me, pity-me, excuse for a bout,' Fitz was saying.

'You've never needed an excuse.'

'You heard about Nolan?'

'Somebody at work told me. You did well not to get involved.'

She could see him getting agitated again. He was walking faster. 'I have got involved. I had to, they were going at it the wrong way. They took everything I could give them, and threw me out again.'

He'd heard of the murder and taken the victim's place. Because he had to. He'd nearly got himself killed last year, had walked into a house filled with gas to talk to a maniac with a box of matches. Because he'd had to. She wanted to kick him. Why did he have to? She walked faster, overtook him, the idiot!

'Look, I'm forty-five years old, and I've just discovered what I want to do with my life. I want to work with the police. When I'm doing that, everything's fine. I feel good, I feel I'm doing some good. When I'm not doing that, I get bored, depressed, things go wrong.' He was now several paces behind her. 'Can we slow down?'

'No.' He was a psychologist, an expert, and he couldn't stop himself from saying something as stupid as that. 'Do you know what you've just said? I bore you. I depress you. Police work makes the difference, not me. I make no bloody difference whatsoever!'

He stopped, she continued walking, he cantered up. 'I didn't mean that.'

'You did.' She followed the path back to the house. 'It hurts, Fitz. It hurts to know that my being there makes no bloody difference whatsoever!'

Things were going to have to change. They'd been through all this once, but she had to go. He bored her, she obviously bored him. Love didn't come into that. Love and boredom were not exclusive concepts. She thought of her work, the relatives linked by some disease, the carers writing off years of their own lives. She was different, she had a choice. There were years ahead, her career was opening up.

Fitz was not going to ruin years of her life. Not another day.

There were a couple of people outside the house, getting out of a car she didn't recognise. A man and a woman. The woman saw her and stopped the man from ringing the bell. It was the young woman from the police, Penhaligon, the one they'd seen on the way back from the hospital. The man with her was the Irishman, Beck.

'We'd like to see your husband,' she said.

Judith didn't react. The matter was going to be taken out of her hands, it seemed. Fitz was going to get his fix.

He trailed up the path, looking taken aback at their presence. Perhaps, thought Judith, trying not to look pleased, trying to suppress the smug little smile he saved for when somebody crawled back to him.

Penhaligon pointed to the male officer. 'Jimmy's got something to say, Fitz.'

Fitz raised an eyebrow. 'Let me guess. Bollocks?'

'It looks like you were right,' said Beck.

The smug smile won through. Fitz indicated the house. 'I'll just get my ciggies.'

Judith stormed after him into the hall. He was using this, not bothering to cover his glee, using it to get back at her. There was a solution. Her plan would have to be revealed now, because things were not going to go on as before.

'Look,' he said, picking up his cigarettes from the hall table. 'They pay me. Think about it practically. We could do with the money.'

She kept her voice level. 'I'm not going to leave again, Fitz. It's unfair on Katie, her life gets disrupted.'

His smile faded. Good. 'I'm not with you.'

'Fitz, I want you to leave.'

'I'm just about –'

She had to say it. Despite what he might think, she took no pleasure. 'For good.'

It wounded him. He blinked, looked her straight in the eye. She didn't move, kept her face still. No game.

He left, slamming the door.

Judith walked back to the dripping kitchen.

Fitz summed up Clare Moody with a glance around her flat. It wasn't a place that anybody lived in, at least nobody human. Spotless, no clutter, a couple of prints that were just on the wrong side of good taste. Wall-lights, a couple of exotic cacti, matt black furniture. Moody herself they'd discovered on her phone. On the way over, Beck had explained that she'd been found gibbering on one of the minor roads leading out of the city, but made a miraculous recovery. A girl who'd been hurt, now she thought she had power. Whatever happened, that'd always be her response. Here she was, proving him right.

'Fifty grand?' she was squawking. Bilborough sat opposite her, impassive. 'Fifty grand? I escape from the clutches of a serial killer and you offer a lousy fifty grand for the exclusive?'

'He's not a serial killer,' pointed out Panhandle.

Moody stared up at her. 'What?'

'He's got to kill five times before he's classed as a serial killer.'

'Why don't you make us all a cup of tea, love?'

She returned to the phone. 'Charlie, I've got to get back to the *Mirror*. No, it's not an auction, I promised them I'd get back to them, that's all. OK, I'll keep you on.'

She put the call on hold, looked around the room, sneered at Fitz, who realised that he reeked of whisky, and turned back to Bilborough. 'So do I get it? My bodyguard.'

'I'll see if it's possible –'

'No.' She shook her head, her curls bounced. Fitz noticed her freshly applied make-up. 'Do I get a bodyguard? Yes or no? I'm a specific target. If you want my help, you fix me up a bodyguard.'

To the phone again, 'Derek. Sorry to keep you waiting. The *Sun* have offered me sixty grand.' To Bilborough. 'Well?'

Bilborough nodded to Beck. 'Harriman.'

Beck left the room.

Fitz took another look around. He closed his eyes, listened to Moody's voice. 'No, it's not an auction, Derek.' Now there was somebody you could imagine hating. 'You asked to be kept informed.' Her occupation was a part of her, it made her what she was. 'I'm keeping you informed, Derek.' A journalist, a tabloid journalist, responding the way she had been trained. 'Fifty-five, your upper limit? What's going on down there nowadays?'

A former *Sun* journalist, a target. Nolan had been targeted for making assumptions. Journalists make assumptions all the time, filter the truth. The killer didn't like being written off. He was a *Guardian* reader, they'd said he was a racist, fascist football hooligan.

A football hooligan.

'They've offered me sixty-five at the *Sun*, Charlie. All you have to do is put the phone down and forget the matter.'

'What was that number?' asked Fitz.

'Nine six one five four eight nine,' Panhandle responded without hesitation.

'Charlie,' Moody's hackles were rising now, 'Charlie, will you listen? Can I get a word in?'

Fitz turned to Bilborough. 'When was Hillsborough?'

'Fifteenth of April, er, 1990.'

'Eighty-nine.' Harriman, the baby copper, corrected him as he entered with Beck.

Moody put the phone down. She was staring up at Fitz, proving him right again. Here was somebody useless at keeping a secret. A big mouth, who loved bad news and loved news about herself. Today must have been the happiest day of her life.

'Nine six one five four eight nine,' he said. 'Ninety-six people died because of what happened on the fifteenth of April, eighty-nine. Why you? Because you work for the *Sun*, yes?'

Without looking away from Fitz, she asked again, 'Do I get protection?'

Harriman stepped forward. Fitz reconsidered, no, he looked about eighteen, to be fair.

'Not exactly Kevin Costner, is he?' She returned her attention to Fitz. That strong personality, he thought, so far up its own behind. He ought to take her home and show her to Judith: Things could be worse, dear. 'Because I used to work for the *Sun*, yes.'

Fitz nodded and addressed Bilborough and Panhandle. He had it. You could almost convince yourself sometimes, on slender facts, but the truth sounded like the truth. The words of truth had power, he felt that power as he spoke, as a preacher must feel it.

'We're looking for a Liverpool supporter. He's recently shaven his head. He lives alone, but he's got a wife and at least one child. He's going to kill ninety-six people in revenge for Hillsborough. And, if there's any justice in this world, most of them will be coppers.'

They stared at him, ready to disbelieve again. But now he had firm evidence.

To Moody, 'Am I right?'

'Yeah.'

The look on Bilborough's face pleased Fitz enormously. He basked, triumphant, in the short silence that followed Moody's affirmative. They'd been wrong, he'd been right.

They couldn't afford to be without him. Their pride, of that puffed-up self-important kind, had wasted days and led to a killing.

From now they were linked.

He remembered feeling like this three weeks after meeting Judith.

'Jane, let a list of night workers together, narrow it down to blokes changing buses at Purvis Road. Forget the skinheads. Jimmy, I want door-to-door two miles around Purvis Road, OK? A man who's recently shaved his head.'

'Starting now?'

Bilborough nodded. Beck and Panhandle went off.

Moody had switched on the television, unable to keep herself away from an electronic media device for more than a couple of minutes. The early evening news, her picture. Fitz noted her nod at the choice, an extreme close-up, her red lips pouting.

'Earlier today, before Miss Moody's ordeal, Detective Chief Inspector Bilborough of the Manchester police spoke to Sue Edwards.'

'Our objective here has been to gather evidence,' Bilborough's image said calmly, 'using every possible means available to us.'

Fitz grunted and followed Bilborough from Moody's flat.

Saturday morning. Albie got in from work, fed the cat with Whiskas obtained from Scott's, and pulled off his hat. His hair was growing out quickly. His features were softening, the old Albie staring back from the mirror. He took the clippers from the drawer.

He still had plans for Moody. She was going to die. It pleased him that she understood him, that they'd had time to talk. They were equals, enemies, they knew each other. She'd keep.

In the meantime, he'd decided he was going to kill a copper.

His collection of souvenirs was building up. He'd videoed last night's news, wanted to see what line they were taking now. Moody would have talked, she couldn't keep her gob shut. They'd know a lot more about him now. He'd have to move quickly, get things sorted as far as possible.

A new phase was beginning. Plans had to be advanced. He turned on the clipper and raised it. Total reinvention.

He was third item on *Newsnight*. Pushed down the line by some Cabinet scandal and a famine somewhere. That wasn't right. He was more important. He'd got himself front page in all today's papers, a photofit staring out from the *Sun*. THE FACE OF EVIL. It didn't look anything like him. Not a word about his mission. The police were keeping quiet about that anyway. Keeping quiet about his revenge for their spiteful destruction of a community.

He shaved a line from his forehead to the base of his skull, gently rubbing the clippers back and forth and back again.

A photofit flashed up on the screen. His old hairstyle was suddenly superimposed over it. The old Albie again, the mug, taking all the blame, working for nothing. They couldn't have chosen a better way to reinspire him.

He shaved away the back and sides of his hair.

They'd got an interview with the copper leading the case. He looked young, too young for a DCI. David Bilborough. In his office, a United poster over his shoulder. He looked a bit dopey, his ears stuck out. A golden boy, playing the game, following the rules. Everybody's favourite, a success story.

Albie recognised David Bilborough.

About a year ago, that girl who'd been carved up by some maniac on the train coming into the city. Jacqui whatever her name was. Albie remembered Dad sitting in his chair in front of the telly, agonised, shaking his bald head, his hands shaking on his blanket, there was so much evil and pain in the world. There'd been an appeal from the parents, and words from the officer leading the investigation. DCI David Bilborough.

Albie saw David Bilborough almost every Saturday morning.

In the supermarket. Half a mile from here. With his wife. They had a kid. A pretty little success story, pushing their trolley about. The young copper and his missus, happy with their world. They were ignorant murdering scum. It was their sort, locked up in a dream, that were half the problem. They were Albie's enemies.

Albie's head was now totally bald.

It was fate. Odds on, tomorrow they'd be in the super-market as usual. So would he. He knew how coppers reacted. How men reacted. How the golden boy would react if his beautiful dreamworld was threatened.

'Our objective here has been to gather evidence using every possible means available to us. There is a connection between the murders of Mr Ali and Professor Nolan –'

The voice was soft, the accent barely there. He was trying to conceal his past, deny his roots, his community.

Albie's hate was building up. He froze the image of Bilborough, got right up close to the screen. The little dots that made up the picture blurred, thick fuzzy grey lines held them in static. Albie pressed the pause advance button on the remote control.

Bilborough's mouth closing, opening, closing, opening. His pink tongue, clean white teeth, clean white shirt, hair combed just right. Perfect automaton, could only have been a copper. Blanked out, didn't care, just played the game by the rules, would obey any order. An order to kill, to stand back and do nothing as his people died.

Albie paused the image again, held it as Bilborough's mouth opened wide. Could have been a moan, a cry. His dream world destroyed. Brought down to reality. You a copper, you a DCI? I'm going to kill as many coppers as I can, thought I'd start at the top.

His hand jerked up, his arm miming the movement of the blade sliding in, entering, penetrating. Getting the message across.

Tomorrow.

Judith made no reference to her ultimatum when Fitz got back, collapsing on the bed at three in the morning. Saturday usually meant a lie-in for him, but he was up suspiciously early, in time to wave Katie goodbye as she went off to a friend's, and press a fiver into her hand in what he must have thought was a fatherly gesture. He was trying to demonstrate something. Judith was too tired to argue about it. It had been deliberately designed to lead her on, she was certain. Typical of you to twist something like that, he'd say. Katie is my daughter, our daughter.

She was reading the paper, glad to note that his name wasn't being splashed about like Nolan's had been. The killings seemed particularly senseless. Judith tried to imagine what could drive somebody to behave like that.

'I said I'd go down to the station later on,' Fitz said as he entered the lounge. He'd made no reference to last night.

Judith said nothing, turned the page.

Fitz picked up the *Weekend* section and rustled it playfully. 'I'll let you into a secret. Like you and I, he's a *Guardian* reader.'

Her irritation surged up. This was what inspired him. Not love, concern, his family. Messing about in the gore, revelling in other people's misery.

'Dennis Nilsen was a *Guardian* reader, you know,' he continued. 'Wrapped up portions of his victims in it like fish suppers. Hell hath no fury like a liberal scorned.'

She closed the paper. 'You love it, Fitz. This is where you

get your kicks. Not helping the police, that's just the means, the way you justify it. You really wallow in it, other people's dirt.'

He blinked. 'I wallow in it? Maybe. But what about you? You do the same thing, at the Project. What's that, eh? Why don't you admit that? It's just the same.'

'I do not enjoy it, I don't take joy from it –'

He was getting into this now, advancing on her, his finger wagging. 'Other people's suffering, other people's grief, you enjoy the emotional intensity of it all.'

'Crap. It's my job. I enjoy my job, not other people's suffering.'

'Oh yes?' He nodded sceptically. She took that as a sign. Irrelevant hypothetical example coming up. 'I know a magic spell, right? It'll abolish all death, all suffering. Do you want it, Judith?'

'Yes,' she replied honestly.

He picked up the news section. 'No more famine, no more rape, no more murder. You reckon you could live with that? You'd be bored stiff.'

'Well, you couldn't. You regard those things as an intellectual challenge, you adore the release they give you.'

He paced the living room, arms flapping. 'No earthquakes in San Francisco, no planes falling out of the sky. Just Sainsbury's on a Saturday, clean the car on Sunday, and John bloody Major the rest of the week. If that's your utopia, you can shove it.'

Judith stood up, followed him into the kitchen, which stank of sherry. He was not going to get away with that. 'You need crime, Fitz. You need to solve crimes. It's another of your addictions. A cure-all. And you have the bloody cheek to question my motives?'

He poured a glass of water. Laughed. An irrelevant observation coming up. 'You realise we had this argument over twenty years ago? You and your friends having orgasms over Vietnam, sat around a bloody bong loving every bloody minute –'

'That was different!'

'It wasn't. You said it yourself, motive's the important thing, motive counts. What drives people to act the way they do. What's the sensation they crave, what are they getting out of it? What emotional itch needs scratching?'

'Bullshit. You know your trouble? You've never needed anything, you've never gone without. A drink and a smoke, maybe, but anything of substance, food, shelter, you've never needed it. So how dare you talk to me like this?'

She wasn't getting through. He was smiling.

'Fitz, if you were starving in the Third World and I came along and offered food, you'd take it from me. You wouldn't give a damn about my motives, you'd take it and eat it to stay alive. All this agonising over motive, you know what it is? It's bourgeois Western luxury.'

The same argument they'd had in 1974, in his grimy room in Edinburgh, listening to bloody Genesis. It was going to end the same way, she could tell. A reminder of the link. The love, the boredom.

'Come to bed with me,' he suggested.

'Of course I feel good when I've helped people, of course I get a kick out of it. But that doesn't take away from the fact that I have helped somebody.'

'Come to bed with me.'

'Only if you carry me up.'

It was a tradition. Part of his weekly routine. Ruth was waiting for Albie in the estate's playground, a long concrete oblong, watched over by older kids, other parents. She was on the roundabout, screaming her head off laughing. Albie smiled. He waited for the roundabout to stop, watched her shake her head and stumble off, and called her name.

She looked up, saw him. Her eyes widened. She was

terrified, she didn't recognise him. This bald-headed stranger who knew her name.

'It's your dad,' he said. He waved.

'What have you *done*, Dad?' She stared up at him and frowned. 'Your hair's all gone.'

He picked her up, noted the slight resistance as he took her frail body in his loving arms. He brushed away the hair from her forehead and kissed it. Life was strange. Everything on the outside was the same. This time yesterday he'd been at the university, hiding in the gents, waiting to kill Nolan.

'Don't you like it?'

'I think it's horrible, Dad.'

That hurt him, more than he expected. Everything he'd done was for her. He'd hoped that when Dad was gone they'd be able to spend more time together. There was a knot in his stomach at the thought of her growing up without him. But it was going to happen.

That was definite.

He helped her onto a swing.

Life can move so quickly. After years of nothing changing. He stopped himself thinking about what Ruth's life was going to be like. He found it easy to stop thinking now.

The bizzies were going to take him, they weren't that stupid. And he still had things to do. Well, then, let them. Let them think they had him.

Match on Monday night.

They stayed for about an hour in the playground. Albie watched Ruth with the other kids. She talked to them, joined in with everything. When she spoke or suggested something they took her seriously. She was so unlike him. He felt envious.

'Come on, Ruth, we'd better get back to your mum.'

She trailed back to him reluctantly, smiling and waving to her friends. 'Ruth, your dad's a baldie!' one of them shouted.

The block was covered in grime and graffiti. A filthy pen, unfit for animal habitation. There'd been houses here once, street after street. Deliberately razed and converted into hamster cages. The systematic, planned destruction of a community. Turn neighbour against neighbour, breed fear and ignorance and disease. This was his daughter's home. Her childhood home.

'Donkey ride?' he suggested. Another part of the ritual.

She smiled and climbed on.

The stairs reeked of shit and piss. There was almost no light. Rubbish everywhere. Dirty needles, rats. More graffiti. Up and up, Ruth on Daddy's shoulder.

THERE AIN'T NO BLACK IN THE UNION JACK. PAKIS GO HOME. GARY MORRIS IS A CUNT.

Up and up, to the family home.

SUCK MY COCK. RIGHTS FOR WHITES. I SHIT ON NIGGERS.

People were eating cardboard in this place. Old folk too scared to open the front door. Youths in gangs carrying Uzis. Where once there'd been streets, loyalty, friendship. Work.

And Clare Moody was earning a hundred thousand a year minimum.

Albie kissed Ruth's head again as they reached the door of the flat. Because what he was doing was for kids like her. For the future.

Jill's mouth dropped open when she saw him.

'We've been playing on the swings, Mum,' Ruth said. 'Daddy's a baldie.'

Jill waved her in.

'She hardly recognised me,' said Albie, faking good spirits.

'I'm not surprised. What have you done?'

'Don't you like it?'

'I hate it.'

Albie had a story prepared. 'A feller was mouthing off at

work about United. I said if they beat Leeds, I'd shave my head.'

It didn't sound convincing even to him. Albie, the loner, just days after his father's funeral, doing jolly bets and dares with his fellow workmates. But it was the best he could think up.

'You'd best come in.'

He followed her into the tiny kitchen. There was a folded copy of the *Mirror* on the draining board. His photofit all over it. A man with a recently shaven head. Did she suspect him?

No, of course not. He was Albie.

She put the kettle on. 'You look tired.'

'I haven't been sleeping,' he said. He'd rehearsed all this, knew his alibis backwards. 'I thought I'd sleep for a week when it was all over, when he was buried and that, but I haven't.'

'You don't need to work nights any more,' she pointed out. 'You could always go back to the quarry now. They'd need skilled men, always.'

He cringed. He was never going to work again. He had a new occupation.

'I was proud of you,' Jill said. 'The way you looked after him and everything.'

As if there'd been any choice. 'He was my father.'

'I know. But other sons wouldn't have done what you did.'

Other sons brought up in places like this, brought up to have no idea of what family means. She had no idea. 'Look, you hated him, right, so let's forget it.'

'I didn't hate him.'

Albie couldn't believe that. Jill hated what his dad represented, at least. Hard work, sticking with your own whatever happened. And she'd had the guts to break away, for Ruth's sake. It wasn't right for a little kid to grow up around a dying old man.

'I'm sorry,' he said. He took a small envelope from his pocket and placed it on the cooker. Another part of the routine. Nothing outside had changed. 'Here's your money. It's the bare amount. Flat week.'

'Ta.'

She handed him a cup of tea, shook her head and looked away.

'What's the matter?'

'Your *head*.'

So, she knew what he'd done. Something inside her feared that he was the killer. She was keeping it hidden, she couldn't admit it to herself. But she knew.

Albie said, 'It makes me look how I feel.'

Penhaligon had been on door-to-door from nine in the morning. The photofits were laughable, and enough of the residents of the endless terraces surrounding Purvis Road thought it pertinent to remark on that. Ridiculous staring eyes, impish ears. Nolan's students were taking a degree in criminal psychology, they should have known better than to create this gargoyle. All that theory, all those case studies, and the moment they were confronted by the real thing they fell back on medieval prejudices.

She was keeping Fitz out of her mind as much as she could. He was back, and he'd been right from the start. She accepted that, but it didn't mean she had to like it, any more than she liked door-to-door. Jane had decided long ago that the public at large were to be avoided. She must have had three hundred doors opened to her before lunch. A glimpse into three hundred lives, behind bolted doors and mullioned windows, dozens of dreary domestic dramas. The politeness she was faking took her back to her training and the time she'd wasted, waiting for everybody else to catch up.

Another door. 'I'm sorry to bother you, sir. I wonder if you could look at these two pictures,' gargoyle with and without his hair, 'and tell me if they remind you of anybody.'

The occupier squinted at her, the racing page in his huge hairy hand. His vest was untucked.

'Who is it?' shrieked a female voice from deep inside the house.

'If you're so bloody nosy why didn't you answer it, you bone idle bitch?' her husband shouted back.

'I was busy!'

'Well, I was on the lav!'

'You're never off the bloody lav!'

Jane flashed the photofits again. Just ignore them, get on with it. 'We're specially interested in anyone who's had a severe haircut recently.'

'You spend every bloody minute of every bloody day on the bloody lavatory, picking out your bloody horses –'

'Oh just shut your mouth will you, you crying cow! I'm trying to talk to somebody here, right?'

'I wish your horses went as well as your bowels, I'd be a bloody millionaire!'

Jane thought of Bilborough, sat in his office. She deserved promotion. She was sick of waiting.

Beck was on to something. He scented it as soon as the woman answered the door. Her eyes were huge, thyroid trouble probably. They missed nothing. She was in her late forties, wore a black and gold blouse and high heels. The kind of bird whose nose was a bloody pain to everyone she knew but was a godsend to the processes of law enforcement.

'I'm sorry to bother you, madam –'

' 'S'all right, chuck.' Giving him a look up and down, classifying him. 'No bother.'

'I'm a police officer. I wonder if you could tell me if you know of a man in this area that's recently, just in the last few days, had a very severe haircut.'

Immediate response. Excellent. 'Severe, you mean shaved, like?'

'Yeah.'

She pointed a painted nail. 'Well, there's the bloke over the road.'

Beautiful, beautiful. This was it. 'Which house?'

'Thirty-seven. There's one of your girl's over there now, look.'

A uniformed WPC was knocking at a brown door. 'Is he in?' Beck shouted across.

The girl shook her head.

Beck held up the photofits. 'Could that be him?'

The woman cackled. 'That could be anybody, love. Mind you, it gives you flexibility, that, doesn't it. For stitching people up.'

Beck looked into the hall behind her. 'You've got cobwebs on your coving,' he told her and walked away.

He moved his car round quickly from the next street and got out his photocopied list of residents. Thirty-seven Oundle Street, Mr Albert Kinsella. Occupation, shift worker at Armitage & Dean's. On the Purvis Road interchange. Beautiful. The name was printed twice for some reason. Computers cocking up probably.

An arrest by tonight, as soon as the bastard got back. His reputation restored. Bilborough was going to regret what he'd said, the accusation he'd made. Beck was going to set the thing straight, bring the bastard in, and they were going to have to deal with it.

Judith watched Fitz cleaning his teeth, singing through a mouth full of toothpaste. His shoes were tapping up and down. He thought it was enough. One wave of the magic wand and everything was made all right. The sex had been fantastic, yes, but the effect wasn't lasting. Judith could feel the smile dropping from her face. The experience had reinforced what she already felt. There was a strong link between them but in the end that wasn't enough.

'I'm just off to the station, then.' He waggled his fingers. His 'little-me' wave. 'Bye.'

He was off. To play with the police. For him, everything was now in its proper place. A nice gory murder to solve, and the little woman twisted round his finger. He'd already forgotten her demand.

'Bye,' she called. Meaning it.

Katie's life was going to be disrupted again.

Albie was fantasising about the death of David Bilborough. On the bus back from Jill's he'd gone upstairs, sat right at the back, and planned it. Everything was going fine. After that, he had something special lined up, forming in his mind.

Back home, he was just putting his key in the lock when a voice over his shoulder said, 'Albert Kinsella?'

Albie turned. Christ, it was that Irish copper, the one that had been on the bus. 'Yeah.'

'Detective Sergeant Beck. Have you got a minute?'

'Yeah.'

The copper knew. It was going to happen now, before he could get to Moody. Unless he took this Irish bastard, right now.

'Can we go inside?'

Shit, the pictures on the wall, the souvenirs, Ali, Nolan, the pictures on the front room wall.

'I'd sooner talk here.'

Thick Irish bastard really reckoned himself. That stupid bloody moustache. 'I'd sooner talk here.'

'I'd sooner talk inside please, Mr Kinsella.'

Albie forced himself to think straight. Try and keep him out. Get him away. 'It's in a bit of a mess, that's all.'

'I'm used to it, I'm Irish.'

Albie realised he was going to have to kill Detective Sergeant Beck. It was going to wreck everything, he was going to have to skip Bilborough, advance his plans for Moody. Everything was going wrong.

He opened the door. Looked around the street. Christ, that nosy bitch from over the road, the resident bleeding curtain-twitcher of Oundle Street, was standing in her doorway. Arms folded. Watching everything, the cow. Even if the Irishman hadn't told his mates what he was up to, she was there. Albie's plan was falling apart.

He had to think. Really think, quick.

Into the hall. He could keep the bastard here, just inside. 'What's it about?'

'Are you married?' Beck pushed past him, heading for the front room.

He was going to have to die.

'No,' Albie replied.

'Divorced?'

'No.'

Into the front room. Beck walking over to the window. His back to the souvenirs. The eyes of smiling Ali and photocopied Nolan on his back.

'You live alone?'

'Yeah.'

Albie moved his hand up behind him. He had to get the pictures down. His fingers touched the wall, felt the raised line where rolls of wallpaper met. Up, up.

'What's this about?'

'There's nothing wrong with it.' Beck still had his back to Albie.

Albie couldn't find the pictures. He brought his hand down. 'Sorry?'

'You said the place was a mess. Looks all right to me.' He took out a packet of cigarettes. 'D'you mind?'

The little Irish twat thought he was Columbo. 'No,' said

Albie. 'Er, what's this about?'

'We're interviewing men who've recently had their heads shaven.' He was looking about, searching for something. He hadn't seen the back wall yet, but any moment, any moment, any moment.

He took a match from Albie's scoreboard, struck it on his shoe, lit up.

Albie shook with panic and anger.

And he produced a plan. The idea came rushing into his head as if God had whispered it in his ear. The way out.

'I haven't had my head shaven,' he said, pulling off his hat.

'Then you're in for a shock when you look in the mirror.'

Albie smiled, laughed. This Irish bastard wasn't smart. He was out to prove something, make a big arrest. He'd walked alone into the home of a man he suspected strongly of being a killer. He was a prat.

'It fell out,' said Albie.

He opened the top drawer. The bayonet was there, sheathed in a tea towel that proclaimed the Six Wonders of the Isle of Wight. Still an option. The thick Irish prat, the patronising little bastard, deserved it. But it was safer to try his idea.

He took a bundle of letters from the back of the drawer and handed them over. 'I've got cancer. I'm on chemotherapy. I'm an outpatient at Stonefield.'

The Irish bastard's face fell. All his confidence and smugness were wiped away. 'I'm sorry.'

Albie had always thought the bizzies were a bunch of simple sods.

Beck looked down at the letters, guilt writing itself over his features. Guilt and a kind of disappointment. No big arrest for him today.

Albie turned and tugged down the pictures. They fluttered to the floor.

Beck turned. He'd seen nothing.

'You're not working, then?'

'I'm on invalidity.'

Beck waved his cigarette in the air, looking for an ashtray.
'I'll put this out.'

Albie proffered the cat's saucer. 'It's OK, honest,' he
said.

'I want to.' Beck stubbed the cigarette out. He looked
over Albie's shoulder. Smiled. Soft-headed git. 'Kittens.'

'I should've got rid of them but I didn't have the heart.'

Beck knelt down and patted one of the kittens. Its paws
curled around his finger, its sharp teeth showing as its sleep
was disturbed.

Albie imagined splitting Beck's head open. Simple-
minded Irish bastard copper. Went gooey over a basket of
kittens, but would leave a pen full of humans to die, just
stand back and watch. White working-class humans, lower
than any form of animal life.

'Thanks, anyway,' said Beck, standing up. 'Sorry to
bother you.'

'It's OK.'

Beck left the front room, treading over the photocopy of
Nolan as he passed.

'Where are you from?' he asked. Small talk to hide his
guilt.

'St Helens.' He could hardly believe it. Beck liked him.

'Liverpool supporter?'

'Everton.'

Beck laughed. 'Well, it beats chemotherapy, I suppose.
Just.'

Albie forced a smile. He thought of Dad sat in the front
room, moaning, moaning.

'See you.'

And Beck was gone.

Albie walked slowly back down the hall, shaking his head

and shivering. It was hardly believable. He remembered reading about Peter Sutcliffe, how the bizzies had had him in three times before they got him. But that was the sort of person the job attracted, he supposed. Thick sods who wanted power.

He picked up the pictures and pinned them back up on the wall. Beck's dirty footprint was smeared over Nolan's face. Beck had left a gap in the scoreboard, taken a match. Beck was a thick sod.

Another target.

And tomorrow . . .

SIX

Fitz spent the afternoon at Anson Road, reading over statements from Ali's customers and Nolan's students. Nothing new in them, and no new developments. Beck and Panhandle were out doing door-to-door, and Bilborough had avoided him, head down on his paperwork. But Fitz was in a good mood, swapping jokes with Skelton, keeping the office entertained. He was on form, felt no need to gamble and little urge to drink. A fulfilling job in hand and great sex with Judith. It was startling the way that things could turn themselves around so quickly. Most pleasing.

He got back home at about seven. On the way he'd thought of getting a bottle of wine for them to share, but decided against it. Probably a bit soon. Better to build on territory already gained.

He slammed the front door and called, 'Upstairs. On that bed. Stark naked. Right now.'

There was no reply. No lights on. She was out. Odd, she hadn't said anything.

The living room was empty. The couch had gone, the plants had gone, the fixed unit shelving had gone. Burglars, thought Fitz. But no. Burglars would have taken the video and the stereo, not a range of tropical cacti and a collection of the complete works of Trollope.

She'd left him.

He couldn't even sit down. She'd taken the sofa, there were dust marks on the carpet where it had been. Fitz turned on the light. It shone brightly because she'd had the lampshade off as well. Stripped the place. A professional removal job. She must have had it planned before their big argument, before the sex. Devious woman.

Upstairs was the same. She'd taken the bed, all her clothes. Katie's room was totally bare.

Fitz sat on the toilet, his head thrown back. Shock was best dealt with slowly. Allow yourself time to sort out your reaction, identify your emotional responses and trace them back. Construct a strategy, visualise the options.

Food first. The cupboards were bare, the freezer empty.

He heard Mark's key in the door. Waited in the kitchen. 'Bloody hell!' he heard his son say.

The door burst open and Mark entered. 'What the bloody hell's going on?'

'It's a little test, Mark,' he said. 'An experiment. On the rare occasions you decide to come home, your mother removes certain objects from the house. To see if you notice.'

'She's left again, hasn't she?'

Fitz passed him an envelope that was lying on the kitchen sink. 'You tell me.' He left the kitchen.

'Where are you going?'

'To get some food.'

Mark followed him to the supermarket, walking ten paces behind and swearing at his back. It wasn't his concern. He was nineteen, legally an adult. Fitz took a basket and stalked the aisles, tossing in whatever came to hand, temper rising. He had an impulse to drop the basket and shout back, but suburbanites were lurking so he didn't.

'You tosser,' he heard Mark say again over his shoulder. 'You tosser. My father is a tosser.'

Some of the other shoppers looked over and giggled. Fitz glowered at Mark and headed for the checkout.

Mark came close. 'Is Mum ever going to come back now?'

'It's got nothing to do with you,' Fitz told him, slamming down the next customer please divider.

'It's got plenty to do with me.'

'It hasn't.' Fitz noticed the woman next in the queue peering at him. 'And keep your voice down.'

'I won't. She's my mother, and she won't come home because of you. So the way you're acting is affecting me. Right. And Katie.'

As if he ever spent more than two consecutive minutes in the house. Fitz unloaded his goods onto the conveyor. 'And you feel strongly about that, do you?'

'I do, yeah.'

'This is the express checkout,' said the woman, pointing perkily up at an orange sign. 'Eight items.'

'You don't, Mark,' said Fitz. 'You'd go with her if you did. You put your mates before her, you put your local boozer before her. You treat the house like a bloody hotel and treat her like a skivvy.'

Mark shook his head. 'You really believe that?'

'I know that.' Fitz threw his basket onto the pile beneath the conveyor.

'Eight items,' said the woman, finger stabbing.

'I'm not going with her 'cause I want her to come back. Right? If I stay, it means she's got to keep in touch. That's why I'm not going with her.'

'I don't believe you.'

'Of course you don't. You like to think the worst of everybody.'

'Crap. I think realistically.'

'Eight items,' said the woman.

Fitz turned on her. 'I've only got eight items.'

'You haven't.'

Fitz jabbed a finger at his shopping. 'Three bottles of whisky constitute one item.'

'Three items.'

153

'One item, one item. Two loaves of bread constitute one item. Two dozen eggs constitute one item.'

'Two items.'

Fitz picked up a packet and waved it at her. 'Six frozen lasagnes constitute one item.'

'Six?'

The entire supermarket was looking over, laughing. Who cared. Who bloody cared. Suddenly the human race looked an impossible prospect. 'Four Cornish pasties constitute one item! And three bastard steak and kidney pies constitute one item!'

'Could you call a supervisor, please?' the woman shouted over his shoulder.

Mark pushed past him and left the supermarket.

'Oh, for God's sake.' He pressed his face up to the woman's, enjoying her startled look. 'Three million on the dole, hospitals falling down about your ears, beggars, muggers and God knows what around every bleeding corner. Haven't you got anything better to worry about?'

Penhaligon was in at 7.30 on Sunday morning, going through the door-to-door reports and feeding anything relevant, not that there was much, to her computer. Alone in the incident room, she made cup after cup of strong coffee. The phones were silent, the city beyond the high gridded windows still and lying in. It crossed her mind that this was unauthorised overtime. She probably wouldn't get paid for it.

It didn't matter. The job was enough. She could do it better than anybody else here, and was. Her eyes, straining from the bright white lettering of her screen, flicked regularly over to the glass front of Bilborough's office. The football posters made the place look like a kid's room. The boss set the tone, and yes, the tone was like a schoolroom. She'd change that.

There was a cough from the doorway. Fitz.

'Missus chucked you out again, has she?'

'I just can't keep away from you, Panhandle.'

'I'm working.'

He picked up the bundle of statements on her desk. 'So am I.'

'I've already been through those.'

'Well, I may as well make myself useful.' He flicked through the papers. 'This all of it?'

'Apart from Jimmy and a couple of the others.' She looked up. 'We're assuming he's a Liverpudlian.'

'Are we?'

He was ahead of her. 'He's a Liverpool supporter, Clare Moody said he's got a Liverpool accent.'

Fitz nodded, waving his finger in a circular motion, unravelling her train of thought. 'But Clare Moody's from Colchester, so a Liverpool accent to her could mean anything from Southport to Newton le Willows. I know.' He sat opposite her and poured himself a coffee. 'I've been through all that. But he's Liverpudlian. He's too genuine to be anything else. He knows what it's like to have your people shat on, Panhandle. Hillsborough would have been the icing on the cake.'

'But it's taken him six years to react.'

Fitz waved a hand. 'Six years or six minutes. All that pressure, building up, building up. Trying to keep it hidden, reading the *Guardian*, acting your part like any other reasonable member of society. When you know the whole bloody world's gone crazy.'

'Do you feel sorry for him?'

Fitz shook his head. 'I know what's going on in that mind.'

Some time off at last, and Bilborough was going to enjoy it. He and Catriona had decided to take Ryan out to the Lakes this afternoon. The weather was holding up. Lying in until

155

9.30 was blissful. Catriona had given him a worried look when she saw him reach for his radio, but it was only a routine call, to see if anything had happened. And if anything had, they would have called him. Yes, Jane was going over the statements taken yesterday. No, nothing much had turned up. Clare Moody was complaining about Harriman already. Apparently he kept falling asleep.

Catriona heard him laughing as he put the radio away in his jacket. 'What's funny?'

He put his arms around her. 'I don't want to talk about it. Any of it. I just want to forget it.'

'I understand.'

He watched as she changed Ryan's nappy and dressed him. Fitz was wrong. This was the stuff of life. Building a home, rearing a child, minding your own business and doing the best you could. He wasn't evading his responsibilities, he welcomed them. It was people like Fitz, poking their noses where they weren't wanted, that caused half the trouble in the world.

He tapped his car keys against his leg. 'Can we miss the shop today?'

'Why?'

'Well, we'll have to come back here and then go out again. It'll mean taking the car out twice.'

'I can't go in the week. Does it really matter?'

He smiled and got the car out. It didn't matter. He just needed to spend time with them, doing ordinary things, keeping his head straight.

Jimmy, Jane, Fitz and the shaven-headed monster of Manchester could wait.

Fitz was reading the Sunday papers. A long piece in the *Observer* about the sociological and psychological significance of the killings. All of it nonsense. The journalist wasn't working from the full facts and her conclusions were wrong. He suppressed feelings of jealousy. It should be his name, he thought, under that headline. Interesting. He felt proprietorial towards a murderer, a person he'd never even met. At the moment he cared about that more than Judith's abrupt exit. 'I make no bloody difference whatsoever,' she'd said, and he'd denied it. But he'd slept soundly, coped with the initial shock very well. Suspiciously well. Almost proving her right. The police work, just sitting here in the thick of things, was enough to uplift him.

He watched Beck reading his notes through to Panhandle. There was more tension between them than ever before. Had he tried something on? No. He was a bit slow, but not dumb enough for that. He was an all or nothing man. A tendency towards explosions. Fitz remembered that countdown the other night in Purvis Road.

'Sloane, Jennifer. Thirty-two Oundle Street. Out.'

Panhandle's eyes flicked to her print-out of residents. 'She's got a son of nineteen.'

'Moved out a year ago,' Beck said patiently. 'Mrs Sloane herself is visiting her mother.'

'You've checked on that?'

Beck sighed. 'Yes. She's in Ormskirk, he's in bloody Barcelona.'

'How do you know that?'

'The woman in 24 is looking after the house, she's got the only bloody key!'

'OK, OK.'

Fitz turned his eyes back down to the newsprint. There was a very bad relationship. Fatal in this kind of work, having to stop and question each other's level of competence all the while.

'Thirty-four Oundle Street, no one resident. Thirty-six, ditto. Thirty-eight, Mrs Pauline Douglas, seen nothing suspicious.' He flicked his notepad up. 'Oh, and I also

157

waited a bit and saw a bloke over the road who'd been out. Kinsella, Albert.'

'Two Ls?'

'Yes. Thirty-seven Oundle Street.'

Fitz sensed something. He looked up. A small bar of light on Panhandle's screen was flashing. NW, NW, NW. 'He's on one of other lists, too. Night worker.'

Beck sighed again. 'He's in the clear.'

Panhandle's fingers flashed efficiently over the keyboard. Fitz saw Beck's shoulders hunching. Stupid masculine aggression.

'Kinsella, Albert John,' Panhandle read off the screen. 'He works nights at Armitage and Dean's.' She consulted another printed list. 'It's on one of the Purvis Road bus routes.'

'Look, he's been off sick for two months. He's got cancer.'

'Did you check?'

Beck was holding himself back. 'Yes.'

'With the employer?'

'He showed me letters from the hospital. Don't teach your grandma how to suck eggs, love.' He closed his notebook and strutted back to his desk. 'The bloke's got a cat and kittens, for God's sake. He wouldn't harm a fly.'

Fitz watched Panhandle, saw her brain ticking over.

She dialled a number, waited, became tired of waiting, and put the phone down.

He walked over. 'No luck with the employer?'

'It's Sunday.'

'You and Jimmy don't seem to be getting along.'

'Shut up.' She looked past Fitz. A WPC had entered, ready to report. He nodded and slunk back to the paper.

'We're going to get some chocolate,' Bilborough told Ryan. 'And we're going to get some cornflakes, and we're going to get some crisps.'

Ryan was singing and smiling. He had clear blue eyes. A wide smile, perfect teeth. Such joy in there. Nothing like kids to delude you into thinking there was hope for the world. Propped up in the trolley, he reached out to play with Bilborough's chin.

He was trying to talk, to find his place, to make his mark on the world. He was growing so quickly. They'd been hoping for a girl, to start off with. Less mess, less aggression. But Bilborough knew, just knew, that Ryan wasn't going to be any trouble. Catriona's girlfriends from the ante-natal classes complained jealously of his quietness. Bilborough remembered his dad had thought the same thing about him. Usually when they were over at the match, his throat aching with all the hollering, he'd shake his head and say, 'David, you were such a quiet little feller.' Voice full of pride.

It wouldn't be long now until Ryan could come along to the match. Catriona was hardly interested, and his old mates had all seemed to drift away.

'Oo ah, oo ah,' he told Ryan. 'Oo ah, Can-to-na.'

Ryan laughed.

Bilborough looked up, expecting Catriona to be walking back up the aisle to the trolley.

She was standing right up against one of the shelves, a jar of pesto in one hand, a packet of pasta shells in the other.

Her face was stretched with terror.

'That man,' she said. 'David, that man.'

Bilborough registered another presence in the aisle. A little fellow in a woollen hat. Walking back slowly towards the checkouts.

'That man. He touched me, David. He touched me.'

The little fellow smiled. He looked like a rat, a gargoyle. He took off the hat. There wasn't a hair on his head. His eyes were huge, staring, insane.

He looked exactly like the photofit.

'He touched me.'

Ryan was still laughing.

The little fellow was still walking backwards. There was an invitation in his eyes.

Come and get me, copper.

The bastard.

He turned and ran off, wiry and nimble.

Bilborough couldn't let him get away. Catriona, he'd touched Catriona.

The little bastard was dodging through an unused checkout, he skipped over the chain blocking the end. There was no time to call control.

'Wait in the car,' Bilborough told Catriona.

He took off after the little bastard, jumping over the chain. Checkout girls staring at him, shoppers rolling their eyes, barcodes beeping.

Bilborough saw him. Running up the steps at the back of the car park. Christ, this area was built-up, he could be going anywhere.

Out into the car park, across and up the stairs. An alley. Abandoned trolleys. They'd slowed the bastard, he'd had to slalom around them. Bilborough kicked them away to either side and pushed himself on.

Church bells were ringing nearby.

Out of the alley, into the street. Houses on either side. There he was, turning a corner. After him.

There was nobody about, it was Sunday. The little bastard had slipped up there. He turned more corners. Led Bilborough along more streets, up another alley. More streets. All the same. A bloke washing his car.

The bastard was still in sight, taking fearful glances over his shoulder every few seconds.

Another street, another empty street. And down a back alley. Bilborough followed. Saw the bald head darting behind a door. Into a yard.

Bilborough stood before the wooden door. He had the bastard, run to ground. Could call control? No. What if he went out the front?

He entered the yard. Tidy, very ordinary. Windowbox on the kitchen window. Washing on the line, tee shirts and y-fronts.

Back door open. He walked through. A quick arrest, twist the little bastard's hand over his head. Call Jimmy and Jane. It'd all be over. Some rest. Brilliant, over by tomorrow night, he'd make the match.

Kitchen tidy and ordinary. A saucer of milk on the floor.

It was dark in here.

Not a sound. The little bastard must have gone out the front.

One look around the house.

Into the front room. The door was open. The curtains were drawn. A few ornaments. A big old record player, a schools football trophy. On the mantelpiece, something weird. Matches stuck into a crib board, it looked like.

He looked round. On the wall facing outwards, in full view of anyone if they bothered to look in, two pictures were pinned up.

Shahid Ali, the picture from Moody's front page exclusive. And Nolan, the photocopy. The souvenirs.

Fitz was a genius.

The door to the hall closed.

Bilborough jumped.

Christ, the little bastard had been standing behind the door.

He was stood there, those mad eyes bulging. He lunged forward, there was something in his hand, he lunged right forward.

Bilborough felt the bayonet as it slid deep inside his body. Right in, deep inside, piercing the skin, going further, pushing right in.

161

The pain, the surprise. The mad eyes, staring at him. Mad and curious. Enjoying this. No, no. The little bastard.

The blade was withdrawn.

Bilborough screamed and his legs gave way.

It was dark in the room. He clutched the wound. His hands were wet, his shirt was wet, his own blood. He had to press on the wound, keep it closed. The wound was huge.

His head jerked up and down. His breath wouldn't come, there was a hole in his lung. He could feel it, a new and disgusting sensation, but he knew what it was.

He was going to die.

The little bastard.

The ceiling was yellow. Tiny stalactites of Artex. His shirt was sticky against his back, against his jacket, against a carpet that smelt like his granny's.

He was crying.

The little bastard was moving about, hardly making a sound. Bilborough looked over. He was cleaning the blade with a tea towel. He wrapped it up, put it in a canvas bag. A canvas bag he'd had prepared, Bilborough realised.

The entire thing had been planned. His death had been planned.

He watched as his killer took down the pictures from the wall. Dangled them in front of him and smiled. Pleased with himself, truly enjoying this.

The pictures were put into a plastic folder and tucked into the bag.

'You're a DCI, aren't you?' he asked. The voice was almost gentle.

Bilborough nodded.

'I'm going to kill a lot of bizzies.' He walked behind Bilborough, stood at the mantelpiece. Bilborough heard him strike a match. 'But I thought I'd start at the top.'

Only ten minutes ago. The supermarket. Oh God. God help me.

Bilborough whimpered, 'Please, please help me.' His voice, high-pitched gargling. There was blood in his mouth.

'I'd like to, but I'm a bit pushed, y'know what I mean?'

'I've got a wife and child.' The blood gushed up and over his lips, his mouth was thick with it.

'I had a wife and child once.'

The little bastard moved back into view. Smiling. Bilborough watched as he picked up his canvas bag and a large cardboard box with a kind of handle on it. A pet carrier.

Something was moving inside the box, making mewing sounds, baby sounds.

The little bastard left the room. Bilborough heard him leave the house, pulling the front door to.

He pulled out his radio. It wasn't going to do any good. Not for him, it wasn't going to do any good. He was going to die. But there was a job, his job, he had to do it.

'Bilborough to control.'

'Control receiving.'

'I've been stabbed.'

'State your position.'

Shit. He had no idea. It was just a house, an ordinary house. All the streets around here. 'I don't know my position. I chased a man, I'm in his house.'

'Can you see a phone?'

Obvious, but he hadn't looked, couldn't think. Pressing hard on the wound with one hand, he sat up. No phone. He had to get out, along the hall and out the front door.

'No. I'm going to the front.'

Fitz barged past the crowd of officers gathered around the radio operator. Panhandle and Beck were right behind him.

'I'm losing a lot of blood,' Bilborough was saying. It was hard to tell it was him. 'Moving makes it worse.'

Fitz realised that nobody else had a clue what to do. The shock on their faces, they couldn't think. 'Letters, envelopes, anything with the address on.'

'Are there any letters around? Envelopes?' asked the radio operator.

'No. Every time I move it opens the wound.'

Fitz glanced at Panhandle. She was trembling.

'Stay still, stay still,' she shouted. 'Press on the wound.'

They heard Bilborough's breathing. Short breaths, gurgles. A scream as he moved.

'How bad is it?' asked the radio operator.

'I'm dying.'

The front door was open. Bilborough crawled along the hall, leaving a trail of blood. Their voices were getting further away. He was leaving them behind, it really was like people said, it felt like he was leaving. A waving goodbye from a train feeling.

Fitz, the mad bugger. Jimmy. His old mate. Why had they rowed, what did it matter? Jane, beautiful Jane Penhaligon.

He pushed himself on.

'I'm in the hall.'

Fitz's voice again. 'Where did you chase him from?'

Of course. Nobody else would've thought to ask that. Fitz, right again. 'The supermarket at Bridge Road. We ran for about half a mile.'

'All units proceed to within half a mile of Bridge Road. DCI Bilborough badly wounded. Exact location unknown.'

He stretched out to pull the door open. The wound slipped from his grip, burst open. Organs slipped forward. He was a mess inside.

'I'm at the door.'

Jane. 'Don't try and move any more.' Always so bloody practical.

The little bastard couldn't get away. They had to get him, without his input. 'He's bald, denim jacket, slight build. About five foot five.'

164

The morning sun on his face. The tears were streaming down, mixing with the blood.

'Get the bastard.'

He grabbed the wound again, screamed as he fell forward and on to the street. And over.

'Is there a street sign?'

There was a kid. About ten. Walking up. He saw Bilborough and backed away. Terrified.

'Help me. Help me . . .'

'Is there a street sign? A street sign or landmark, shops?'

The kid ran away. Ran down the empty street.

'Is there a street sign or landmark or anything like that?'

Bilborough's head fell against the tarmac. His ear on gravel. Blood pouring from him.

'Nothing. There's not a soul. There's no one in the street. Not a bloody soul.'

Fitz found Bridge Road in the *A to Z*. Looked around the neighbourhood, tapping his finger against the page. He found what he was looking for.

Oh Christ. He wasn't even going to think about what this was going to mean.

'Did he have a cat and kittens?'

Beck jumped. His face purpled.

'Did he have a cat and kittens?' the operator repeated.

'Yeah.'

'Oundle Street!' Fitz roared and followed Panhandle as she ran from the control room.

'This is evidence.'

There was a job to be done.

'This is a dying man's statement. I know what a defence lawyer will try and do.'

Penhaligon's car screeched out of Anson Road. Fitz was

beside her, using the *A to Z* to navigate. She turned on her radio.

'I'm of sound mind. I'm frightened, yeah, I don't want to die. I'm frightened, but I'm thinking straight. He had a photocopy of Nolan on the wall.'

She glanced at Fitz. He closed his eyes and muttered something.

Beck followed Penhaligon's car in his own. He was sobbing. Oundle Street. Number 37, Kinsella, Albert John. He wouldn't harm a fly, he was on chemotherapy. He was on fucking chemotherapy.

'He fully intended to kill me. He stabbed me. I can't get up the bloody steps. He stabbed me in cold blood.'

'Are you listening, Jimmy? I want you to get this bastard, Jimmy. OK? Get the bastard. For me and Catriona, get the bastard.'

Beck put his foot down on the accelerator. No. Bilborough wasn't going to die. He couldn't die.

If he died, Beck couldn't live.

'Catriona,' Bilborough whispered. The pain was fading. Replaced by something stronger, a mighty hand on his forehead, pushing him down into folds of yielding earth.

'Oh God, Catriona.'

Waiting in the car back at the supermarket. Waiting for a day out. Waiting with Ryan.

'What are we going to tell her?'

All those years ahead.

Fitz could tell Bilborough was dead. The blood was running out of him, into the gutter. He was staring up at the sky, the radio in his hand.

Fitz studied Panhandle. This was going to shake her badly, really change her life, everything from this moment altered.

166

'Boss?'

She addressed the corpse. Fitz stayed back. She didn't need sympathy or any of that crap, there'd be no help in that. Least of all from him. She was going to have to work it out for herself.

'Sir?'

Another car screeched up. Beck got out. Red-faced and sobbing.

Panhandle knelt by the body. He knelt beside her, shaking his head.

Fitz watched them.

Panhandle noticed Beck. She slapped him hard, grunted, snarled. Slapped him again, harder. And again. He tried to grab her hand.

He embraced her, pressing her body to his. Any moment now, thought Fitz, Jimmy Beck is going to make one of his requests. Half of those tears were for himself. And Panhandle, how's she going to react? How long will it take her to get over this and move on up? To use it like she uses everything else, for her own advancement?

'Please don't tell anyone,' Fitz heard Beck whisper. 'Please. Please.'

SEVEN

Albie hadn't been out this way for five years. The bus times hadn't changed. The limited Sunday service left Purvis Road at ten past eleven and at the same minutes every hour, punctually.

David Bilborough's face stayed in Albie's mind as he watched the grey city thinning away. The blood that came from his mouth and nose, his little whimpers. He'd died without dignity and that was what made it good. Shame not to be there at the last gasp, but he'd have missed the bus otherwise. It was the only punctual service in the city. Albie took a peek in his bag at the photocopy of Nolan, taking strength from the glimpse.

But Ali and Nolan had been just the start. Preliminary practice for Albie. David Bilborough had really satisfied him because it was real, direct revenge. The way Albie felt now was beyond anything. It was beautiful, because he wasn't thinking at all. There was no need. He had become the catalyst, the instrument.

It was right that he was going back now, using his past to make the future.

The police force is a machine, thought Charlie Wise as he was driven into Oundle Street. An efficient device. One component wears out or gets broken, needs replacing, and a spare part is found.

He'd been waiting for his new assignment for only two weeks, had been in Manchester only a month. The transfer from Merseyside had been in the works a few years. The wife was spending more and more time with her family here, Wise needed a change. The move had been made, but he hadn't expected the new job so quickly. Didn't welcome the circumstances, either. Dragged from the bath on Sunday lunchtime by the Chief Super. Told that young Bilborough had been murdered, died in the flaming gutter, a victim of the skinhead monster. There was a choice, that was made clear. It'd be difficult but they could find somebody else.

No chance. Wise had met Bilborough a couple of times. A great lad, young, successful, wife and kiddie. He'd take pleasure in putting the scum away.

'They mustn't have time to think, Charlie,' Allen had said over the phone. 'You know what's it like. I'll take you in now. Right now. We've got to move fast on this bastard.'

Bilborough's body was being zipped up and carried off. There was a lot of blood. The yellow tabards of the scene of crime fellers were daubed with it. Ghouls at both ends of the street, oohing and aahing behind the tape.

Allen pointed. 'That fat feller, he's Fitzgerald, the psychologist. The girl with him, that's Jane Penhaligon.'

The girl's hands and jacket were blood-stained where she'd touched the corpse. Her face was blanked-out and turned down. She was looking at the houses opposite, not seeing anything. The fat bloke came over to her as the body bag passed by and embraced her. Just for a second. Then she almost pushed him away. A slight pressure of the hand.

Allen stopped the car and they got out. Over thirty years in the force, Wise knew it was best not to let your emotions show. Do your duty, do it quickly and efficiently. He had to set the tone for their response to their boss's death, and that was going to be difficult. Keep them occupied, that was the best approach. Keep the machine operational.

A short fellow with a thick moustache walked forward.

He'd been crying and there were bloodstains mixed in with the tears.

'DCI Wise, DS Beck.'

They shook hands. There was nothing in Beck's handshake. The life had gone out of the bloke.

'You were close, yeah?'

'Yeah.' The muscles on Beck's forehead tensed. Wise didn't want him to start crying again.

'I'm really sorry.'

'Thanks.'

Charlie tapped him on the shoulder. 'You feel up to sorting this out?'

Beck's eyes kept flicking over to the open door of number 37, the dark hallway beyond. The sticky black trail over the porch. 'I want to, yeah.'

He walked slowly over to the house.

'I rang David's house but there was no answer,' said Allen.

Jane exchanged her bloodstained jacket for a uniform coat offered by a WPC and muttered, 'Thank you.' Then she turned back to Allen. He was staring straight at her, concerned.

She couldn't let him see her like this. Already she'd almost given way before Fitz. It was so unfair. So public. She wanted to be alone. Sort out her feelings and get back.

But Allen mustn't be allowed to think that she couldn't cope. She hated herself for it, but he was important in her life, crucial to her career. Even now she couldn't put that aside.

'I said I rang David's house and there was no answer,' Allen repeated.

Years back, in her sixth form, Jane had been seeing a lad. Nothing serious. They split up. It didn't matter, just a fling, who cared. A few weeks later he'd been killed in a car crash. People had surrounded her, offering their sympathy. But she'd felt next to nothing. She'd cried a bit at the funeral, but she'd been thinking all the time what a bastard he'd been to get himself killed the week of her mock A levels.

But David Bilborough had been cute. She was never going to ruffle his hair, play with his hands, let him have his way if he ever tried it on.

She didn't want to think about Beck or Fitz for a long while.

There was a job to be done.

'His wife'll be at the supermarket,' she told Allen. 'He ran here from the supermarket at Bridge Road.'

Allen nodded. 'I'll go over there. You should go home. Do you want somebody to come with you?'

'No. I'll come with you, sir.'

Beck looked around the front room. He'd been standing here less than twenty-four hours before. Cracking jokes with the bastard, cooing over his bloody kittens.

But it couldn't be right. He'd seen the letters, he'd stood and read the letters from the hospital. Procedure had been followed. It was a fluke, he told himself. You couldn't be expected to check everything out.

He wanted to set fire to the place. He wanted to die.

And Penhaligon, rolling her eyes and sighing at him when he'd brought the reports in, telling him that checking the till roll was obvious. Patronising bitch thought she knew it all. Her and Fitz, super-brains. So efficient, superior.

They knew. They were going to hold it over him forever. Even if they kept the secret. Years ahead, whenever this business was just a distant memory, when the boss was just a photo on a wall, Penhaligon was going to remind him about it every time they were in the same room. Just by being there.

The Forensic team were working away, sorting things into plastic bags. Their backs were to him. A packet of their surgical gloves were lying on top of an armchair. He took one and reached for the handle of the drawer.

The new DCI put his head around the door. Beck had hardly noticed him when they'd been introduced. Amazing they could get someone so bloody quickly. Nobody was expendable.

Wise was huge, bearded, a teddy bear in glasses. He looked irritated. 'There's a gang of kids in the alley. Could you get rid of them, seal it off, yeah?'

'Yeah.'

Wise nodded and pulled his head out.

Beck reached into the drawer. The letters were still there, the name of the hospital across the top. Evidence for his case against himself, against his guilt. Fitz was wrong, there was no shaving of heads involved, the bloke's hair had fallen out because of the chemotherapy. And Penhaligon's rage at him was misplaced, because the bloke had been ill and was off work. He'd fouled up because of misinformation, Fitz's assumptions.

He put the letters in his pocket.

Wise's shaggy head reappeared. 'And there was a lad in the street, apparently. Could you find him, get a statement?'

'Right.'

Wise stared at him. 'Are you OK?'

'Yeah.'

'Well, when you've done that, go and have a pint.'

As Jane walked towards the supermarket with the Chief Super, towards the main doors which were now crowded by Sunday shoppers, jumping jammy-faced children and their shell-suited parents, she saw Bilborough's car. There was somebody in the passenger seat. Catriona. Jane watched her as she turned her head, looked around, her lips pursed anxiously. She was bouncing Ryan on her lap.

Jane wished to be somewhere else. Anywhere else.

The amount of times Bilborough had asked her to handle

the relatives. The poor sod.

She walked towards the car, every footstep a report, sharp on the tarmac, counting down the seconds. Catriona saw her in the mirror and turned, eyes large. Fearful.

Jane opened the door, sat in the driver's seat. Bilborough's gloves on the dashboard. A half-eaten packet of mints. She'd done this so many times, broken the news and then just walked away from it.

'That man's hurt him?'

'Yes.' Say it, say it.

'Badly?'

'Yes.' She couldn't.

The baby gurgled, waved its little hand at her. Jane felt tears welling up. She let them out. Caught a glimpse of her wrecked red face in the overhead mirror. What did she matter?

Allen, in the back seat, rested his hand on Catriona's shoulder. His eyes were reddening.

'I'm sorry, Catriona. David's dead.'

Jane watched Catriona crumple. Her shoulders fell and she pressed her head back against the rest.

'I want to go home. I want to go home now.'

Allen nodded to Jane. She slipped on her seatbelt. Absently, Catriona did the same, pressing the still smiling Ryan to her breast.

They left the car park.

Albie walked into the quarry without being challenged. The Sunday shift was notorious, the boys spent half the day watching telly in the hut. He squeezed himself through a gap that ran between two high sides of rock and did a survey. Turned his head from side to side.

The siren sounded.

He used to play a game when the siren went off. See how close he could get to the blast. Half the fun was in winding the other blokes up. They thought he was a nutty scouser anyway. Used to put his Walkman on, Vivaldi or Rossini were best, and then walk right up to the edge of the danger area. Watch that wall blow, millions of years of geological history turned to dust in seconds. It proved that things could be changed overnight with the right power. Shook the dust from his hair, walked back to the hut. The foreman had given up trying to stop him. Besides, he'd never gone too far, it was just like a game of chicken.

Albie followed the siren. Thirty seconds.

He started to hum. Mozart, oboe concerto in C Major. *Adagio non troppo*. Good for concentration.

The charges blew. The rock wall crumpled, caved in. The noise stung Albie's ears.

He smiled.

With that force he could achieve anything.

Over to the storage hut. In five years, the topography of the quarry had been blasted into a completely new shape, but Albie had worked in the place long enough. It was no problem. He judged his location not by landmarks but by measuring his distance from the main road and counting his footsteps. Walking in a straight line. He remembered it all. Could have been yesterday.

He heard a van driving up. Didn't turn round, kept walking towards the hut. Nothing was going to interfere.

Door of the van slammed. Heavy booted feet crunched over gravel. A big bloke, then.

'What are you doing?'

Albie turned. Big ignorant musclebound idiot, checked shirt and hardhat. Not important.

'Mind your own business.'

'It is my business.' Coming closer. Clenching his fists, dumb ape. 'What are you doing?'

Albie put down his canvas bag gently. He felt nothing. This was like a job, like filing, something you had to do to

175

keep the whole operation running smoothly. Sorry and all that, old chap.

His head was splitting. The blast, he'd been too bloody close. It was in his ears, right inside his brain. Pounding.

'Come here or I'm calling the police, mate.'

'I kill police,' said Albie. He drew the bayonet out and had the bloke. Over in seconds.

An acceptable casualty.

There were keys on the bloke's belt. Albie recognised the ones he wanted and set to work.

Beck slipped past Wise, ignoring the hairy hand of comfort. He went straight to the car, trying to fight down the stabbing tightness in his chest. There was an urge building. To take his hands from the wheel, raise them to his face. Let the car go where it wanted. An end to all responsibility. Put the full stop on all this bad feeling. Crush himself in the wreckage.

The first letter. 'Dear Mr Kinsella. As agreed an appointment has been made for you to attend Dr Enright's clinic for chemotherapy treatment. Your appointment date is Friday February 10th 1995 at 09:45.'

Half of the proof he needed.

It took him quarter of an hour to find the admin office of the hospital. Another ten minutes to get the door opened. Just one bloke in there. Young, in a cardigan, thinning hair. Lisping and effeminate. 'You're lucky to find me here. It's Sunday, you know.'

Beck looked at the shiny head. This creep was going back to his Mum and his boyfriend tonight, no guilt, no worries. The world was still turning. For them.

The boy's long fingers flicked over the keyboard, signing on. 'What do you want to know, then, constable?'

Thought himself clever. An image entered Beck's head. The screen dropped on that shiny head. 'Albert Kinsella. Two Ls. Thirty-seven Oundle Street.'

The screen flashed NO PATIENTS REGISTERED FOR DETAILS GIVEN.

Beck patted his pocket, checked the letters. They had to be real.

Another attempt, a different register. A flashing D in the top left hand corner of the screen.

'He's dead,' said the lad.

'I spoke to him yesterday.' Beck produced the letters, shaking in his hand.

The lad cast a glance at the letters, nodded. 'Well, they're genuine.'

None of it made sense. 'Early thirties, yeah?'

More information scrolled up. 'Died March 18th this year aged sixty-nine.'

'His son. I spoke to his bloody son.'

A girlish titter from the lad's thin wet pink lips. Weren't the police a bunch of clots. 'Possibly.'

Beck snatched the letters back. The evidence against him. The proof of his incompetence. His contract with destiny. In every crease, in the folded corners, the neatly justified paragraphs. The highlighted date. A thing of significance.

'With people like you on his trail, Lord Lucan must be worried sick,' the boy said, switching off the screen.

Jane had to break a small window at the back of Bilborough's house. Catriona hadn't taken a key to the supermarket.

The house was clean and silent. She'd been here a couple of times before, sneered inwardly at the suburban trappings, the Phil Collins CDs and MFI shelving. The carpets were springy. The place smelt of detergent.

In the hall there was something new. Must have been a recent addition. A black and white photograph of Bilborough's office at Anson Road. He was at his desk, smiling. She was on his left, smiling. Beck to his right, smiling.

Jane couldn't remember the photo being taken. It was the

kind of sentimental gesture she ignored.

The shapes of Catriona, the Chief Super and Ryan were behind the frosted glass of the front door. Silent. Waiting for her. But first one more look about the house. A look at what might have been. What she had secretly plotted to diminish.

'He touched me,' Catriona told her as the door opened.

'Sorry?'

'That man. He touched me.'

The radio in the quarry foreman's van was tuned to Radio 2. So much for the muscles.

Albie hummed along to 'A Walk in the Black Forest' and was surprised to find that he remembered all the words of 'Welcome Home' by Peters and Lee. There was a wave of noise over it. A scraping noise over everything. When he moved his head from side to side the noise roared like a huge dirty wave breaking.

The van slipped back into Manchester without any trouble. He'd had a provisional licence once but had bottled out after a couple of lessons. He couldn't imagine why, driving was easy, even on Sunday with all the happy families in their Volvos heading for the Lakes.

A quick glance over his shoulder now and then. The foreman's body, bleeding over old rugs and blankets. Eyes open and glazing over.

Albie wanted to talk to somebody.

'Sorry, mate.' He laughed. 'But you were in the way, like. And I'm a bloody hooligan. I'm a nutcase. I've killed a copper. I'm a menace to bleeding society. 'Cause it's about bloody time society got menaced. And who did you vote for, eh?'

That scraping noise, pressing on his forehead. It was like voices, screaming at him. Begging for him to continue, to press on, to get things sorted.

Back to the allotment, and time to set the plan in motion.

He couldn't hang about. Even that stupid Irish bastard would think of checking here in the next couple of days.

He parked the van with the back doors right up to the shed and set about moving the body. It was like they said, people were heavy. The most difficult bit for any killer was getting rid of the body. Especially if you hadn't planned ahead.

But Albie was a meticulous planner.

Catriona still wasn't talking. She ran herself a bath and locked herself in with Ryan. Jane stood on the other side of the bathroom door. Baby cries and splashing. And then a moan, a growl of anger from Catriona. The private grieving. Usually Jane was well away by this point.

That moan haunted her, tugged at her guts. To be that close to somebody, close enough to live with them, ignore their faults, love them whatever, do everything together. Noble or stupid, such intentions had never occurred to Jane. It was a kind of autism. Her function on the social level was minimal, means to an end. Men, take them or leave them. Friends, fun to be around, occasionally. Her family, dragging on, dragging her backwards. Through all of it she'd been scratching at surfaces, never reaching the point. She'd never been anyone's best friend, the love of anyone's life.

Up to now she'd thought that didn't matter.

Fitz walked slowly from Oundle Street to Bilborough's estate. The lines of terraces, street after street of them, gave way to a large park. He sat on a bench, watched some kids playing, smoked away. His mind emptied. Most strongly he felt regret, similar to when something particularly nasty comes on the news. Damn, you think. Then push the little pain aside because things need doing. Except this time the lump of regret remained.

There was something else. Bilborough's description of his killer, the way the bastard must have planned it all. A few hours ago he'd been sat with Panhandle in the office, almost trying to apologise for the bloke. It's different, he thought, when it's somebody you know stabbed in the side, crawling along the gutter crying for help. That's why there are police, that's why there are psychologists. Specialists who can come in and deal with the problem because of their detachment.

Ultimately, it was his job to help people. In his leisure time he was free to destroy himself, burn his bridges, drive his wife and kids away forever. He was on duty now, and Catriona needed the help he could give. And Panhandle, when she let him get close enough. In a few days' time, then.

When he arrived at the house, the baby was toddling about the living room unsteadily, in a romper suit and wee red boots. Bilborough and Catriona were the sort for marriage and child-rearing. Salt of the earth. The backbone of England. Get yourself a good job, get yourself married, get yourself a kid, and die. Serve the state, back up the others who are never going to live your way.

Catriona needed to go over what had happened. To repeat the events of the day in detail before she could move forward. Fitz watched Panhandle as Catriona talked of the planned day at the Lakes. Her eyes were cast wistfully down at the rug, she hugged a cushion unconsciously. She was thinking about Bilborough, wondering if she could ever have set up home with anybody. Of course not, she didn't have the patience.

'That man,' said Catriona. 'He used me. When he touched me. He knew how I'd react, how David would react. I was nothing. Just something he used to kill David.'

That needed attention. Fitz was glad he was here. His advice was practical, what people needed in these circumstances. No soppy sympathy. Just lay it out simply and stick to the facts. 'He didn't use you. He used the fact that you loved each other. You've nothing to feel guilty about.'

A couple of moments passed. Catriona nodded. She regarded Fitz directly. He was used to being scrutinised for what he said. 'You fell out with David,' she said.

So Bilborough took his work home. 'Yes.'

'He told me about it. He used to come home, get straight in the shower. He swam through filth all day, he said. Had to wash it off, didn't want to tread it through the house.'

Fitz was struck by guilt. His argument with Bilborough, his accusations of bunker mentality, et cetera. Had compared him to an SS officer, insulted his wife and child. It had all seemed so telling at the time, as he stood in the office loving the sound of his own shout. He'd prepared that speech, mouthing it to himself over and over during the time of his exile.

Other people's discomfort. His motive?

'He wouldn't lock up an innocent man,' said Catriona. 'He wouldn't do that and come home to us.'

If she wanted to go on believing that, if she wanted to keep the facade intact, fine. Some things were better left unsaid. Covering the truth. It was what made marriage, and civilisation, work. For some, anyway.

'I know,' he said. 'I was wrong. I'm sorry.'

In the shed, Albie worked as he had always worked. Shutting out external thoughts, concentrating on the matter in hand, swift and efficient. Ten O levels, three A levels, the quarry, Armitage & Dean's, his revenge. Industry and application.

The scraping noise was thinning out, being replaced by a high constant tone, an atmospheric squeal.

It helped to block out thought.

The foreman's body was buried in under an hour. Albie patted the earth with the flat side of his spade, smoothing it level, and shook the dirt from his gloved hands. The foreman's body was not alone beneath the soil.

• • •

Beck was back at Anson Road before two in the afternoon. There'd be time to think later, he'd decided. The most he could do, for everybody's sake, was to get the bastard, quick. To fulfil Bilborough's request.

The incident room was packed with officers. The phones were ringing constantly. Mostly the press. A young copper with a bright future, lured away from his wife and kid and stabbed in the gutter. A tabloid dream. And they didn't know the half of it, the full saga of betrayal and deceit. Nobody could ever know.

Beck looked through the glass partition into Bilborough's office. In the last few days, after the argument, Bilborough had been treating him like a dog, making it obvious to everyone by giving him those pissy jobs.

He could resign, get out now. But that would be handing Penhaligon everything she wanted on a plate. And he wasn't giving any ground to her, even now she had the ultimate weapon to use against him. She could patronise him as much as she wanted, she was going to patronise him, but he wasn't going to give her the satisfaction. He was a good copper, Bilborough had recognised that before she'd come along. She might be efficient but she was bad for the atmosphere, too openly ambitious, too smug, full of herself.

Beck wanted to bring her down.

Skelton waved a phone over at him. 'It's Clare Moody.'

'What does she want?'

'She'd like to speak to someone about DCI Bilborough's death, sir.'

The interfering cow. 'Tell her to piss off!'

Skelton waved the phone again. 'It's DCI Wise for you, sir.'

Beck took the call. 'Sir.'

'Now are you all right there, Jimmy?'

'Yeah.' Already he was being patronised. 'Yeah, I'm fine. Have you turned anything up?'

'I've turned up a wife and kid for this Kinsella.'

So the bastard had lied about that as well.

'Divorced about five years ago. She lives at 85, Court 4, Sandringham Towers. You know where that is?'

'Yeah.' Beck scribbled down the address in red pen. A wife and kid. Kinsella, who'd killed Bilborough, had a bloody wife and kid. 'It's on one of the big estates. I'll get right over there now.'

'Watch it, Jimmy, go gentle,' said Wise. 'I'll meet you back at the nick, OK?'

Beck put the phone down. He folded the piece of paper on which he'd written the address. Kinsella's wife. He needed to see her, to make it very plain how he felt about her loving husband. Very plain.

'Skelton, I want a couple of cars and a warrant. Now.'

The place was as he'd expected. The sort of neighbourhood where scum and sewage were bred. He was out of the leading car before it stopped outside Sandringham Towers, running for the lift. Naturally the thing had been vandalised. He raced up the stairs after his officers. Pounding up through levels of the unlit, shit-smeared vertical hovel. Two steps at a time, his heart beating against his ribcage. He wished for a gun. Kinsella might be in there, shagging his wife, surrounded by filth like the filth he was. Getting off on Bilborough's death like that Tina girl had got off on George Giggs's death.

If Kinsella was in there Beck was going to kill him. No question. With his bare fucking hands Beck was going to rip Kinsella apart, piece by piece.

He forced his way to the front of the crowd of officers as they reached the eighth floor. Strode along the balcony to the door of 85. Knocked hard.

The door opened. A woman with long dark hair. Kinsella's wife. She looked dumb, sewer filth. Dumb cow.

'Police!' Beck shouted.

His men swarmed in behind him, invading, pushing in, violating as her husband had violated. Revenge. The place was tiny, not big enough for a family of rats to live in. The whole block should be fumigated, cleansed, the scum residents flushed out.

'What's going on?' Beck heard the woman wailing. 'What's going on?'

'We're looking for your husband, Mrs Kinsella.' He surprised himself. Despite all that had happened the training was strong. That politeness came almost instinctively.

Where was the bastard?

Beck burst into the dingy kitchen, checking every corner. He heard a kid screaming and shouting somewhere else in the flat. He opened drawers at random, searching for the bayonet.

'I haven't got a husband,' the woman screamed.

'Ex-husband.'

She tried to close the drawer. 'You won't find him in there.'

'Would you move away please, Mrs Kinsella?'

'I haven't seen him in years!'

'You're lying!' Beck shouted.

She bellowed at him, 'Will you all get out, please? Would you all just get out of my bloody house right now!'

Her house, get out of her house, leave her alone. The bitch.

Beck grabbed her, threw her onto her poxy flea-bitten sofa. 'Just sit there and shut your bloody mouth!'

Carefully, with the utmost concentration, Albie continued his task. A range of materials was spread on Dad's workbench in the shed. Ordinarily available to any householder, handy objects that the careful home owner keeps about. Padded envelopes, stamps, clothes pegs, drawing pins, lengths of wire cut to precise lengths, batteries. Also substances obtained from the quarry.

The wires were pinned to the clothes peg. One wire he connected to the points on the top of a battery. The other wires led elsewhere.

He clicked the clothes peg. The pins clicked together, the percussion of the click barely audible.

Satisfied, Albie clipped the peg onto the top of a seed packet.

A high window overlooked the interview room on the first floor at Anson Road. It was gone five and still light, every corner of the bare whitewashed room visible. Charlie Wise sat at the desk. The folder containing statements from some of the supermarket shoppers and the kid that had run from the dying Bilborough lay open on his knee. Records on Kinsella were a problem. He'd been so law-abiding it hurt. Never bothered any government agency, never claimed the dole, never claimed housing benefit, never been in trouble with the police. There wasn't much to glean from the house, apart from a stack of classical records and cassettes. All they had so far was his application form for the night job at Armitage & Dean's. The handwriting was cramped, downward-slanting, restricted lower loops. Charlie's wife was into graphology. Up until now he'd thought it was daft.

Any further information in support of your application. You may continue onto a separate sheet if necessary: *I am interested in working nights because my father is terminally ill and needs constant attention during the daytime. I am his only surviving relative.*

Just the bare facts, no plea for sympathy. The dutiful son. Charlie was almost touched.

He took off his glasses, rubbed his eyes.

185

Jane Penhaligon was behind him, still staring into nowhere. A chestnut-coloured blur. He put the glasses back on.

'Do you want to go home?' He addressed her firmly, making it clear that the query related only to the efficiency of their operation. There was a risk she might misinterpret his concern. Nothing worse than being patronised, particularly for a female officer. Charlie had been on courses.

'No. I want to continue working,' Penhaligon replied. 'I want us to catch Kinsella.'

She was trying to make sense of the death, a common grief reaction. When you lose somebody close you hurry to put the loss into place in your life. The numbness fades and the brain kicks back. Charlie had been on grief management courses too. Determined and ambitious Penhaligon might be, but there was a heart somewhere.

'I don't want to think about anything else, sir,' she said.

After a little commotion at the door, Beck, collar pulled to one side, arrived with Kinsella's wife. The woman was tall, dark-haired. In Charlie's experience people reacted in one of two ways to the police. Either they froze with fear or looked wary. The frightened ones were almost always innocent. Wariness was a signal in itself. Jill Kinsella looked thoughtfully around the room, her hands folded on her lap. She took the seat opposite Wise and looked over his shoulder, at Penhaligon probably. There were a few seconds of quiet.

'Mrs Jill Kinsella.'

'Yes.'

'We want to ask you about your husband.'

'He's my ex-husband.'

Charlie reconsidered. He knew, just knew, that she had no involvement in the murders. Her wariness was motivated by something else. She was keen to put her husband in the past, distance herself from him. He hadn't abused her or ripped her off, they'd checked with the DSS and the neighbours.

186

Theirs was a model separation, a divorce settlement agreed upon with alacrity, no complaints about the maintenance payments.

She still loved the feller. Wanted to protect her man.

'Can you tell us when you last saw your ex-husband, Mrs Kinsella?'

'His name's Albie.'

'When did you last see Albie?'

She sighed. 'He comes round of a Saturday. Every week.'

'Did he come round yesterday?'

'Yes.'

Beck spoke. 'You told me you hadn't seen him in years.'

She didn't reply.

'Why did you lie?' asked Charlie.

'I'd like to see my child.'

'She's being looked after.'

They were getting nowhere. Charlie contemplated the tough approach. There was a folder full of photographs on the table, the cover embossed with the emblem of the Manchester Met. Inside, enough to make an average citizen sick. One flick of the wrist and the folder could be open.

Beck leapt in before Charlie could decide. Bad behaviour, even in these circumstances. Have to watch that. 'Your ex is a killer.'

She tensed, bit her lip. The worry she'd been pushing down surfaced. She was genuinely afraid.

'I don't believe you.'

'He's killed three people.'

'I don't believe you.'

Charlie took his hand from the photograph folder. 'Your husband's recently shaven his head.'

A shrug. 'He was wearing a hat. I didn't notice.'

They weren't going to get through to her soon, and they didn't have time to fiddle about, her precious Albie was out there, roaming free. The press coverage Wise had authorised

187

would tighten the net, but Albie had shown intelligence and nerve in all his activities. He wasn't stupid. They'd need somebody clever to get through to him.

He collected Jimmy Beck and strode back up to his new office. It was full of Bilborough's things, emotional triggers. An irritation. Charlie had to set the tone for the investigation, the clutter wasn't helping.

'This man Fitzgerald, the psychologist. What's he like?'

'Crap,' said Beck eloquently.

'Yeah?'

'Yeah.'

The Chief Super had told Charlie about the rift created over the Cassidy business. It was unimportant. Fitzgerald might be a pain but if Bilborough had listened to him earlier odds on he'd have lived. And anything that increased the efficiency of the machine had to be tolerated.

He found Fitzgerald's number and started to dial. 'And pack all this footie stuff into a box,' he told Beck, nodding around the office.

Beck looked as if he was about to faint.

When the phone, on the floor of the stripped bare hallway of his house, began to ring, Fitz was unsurprised. He was sat on the carpet in the living room, watching *Masterchef* with disdain as he washed down a couple of lasagnes with whisky.

'That combination of cinnamon and citrus fruits is slightly tart for my tastes,' said one of the judges.

Fitz pointed a finger at the screen and belched. 'You have no idea what life is about!'

He picked up the phone. 'Menswear?'

'Dr Fitzgerald. This is DCI Wise. I'd like you to come over to the station.'

They hadn't got him, of course. 'Have you got him?'

'We'd like you to talk to his wife.'

'I'll come right over.'

Talk to the bastard's wife. Not much point in marital guidance there. A bit too late for that. Everyone needed a bit of marital guidance, for the sake of the human race. All the real bastards in history were failures in loving. They went around spoiling things for everybody else just because they couldn't get it right.

Fitz swallowed. He'd assaulted Bilborough's marriage, wife and kid, standing in that office, pointing the finger. And then along came Albert Kinsella to finish the job. The revenge of the rejects.

He put on his coat. Went to switch off the telly. The news had come on. 'The death of DCI Bilborough,' the newsreader was saying, 'has already led to calls from backbench MPs for the restoration of capital punishment for the killers of policemen.'

Hate building on hate.

The new DCI, Wise, had already cleared out Bilborough's stuff, Fitz noticed. Here was a man who liked to establish his territory. Where Bilborough's habit had been to lean back from the desk, Wise leant over it, swamped it with his bulk. Not flab, thought Fitz a little enviously. Very firm. The glasses were about an inch thick, making him resemble a myopic mammoth. The big shaggy head was down, reading through a mass of reports.

He glanced up at Fitz. 'Sit down.'

Fitz sat. Wise went back to reading. Gracious, that was tedious and obvious. He thought of Mark complaining about last year's summer job, he was being treated like he was still at school. The boy had a surprise coming. You never leave school.

'You've made your point,' he said after a few seconds.

'Come again?' asked Wise, not looking up.

'You're in charge. Point made.'

Wise tapped one of his fingers, a hairy sausage, on the sheet before him. 'I'm reading about you.'

'Ooh. Are there any dirty bits?'

Far too flippant, Fitz knew. But Wise hadn't known Bilborough. The loss wasn't personal.

At last Wise closed the file. 'You've had results.'

'So have Arsenal.'

'Your results are my results. OK? I get the brownie points, you get some money.'

As Bogart, Fitz said, 'This could be the beginning of a beautiful friendship.'

'I doubt it, lad.' Wise stood up. 'The wife isn't talking. She isn't giving anything away.'

'There are things I'll need,' said Fitz.

Wise handed Fitz an unlabelled audio cassette and nodded. Fitz said thanks, put the cassette in the machine. It was dark now, and the interview room was lit by a line of fluorescent strips. Jill Kinsella sat opposite Fitz, staring at the floor. He'd read all the details Wise had dragged up about their relationship. Nothing had surprised him particularly. Only a person like himself, on a crusade to look for the worst in everybody, to bring everyone down to his own level, would have been sceptical about the motives of this poor selfless lad.

Protective instincts. Her desire for natural justice, concern for poor Albie. It had to be overridden, the stakes raised.

She believed she knew Albie. Nobody knew Albie.

Fitz pressed Play. He'd warned Beck and Panhandle what was coming. The spools whirred, clearing the blank strip at the start of the recording. The hiss of static. Then.

'This is evidence. This is a dying man's statement. I know what a defence lawyer will try to do.'

Fitz opened the folder of photographs, turned them to face the woman. He could feel the eyes of Beck and Panhandle on his back. They weren't looking at each other, he'd noticed.

He turned the photographs in the binder. Shahid Ali, lying beside the counter. A close-up, the *Guardian* and teabags behind his head. Blood pouring from his mouth. On the mortuary slab, naked, the cleaned wound in his side gaping.

The woman shuddered, shook her head.

'You can't believe it, Jill. Hmm? Not Albie, not your Albie. Albie's got principles.'

'I'm of sound mind. I'm frightened, yeah, I don't want to die. I'm frightened, but I'm thinking straight . . .'

Fitz heard Panhandle shifting in her chair.

He turned more pages of the folder. Nolan, dripping blood on the floor of his office. His twisted face on the copying glass. On the mortuary slab, beard crusted with blackening blood.

Jill closed her eyes.

Fitz raised his voice. Nearly there. 'Albie's worked nights for years. Turned up the money every single week. Not thinking of himself. Even after you separated, the money was there. Every week. Not Albie.'

'He had a photocopy of Nolan on the wall. He fully intended to kill me. He stabbed me.'

Bilborough screamed. Jill's eyes opened. A flash of terror passed over her face.

'I can't get up the bloody steps. He stabbed me in cold blood . . .'

Fitz took a drag of his cigarette. He was getting close. Albie's principles needed to be teased out, isolated. Firm convictions are built on shaky mental ground.

'And even if he did do it,' Fitz continued, flipping over the first photograph of Bilborough. From above. His midriff soaking bright red. 'Even if he did do it, you'd understand, you'd know why he did it. We wouldn't. We'd simply look at these,' now from the ground, Bilborough's white face

191

pressing the tarmac, 'and these,' a wide shot with the brown door of the house clearly visible, 'and we'd send him down for life. Eh?'

Nearly there, she was climbing the emotional ladder. Rung by rung. The summit in view.

'Are you listening, Jimmy? I want you to get this bastard, Jimmy. OK? Get the bastard. For me and Catriona, get the bastard . . .'

Fitz felt Beck's reaction to that. So big it had legs. Crossing the room like a great hairy spider.

Time to get in.

'Jill, did Albie have a bayonet?'

She choked.

'Catriona. Oh God. Catriona. What are we going to tell her?'

A sob from Panhandle. Nice theatrical effect he hadn't planned on, but it added nicely. She was going to resent him even more for this. Putting her through the grinder. But it was the only way.

And the capacity to realise that, Fitz thought, was what made him unique. And proving that was good for the self-esteem.

'Didn't you find the bayonet strange? Didn't you ever feel like saying excuse me, dear, I can't help noticing there's a bayonet sticking out of your trousers. Is there a reason for that –'

'It was his father's.'

Fitz stopped the tape. Success, priorities shifted. It would have taken Beck, Panhandle and the myopic mammoth half a day to get this far.

'Please go on.'

'He didn't walk round with it. He kept it in a drawer.'

'Cutlery?' Facetiousness annoys the hell out of people. 'Where did you meet?'

She looked away.

Fitz pulled out another set of photos, selected from Bilborough's office. Go for the strong emotions. Death, despair, life, happiness. The woman had a daughter, loved her husband. Appeal to those feelings. As he displayed the first photo he felt the old heartstrings tug, his stomach squeezing. A beautiful young woman, smiling, eyes full of hope and happiness. He pushed down the reaction. This was no time to get soppy.

'This is DCI Bilborough's wife, Catriona.'

A blond-haired baby boy, standing uneasily, an adult supporting his hand.

'This is his little son, Ryan.'

The third photograph. Fitz kept his eyes off it, it had almost had him bawling when he'd seen it in the office. He looked straight at Jill Kinsella.

'And this is all three of them together.'

Back to the police folder. The view from above. 'And this is DCI Bilborough lying dead in the street; where did you meet?'

'The Lakes.'

At last. She was weeping. 'On holiday?'

'No. I was working in a hotel. He was working in a quarry.'

'You still love him?'

She nodded.

'What went wrong?'

She didn't answer. A powerful, deep-rooted insecurity. He was getting closer. Guilt? Not quite. Shame? More likely.

He glanced at the papers provided by Wise. 'You left him in May '89?'

She nodded.

'A few weeks after Hillsborough?'

Here was the block. The shame. She couldn't reply.

'Tell me about it.' Fitz put all the humanity he hoped he possessed into his entreaty. 'Please?'

She shook her head. Sickened with herself. Fitz began to understand why.

Her shame could never match up to Albie's.

'Is that what Hillsborough means to you?' he persisted gently. 'Not the deaths of ninety-six people, but the end of your marriage? So much death. Even the deaths of people you know. And you can't grieve. The end of your marriage, that's all it means. The end of your marriage.'

She wept openly. Opened up for inspection.

Now to encourage her, bring her back. Coax out the truth. 'And it makes you feel selfish, sick, as guilty as sin.'

She sat up.

'Saturdays. He'd go out to the match. Him, and his dad. I went out all day with my friends. It was an arrangement. Every week of the season. My Mum minded Ruth.'

Fitz nodded. Trust me.

'I got back late. He was in bed. He was acting strange, but I was half-pissed, I couldn't tell.' She shivered. 'Then. The morning. The papers. Those photographs.'

Fitz thought back. Judith lying beside him, turning the pages in disbelief. 'Aren't they thinking of the relatives? This is sick.'

His clever response. 'The spectacle of human destruction, the horror, we need to see it. All of us like to hear the screams.' He was a pillock. There was no excuse.

Jill went on. 'He'd been trying to ring me all Saturday afternoon. And Saturday evening. He thought I'd be out of my mind worrying. I told him, I didn't know anything about it, I'd been out with the girls. He said, "All kinds of people dead and you're out with the girls."'

Significant. Nobody else's feelings had ever matched the intensity of Albie's. Spark to a flame. The slow burn.

'I told him I didn't even know!' she shouted.

Fitz lit another cigarette, offered her one. She shook her head.

'He was depressed. Depressed isn't the word for it. There's no bloody word for it. I took him for a walk. It was a sunny day. There were people lying on the grass. He went berserk. "People lying on the grass." That's all he kept saying, all night. "People lying on the bloody grass." '

The isolation, thought Fitz. Constant but bottled up and boxed away. A wife and a kid, duties as a father. A slim support. The sort of personality that needed responsibilities, a social framework. Conscience, good behaviour, the line between right and wrong. That was Albie's prop. Whittled away over the years, then kicked right away by Hillsborough and its aftermath.

Jill raised her head and sneered. Lines of pain creased her brow.

'And then the *Sun*.'

'Yes?'

'That front page. He wanted to kill them all, kill all of them. Everyone who worked on it. Set fire to the place, blow it up. He couldn't believe it, nobody could believe it. How could they say what they did? Why? On the radio, people phoning in. All that anger, all that grief, and . . .'

Her head fell. Fitz knew this was it. The confrontation she had been avoiding. The proof. Her voice cracked.

'He told me. He just told me. He'd screwed two women. Behind my back. Told me when, where, how. Shouting. I asked why, I mean, if I didn't know, it didn't hurt me, so why was he telling me this.

'And he said, "Why not? What does it matter? Nothing matters. Why not?" '

EIGHT

His head aching, Albie finished his work for the day and snapped off the lamp on the benchtop. A light in the window of the shed might attract attention, he reasoned. Only one night in the open. He could have moved on, but it was probably safer to keep still. Couldn't be taken yet. There was an old sleeping bag rolled up in the corner and he'd be warm enough with his jumper on.

There were things of Dad's all around the shed. Pinned up was a photo from a couple of years back. Albie, hair over his collar, his arm around Dad, in the allotment.

He unpinned it. And wept.

It signified everything.

For you, Dad, all of it. Because of what they did to you. I had to change, I was forced. I never told you, couldn't tell you, half of what I felt. About anything.

I want you to understand.

It was getting late. Fitz viewed Jill Kinsella dispassionately in the apricot glow of the desk lamp. She'd know Albie's habits, the predictable patterns of his behaviour. A fair idea was firming up in his mind, and her reaction to his next few words was crucial.

'You didn't try to patch things up?'

'I couldn't. Not long after I left, his dad got sick, moved in with him. I'd call round, every Saturday. Religiously. But I'd feel excluded. They were there. At Hillsborough. I wasn't.'

Encouragement for Fitz. Albie's dad, the last responsibility. He'd clung to it, unconsciously welcomed it. The final chance to demonstrate his values. The link between father and son, the link forged in the football stands.

'Every Saturday? They stopped going to the match?'

'Yeah. Albie wanted to go, but his dad wouldn't. And Albie wouldn't go without his dad.'

'His dad died a week ago?'

She nodded. 'I was relieved. Albie hated me for it. He was relieved too, I know he was. But he was his dad and he loved him so he couldn't admit it.'

A week on his own. The final link broken and all the bad feeling, all the hate, released. Albie wasn't going to be able to cope alone. Fitz considered a moment. Yes, he was certain now. Dad was going to make a comeback, in Albie's head.

Jill looked at her watch, checked it against the clock on the wall. 'I'd like to see my child, please.'

Charlie Wise began his second day as DCI at Anson Road by calling everybody into the incident room to lay down the ground. On his way in he'd prepared a few words. They came easily, he meant them.

'You're still working for him, right? For him, his wife and his son.' He looked about the room, trying to draw them all in. Plenty of eye contact. Group dynamics and management course.

That Fitzgerald was standing at the back, hands in his pockets. Watching the reactions like he was looking at a microscope slide.

'A year ago, you lost a mate, DS George Giggs. Jimmy's told me what your boss's attitude was then. Don't get mad, get even. How do we get even? We catch the bastard. Right, Jimmy?'

Beck nodded. He was twitching, looked as if he was about to fall over. It was starting to get on Wise's nerves.

'What we've got on this man can hang him twice over. We've got his face plastered over every billboard and every TV screen in the country. Every single lead we'll follow up. This man's killed a DCI and there'll be money available. The papers have already put up rewards. So let's get on with it and keep our heads down. OK?'

It worked. There was a murmur of gratitude and the team went back to their tasks, co-ordinating the switchboard, talking to the press. They were a good lot, very efficient. Bilborough had been a good lad.

Except for Beck and Jane Penhaligon. There was something odd going on there. As long as it didn't compromise the efficiency of the job in hand, he wasn't going to let it bother him. Besides, Fitzgerald was a damn sight more irritating.

Wise had a word to the press, going on TV for the first time in his life, just to let the little bastard know, if he was watching, that nobody was scared of him. Frequent requests for an interview came from Clare Moody through Harriman. He ignored them.

Back in the incident room, Fitzgerald was sorting through the stuff Forensic had brought up, carefully bagged, from Kinsella's house in Oundle Street. Jane Penhaligon was silent, taking everything passed from Fitzgerald and applying her efficiency. She was back on form. It was almost frightening.

Stacks of football memorabilia. Programmes, posters and tickets going back years. He opened one at random. Home against Ipswich Town February 24th 1973. On the back page there was a scoresheet. The result had been added in biro by an industrious, downward-slanting childish hand. Two-one to Liverpool. Albert Kinsella, age 9.

There was another folder, the last in a series of scrapbooks brought down from the loft. A sticky label was tacked to the front, the word SIGNIFICANT written on it by Fitzgerald. Like the others it was weighty, crammed with yellowing news-paper meticulously cut out and pasted.

It ended on April 14th 1989. There were two blank pages. Charlie was about to put the folder down when he saw something else peeking from near the back of the book. A scrap of paper.

Pasted in the back was the front page of the *Sun* news-paper dated Wednesday April 19th 1989. THE TRUTH ran the headline.

> Some fans urinated on the brave cops. Some fans picked pockets of victims. Some fans beat up PC giving life kiss.

He remembered driving in to work on the Monday morning after Hillsborough. The city was silent. Absolutely silent. The only sound, weeping in the streets. And then this, a bad case of insensitive reporting at least. A conflict of loyalties for Wise that he'd almost forgotten. He'd been brought up in Liverpool, lived and worked there all his life as a copper, watched the scum rise as hopes faded, as the guts were ripped out of the city. He had no illusions, but it was his home and he'd seen it deliberately left to rot. The old houses knocked down, the neighbourhoods broken up. The past, the strong links, eroded. Kids growing up who'd never see a patch of green, whose parents had no trade to pass down.

That was one of the worst things about this Kinsella. Up to a point you could see where he was coming from. Up to a point.

Wise watched Fitzgerald as he went through Kinsella's family photo album. The trouble was that when he wasn't being impressive and pulling rabbits from hats, he was irritating. Something about him just made you want to punch him. There's nothing worse than an egotist whose opinion of himself is actually correct. He got off on the murders as well. Liked to be involved with the extremes of human behaviour.

Not in an idle gossippy way, but because he seemed to need it to prove himself.

Fitzgerald took a particular photo from the collection. 'His father after chemotherapy.'

Jimmy Beck reached for it.

Charlie had seen it earlier. Kinsella senior had lost every hair on his head. Fitzgerald said eagerly, 'His dad's very important to Albie. All of his dad's pain and suffering. He feels guilty, needs to feel it too.'

Jane Penhaligon held up a finger. 'They never missed one Liverpool game until Hillsborough. Liverpool are playing United at Old Trafford tonight.'

Fitzgerald beamed at her. 'Albie'll be there. He'll take his dad.'

'His dad's dead,' said Beck.

'Exactly.' Fitzgerald stood up, loomed over Wise. 'He's lonely, he needs his dad. He'll be taking his dad to the match. If you want him, you'll find him there.'

The logistics spiralled before Charlie. This time yesterday the main challenge in his life had been choosing between Weetabix and cornflakes. 'There'll be forty thousand at the game.'

'A tenner says he's there!'

'Old Trafford's going to be packed full of coppers. He's mad but he isn't stupid.'

Fitzgerald brandished the cribbage board. Waved it in Wise's face. 'Ninety-six matches. Three dead, ninety-three to go. Kick-off's at 7.30.'

Wise had to hold himself back.

Back in his office, alone, he called the Chief Super. Allen listened patiently as he related Fitzgerald's theory. It sounded more ridiculous to Wise's ears as he repeated it.

Allen sighed. Good, thought Wise. He was going to have some authority behind his rejection. That'd shut Fitzgerald up.

'Set up in the monitor room,' Allen said. 'Liaise with the security officer. Bring in that Moody woman, she's seen him with his hair off, and his supervisor from the factory. Put out ID, posters around the ground. You'll have to get moving quickly.'

'Sir, it's one man's hunch, that's all.'

'He's been right before. Do it.'

'There'll be forty thousand people at Old Trafford tonight.'

'Five thousand. We're only interested in the Liverpool supporters, they'll all be packed in together at one end.'

'Forty thousand or five thousand, sir, it'll be like looking for a needle in a bloody haystack, assuming he's going to be stupid enough to walk in in front of a line of coppers –'

'Do it.'

Wise stuck his head out into the incident room, suppressing his indignation. Keeping his eyes off Fitzgerald he announced loudly, 'We're all going to Old Trafford tonight. Any conscientious objectors, see me in my office.'

There was a murmur of laughter. A good sign. His gaze flicked over Penhaligon, resigned, Fitzgerald, grinning and trying to catch his eye. Beck looked furious. That was getting to be a problem.

He beckoned. 'Jimmy.'

Beck hovered about the doorway of Wise's office. 'Yeah?'

Wise picked up his phone and spoke to switchboard. 'Get me the safety officer at Old Trafford.' He pointed to the door and said to Beck, 'Shut it and sit down.'

'I'll come back later, I'm a bit –'

'Sit down!'

Beck closed the door but remained standing, tapping his pockets.

'What's on your mind?'

'Nothing.'

'You can always take a couple of days off, I knew you were close.'

'It's all right.' He gestured to Bilborough's belongings. 'What are you going to do with all this footie stuff? It meant a lot to him.'

It meant a lot to Albie Kinsella, thought Wise.

'I thought you could pack it up in a box and take it round to his missus, eh?'

Beck nodded. Wise was on the point of openly ordering him to take that time off when the switchboard feller came back on the line, asking if his query was urgent. 'Well, of course it's bloody urgent!'

He sat down aware of Jimmy Beck moving about behind him, taking pins from Bilborough's posters and rolling them up tightly.

In a city anyone can be invisible, thought Albie. The hood of his anorak covered his face. He watched the girl across the aisle from him on the bus reading a newspaper which had a whacking great photo of him on the front page. It was Jill's favourite picture of him, she used to keep a copy in her purse. KILLER OF A FAMILY MAN was the headline. Some of the other papers he'd seen this morning had amused him more, particularly the supposed plea from the highest level that the senseless killer of DCI Bilborough would be hunted down like the beast he was. Wrong on both counts, sir. Neither senseless nor a beast am I. As certain individuals will discover in tomorrow's mailbag. The country's marvellous nationally owned postal service is going to be put to good use before it is frittered away.

Albie hadn't slept for two whole days. Not a wink. Last night, in the sleeping bag, lying on the floor of the shed, he'd been speaking to Dad. It felt silly at first but it got easier the more he said. There was a lot to say.

He got off the bus at the cemetery. The ground was

sodden and the air grey and drizzly. An old woman came tottering along the road, a bright orange hot water bottle held in one of her jittering liver-spotted hands. It took her a minute to walk fifty yards. She was muttering. Talking to somebody who wasn't there. Albie could understand that now. She stopped before an iron tap built into the back of one of the graves and brought the lip of the hot water bottle up to collect the rusty trickle that issued as the desiccating bones in her hand twisted to release the valve mechanism.

It was a cliché, like something out of bloody Dickens. Happening right here before his eyes. Poverty, what poverty. This poverty.

Albie stopped at Dad's grave. There was a temporary wooden cross up. Albie's fury was provoked. Should be a huge memorial for what this man had done. Had risked his life ten times over and never asked for thanks from his countrymen. Buried with help from the social security. Funeral benefit for heroes.

There was a pillar box outside the cemetery. As Albie left he took two padded envelopes from the bag he was carrying and posted them. He heard them drop. No going back.

The old woman tottered past him, hot water bottle slopping over. Her cracked toenails had split open her shoes.

The press were camped outside Bilborough's house, the sky lowering over the pagoda of their umbrellas, keeping themselves warm with cups of Thermosed coffee. Beck, walking along the curve of the drive with the cardboard box full of Bilborough's possessions clutched tight to his chest, watched them laughing and chatting to each other and was reminded of periods of illness. Watch the cheery world go by on its moronic business as your stomach squeezes up every few seconds. The guilty feeling stretched to the tips of his fingers, a thick coil of chain attached to a heavy weight pulling him slowly down. A few feet ahead of him was a muddy puddle,

iece of bread floating rotting on top. He wanted to throw the
ox and himself into the puddle, kick and scream like a little
kid in front of the country's assembled news media. But
immy Beck had never avoided his responsibilities. He made
mistakes, he was not irresponsible.

Avoiding the pleas for a quote, he exchanged nods with
he uniformed officer on duty at the house, explained his
mission, and was admitted by Catriona. She smiled when
she saw him. Beck was transfixed. He couldn't stay here
ong. That picture on the wall, him with Bilborough and
Penhaligon, smiling away. He remembered the day it was
aken, a short while before the Jacqui Appleby business.
Before Fitz.

'His things from the office,' he said, gently lowering the
ox on to the hall rug. He realised there was somebody else
n the house, there was a female voice coming from the
kitchen. A friend of Catriona's talking to little Ryan.

Catriona was looking at him with concern. He couldn't
ear her sympathy. 'You want a cup of tea?'

'No, thanks, I only popped in to drop his things off.' He
despised the sound of his voice, the artificial brightness. To
Catriona it must have seemed that he was bottling up his
grief. The truth was worse. He was covering up his self-pity.
I'd better get back.'

He made for the door but she stopped him, laying a gentle
hand on his elbow. The slight pressure burnt him. 'He had a
icket for the match tonight,' she said. 'Will you give it to
omeone? He'd have liked that.'

'Yeah.' There was nothing else he could say.

She left him alone in the hall. The shapes of the gathered
pressmen outside were distorted through the frosted glass
window built into the front door. The rain was pelting down
now.

Catriona returned and handed him the ticket.

'People say nothing, Jimmy, because they're afraid of

saying the wrong thing. But it's better to say the wrong thing than nothing at all.'

Her words coaxed out his tears. She embraced him like her own child, patting him on the shoulder.

'He was the best copper that ever lived and I'm so sorry he's dead,' he blurted.

The pub was filling up nicely. It was half past six and the jukebox was up loud, the air filled with smoke and song, and every corner covered by Liverpool fans dressed in the away strip. Jane was boxed in, squashed against Fitz's hulk. He had followed her towards Old Trafford, taking the hint that Wise didn't want him in the monitor room at the ground. A minor miracle, Jane reflected.

She was jostled as a lad edged past their table. 'Your boyfriend's a fat bastard, love,' he told her casually. She could tell Fitz would rise to it.

'Get it right, son. I'm not her boyfriend and I'm a *rich* fat bastard.'

Jane could remember a time she would have thought that was really funny.

'Why don't you go up to the monitor room?' she asked him.

'You mean why don't I get lost?'

'There is that.'

He had three measures of whisky in three glasses on the table before him. He finished off the first and started on the second. 'I don't like Clare Moody.'

'You don't like plenty of people.'

'Correct, Panhandle. But there's general dislike and there's active dislike. I actively dislike her. And I'd be no use up there, I'll not recognise Albie when he comes in.'

A new song started up around them. 'L I V, E R P, double O L, Liverpool FC.' Jane had never understood the appeal of football or the devotion of its followers. It seemed to her a part of the secret language of men, used often as a means of shutting women out of conversations. Then, those conversations weren't the ones she'd have been interested in anyway.

'I'm sorry I hurt you,' Fitz shouted suddenly over the racket.

Jane's heart sank. Not now. 'You didn't.'

'I did. I know I did because he told me.'

'The boss?'

'He told me if I hurt you again he'd put my legs in plaster.'

Fitz was using this, dangling it to get her attention. Using her grief for his own ends. She wasn't shocked. 'Go away, Fitz.'

'No!' he shouted back, getting red in the face and looking hurt. Genuinely looking hurt.

'Please go away. I've got a job to do.'

'No!' He lit another cigarette and looked her in the eye. 'Judith's left me.'

'Well of course I'll move in immediately.'

He'd succeeded in his manipulation. The feeling was too strong to subdue. She turned to face him. His face was inches from hers. His breath was rank. 'It's one thing to be stood up at the airport, Fitz. But to be left at the airport by a big, fat, egocentric, middle-aged, married man is a different thing altogether.'

He smiled. 'I don't mind being called big. Not too keen on your other adjectives. Can I explain?'

'I'm not interested.'

He took her by the arm almost aggressively. Keeping his voice sounding as casual as he could, he said, 'It won't take long. You see, I've rehearsed this so many times, Panhandle, I could do it backwards. I was in lust with you and I didn't want to be in love with you because my life's complicated enough at the moment. Falling in love with you would be

207

rather easy. And that's why I didn't turn up at the airport.'

'Once more, with feeling.'

He removed his arm and said, 'You shouldn't feel so guilty, you know.'

'I don't feel guilty, Fitz. If I'm going to have to work with you, then fine, we'll be working together. I don't feel guilty, I just don't intend to make a fool of myself ever again.'

'I meant that you shouldn't feel so guilty over Bilborough's death.'

'I don't. What are you saying?'

Without looking at her he said, 'You saw promotion, Panhandle. Grief and all those other wholesome things, yes, but your boss was dead and you saw promotion.'

'I didn't.'

'You're lying.' He said it without malice. 'Sex, too. You fancy him but he's your boss and he's married so you don't push it, but it might happen quite naturally. One day. And if it does, you'll not put up much of a struggle. But now he's dead and you wish you'd pushed it. He's dead and you're thinking "Life is so short, from now on it's 'seize the day'."'

'Yes, you're right.' He was undiscriminating. His capacity to humiliate could be turned on anybody at any time it suited him. 'And you are an emotional rapist.'

It seemed to hurt him but she didn't trust his apparent reactions. 'I'm saying I understand. All that stuff's better out than in.'

The pub was heaving and there was no point trying to leave. Jane sat back in her chair and tried to keep as far away from him as possible.

The security at Old Trafford consisted of more coppers on horses in one place than Wise could remember seeing, high-tech remote-controlled cameras around every corner inside the ground, other cameras covering the approaches.

The crowd were apparently behaving themselves very well, considering. The full details of Kinsella's case history hadn't been revealed to the media, despite earnest protests from Clare Moody, and it was unlikely that the swell of supporters would suspect the possible presence of the killer in their midst. Not that he was going to turn up anyway. This was a bloody stupid idea on all parts.

The control room operator, Sanger, was a short, gingery man who looked about ten years too young for the job. His hands flicked over every part of the system like a kid at one of those activity centres. He knew every last function of his toy and seemed overjoyed at the prospect of getting to use it for something slightly different to usual. The officers from Anson Road had been posted about the place, each responsible for one area of the Liverpool end.

'See, you've got all of the visitors' seating area covered like this,' said Sanger, who had devised the details of the operation over the space of a few hours and now considered himself a part of the investigative team. 'It's watertight. If he's there we'll have him.'

He flicked around the cameras for Wise with an expression that begged praise. Wise reserved it, secretly wishing himself back at Anson Road doing something sensible.

One of his men, the young black lad, was calling in. 'Skelton to control room. Can you see me?'

Sanger licked his lips, flicked a switch and zoomed in on Skelton's uniform. The bloke had eyes like a hawk. He'd spent the afternoon staring at the picture of Kinsella on the front page of the papers. 'I can see you,' he said eagerly.

'Hooray,' Wise muttered into his beard.

'I see a possible, OK?'

Totally bald. One of a group of about thirty skinheads dressed in the Liverpool away colours. Surrounded by about a thousand more in that street alone, most of them with hoods up or hats on against the rain sloshing down. Hopeless.

'Could you give me your name, sir?' they heard Skelton asking the lad.

The belligerent reply, 'It's Paul Wilkinson.'

Charlie poured himself another cup of tea from the urn at his side, shook in a few drops of cream from a little container, stirred the thin strip of plastic that served as a spoon, and settled back in his chair to watch the crowd.

He could think of better ways to waste an evening.

The Liverpool supporters were pouring out of the pub, giving Fitz a chance to stretch his legs. The door opened and closed, opened and closed, admitting a powerful draught each time. A pathway to the bar was clearing and he was almost at the bottom of his third measure. Panhandle remained next to him, she imagined probably that by not walking out she was making a point. That he wasn't important. A dead giveaway. It was all very circular.

The tension between them was broken as Beck entered the pub. The first and only time Fitz had been pleased to see him. The old habits were reasserting themselves, he noticed. Almost the familiar Jimmy Beck again, only with an extra layer of compensatory machismo. The cigarette was back, half-in and half-out of his mouth, his hair was swept back. He looked somehow comfortable in his agony, yes, a niche had been found for his strongly-stewed insecurities. A new countdown was running.

He sat opposite them, a nod to Penhaligon.

Not more silence. Things really were better out than in. Conveniently the jukebox clicked off, allowing Fitz's voice to carry at a whisper. A demonstration for Panhandle as well. He was no emotional rapist, this was essential therapy. You don't talk about things, you're handing yourself over to them, allowing them control.

'Bald head, chemotherapy, cancer. Anyone could fall for that. Anyone with any compassion. But that's what hurts,

210

eh? Right? A rare moment, you show a suspect a bit of compassion, a bit of pity. But there's no place for pity in this job, Beck. No place for it in the whole bloody world. So. Never again, you're thinking.'

A direct hit. Beck was so easy to read. And now he was going to look up, yes, and ask, yes –

'Have you told anyone it's down to me?'

'No.'

'No,' said Penhaligon.

The pub doors were thrown open and a Scouse voice wailed, 'Any spares? Any spares in here?'

Beck waved to him. 'Hey!'

The lad, tall and gangly, swathed in scarves, loped across. 'Got a spare?'

Bilborough's ticket, of course. Fitz watched as Beck proffered it.

'It's at the Man U end,' said the lad.

Beck leapt up. 'Do you want it?'

'OK, how much?'

'I don't want your money.'

The lad straightened. 'I'm not on the scrounge, you know.'

Beck pressed the square of paper into the lad's hand. 'You wanted a ticket, you've got a ticket. So go! Right? Go and enjoy yourself, enjoy the game!'

He swung away, letting the cigarette fall from his mouth and then stamping on the butt savagely. The lad looked at him, baffled.

Fitz shrugged. 'Haemorrhoids,' he said by way of explanation.

The first time in six years. Albie and his dad were back at the match. Packed in tight with the other sub-human scum, surrounded by snooty bizzies on horseback. Gates about to be opened, it was almost seven. Tension building, shouts and cries. White faces, white men all around. Saved their pittances for this, lived for this. Died for this, were cast out, despised.

The future was coming. Albie could see it forming, he told his dad all about it. This was a point in history, these were the instruments of radical social change. There was hope.

The gates opened, the crowd surged forward. Albie and his dad were caught up in it, swept away. So many faces, so much excitement. The noise, the heat. Above, the stern faces of the bizzies, the fancy cameras, recording it all, regulating it all, controlling it. They thought they had control, they were wrong. Right under their noses change was brewing. The factories were gone, the mines were gone, the communities were gone. But you couldn't kill the spirit of the working man. His hour of glory was coming.

These men were Albie's army.

And through the turnstile. And among the crowd, pushing along the wide corridor. And up the stairs, a vast many-headed animal. Pride and strength in its muscles, rising from a long slumber. And up more stairs. Along another corridor, the roar all around now. Calls answered from all sides, cries of identification.

And through, Albie and his dad, onto the terraces, the first time in six years. Under the floodlights, the perfect symmetry of the ground, the swelling mass packing into the ground, voices united.

United.

The spectators had arrived in the control room, neither the sort you'd expect to see at a match. Kinsella's supervisor from work, who kept shaking his head and saying, 'He was a quiet one, you'd never have expected it,' and the porcine Clare Moody. Her bodyguard, who introduced himself to Charlie as Harriman, looked like a boy scout.

'Now he'll probably have a hat on,' Wise told Moody, trying to make it sound as if he was utterly convinced of the operation's chance of success.

Her eyes narrowed as they swept from screen to screen. 'He could have a veil on and I'd recognise him.'

The teams ran out. Two perfect straight lines formed. Beautiful. First time in six years, the lads standing there, tall and strong. Albie recognised them all, even at this distance.

'It's James in goal,' he told Dad, part of the ritual. 'Yeah, James in goal, Jones, Molby, Ruddock, Dicks, Macmannam, Clough, Redknap, Barnes, Fowler, Rush. Scales, Thomas and Babb on the bench.'

The whistle blows. The crowd roars. Albie's heart soars.

The sound of the future.

The cameras roved over the faces of the Liverpool supporters. Screaming and shouting, leaping and punching the air. Roaring as one, a sea of faces, each a mimic of the next in line, the one above, the one below, the one at a diagonal angle. Wise took a quick look at Clare Moody. Perhaps this wasn't so hopeless. She was hunched forward, absorbing every detail from the screens, her plastic teacup forgotten.

Jimmy Beck came in, hovered about at the back of the room.

What was the bloke's problem?

'What do you want?'

'If he's here,' said Beck, 'I'll see him.'

Trying to make sense of the boss's death, wants to be in for the kill. 'How?'

'I just will.'

'Have you seen him close up?'

There was no reply from Beck.

'Have you, eh?'

'No,' said Beck.

Wise nodded to Clare Moody and Kinsella's supervisor. 'Well, they have, all right?'

The bodyguard, Harriman, toddled back in on an errand from Moody. He handed her an expensive-looking leather jacket and she slipped effortlessly into it without thanking him or taking her eyes off the rows of shifting screens.

'What are you doing?' said Harriman.

There was a tone to his voice that Wise didn't appreciate. 'What's up, son?'

Harriman indicated the screens. 'He bought his ticket in Manchester. He won't be at the Liverpool end.'

'He's right,' said Beck.

Wise stared at him. 'You knew that?'

'I've just realised, yeah.'

'He could be anywhere?'

'Yeah.'

Wise looked around the room. Moody was staring at him with incredulity. Yes, this was going to look wonderful in tomorrow's papers.

Sanger smiled. 'Forget it,' Wise told him.

'I'll spot him.' Beck again, determined, lighting another cigarette. His shoulders were shifting in his suit.

Wise sighed. 'Look, Jimmy, there's forty odd thousand in here, so forget it. Right?'

Beck left the room.

Game was good. Great tackle and we've got control of the ball. Running with it. Great. But too slow, oh come on, give it some.

'Come on John, a bit of effort. Come on. Give it some, move! Give it. Good lad. Go, John, go on, John . . .'

Albie felt the wave of pleasure, the rush of adrenalin. Couldn't keep still, couldn't keep his mouth shut, despite the tossers all around him.

'Come on, lads, you can beat these. These are nothing. These are crap. A gang of posers, that's all they are!'

Around him were the enemy. Above, below, on either side, Albie was swamped by the enemy. Being surrounded gave Albie a warm feeling, a rush.

Voices, above and below and from either side, people, other people, trying to shut him up, close his mouth, stop him revealing the truth, drowning him out.

'Just keep your mouth shut, right, you Scouse bastard, 'cause I've had just about enough of your mouthing off . . .'

Albie raised his voice. Sang.

'Come on, you Re–eds! Come on, you Re–eds!'

To Dad he said, 'They need a bit more passion, Dad, a bit more commitment.' They'd lost the bleeding ball again!

'I'd sooner be a Paki than a Scally so piss off to your own end, eh? 'Cause you've got the wrong accent, you know what I mean? So piss off over there with all your other scrounging idle gobshites . . .'

Louder. 'Come on, this is Man U, for God's sake! *Come on!*' Yes! 'Good lad, Ian, good lad, keep at him, keep at the bastard, he's nothing, Ian, he's crap . . .'

'Have you run out of houses to screw, you robbing Scouse bastard, eh? Piss off down the M62, you robbing Scouse bastard, 'cause we don't want your sort here. Right? Can you hear me? Can you hear me, *you robbing Scouse bastard?*'

Fitz found a payphone just outside the ground and dialled home.

'Yeah?' said Mark's voice.

'Goodness me, you're in,' Fitz shouted. The noise from the stadium was carrying through the broken glass of the phone box.

'Where are you?' Mark shouted back. 'I can hardly hear you.'

'Never mind that. Have you heard from your mother today?'

A short silence. 'No.'

'Do you know where she is?'

'She doesn't want to speak to you.'

The pips went. Fitz riffled in his pockets but found only notes and a collection of coppers. Damn it.

Well, he thought as he left the box and made his way towards the ground, it could wait. At the moment Judith was the last person on his mind.

He was, after all, enjoying himself.

Two strong pairs of arms clamped down on Albie's shoulders. He caught a flash of yellow. Stewards, lifting him up, dragging him away. More of his enemies. He lost sight of the game.

'Eh, we've paid for our tickets, my dad and me, so get off us, OK? We're going nowhere. You're taking us nowhere. We're quite happy where we are, all right? *All right?*'

'We're moving you for your own protection!' They always said that, yes, it's for your own good. Lies. 'If you don't stop struggling, we're going to have to get rough!'

Familiar excuse. Stop struggling while we administer this truncheon to your face, it's for your own safety. Lying bastards, collaborating scum. Albie caught sight of a few people in the crowd around him laughing. They thought he was mad, did they? Thought he was a nutter?

'Get off us! Get off us! Get off us!'

'It's for your own safety, it's for your own safety . . .'

He was dragged out of the stands roughly. They were all shouting at him as he went by, they'd heard the accent and seen the clothes and assumed things. They were his enemies, all of them were his enemies, traitors to their class, they just sat back and copped all the lies, became part of the problem. They were scum.

216

'You're not singing any more, you're not singing any more . . .'

Beck stomped through the empty corridors, sickened, cigarette flashing up and down. Stupid bloody idea, coming here. Even stupider to cock it up like they had. Looking at the wrong bloody end, ridiculous.

But he'd hoped. Craved for one sight of that imp's face in the crowds. His heart was beating against his chest, the great waves of emotion roaring out from the stands tugged at his guilt and self-loathing. The crowd, the composite of faces, in his mind he saw them squealing, burning, covered in their own blood. The whole place folding up and caving in, the stadium going down into the earth, dragging them away.

A couple of stewards were walking towards him, a small feller in an anorak gripped between them, protesting, his dirty-trainered feet scuffing against the ground as they hurried him towards the exit.

'What have we done, eh?' Broad Scouse accent. 'Come 'ed, what have we done?' Something wrong about it. 'What are you throwing us out for?' It was forced, that accent. ' 'Cause we've done nothing, we're not the guilty party, y'know what I mean?' Deliberately muddying up his voice, there were traces of Lancashire in there. 'We were the ones getting the stick, all through the game.' Liked playing a victim, this bloke, liked a bit of persecution, liked to be roughed up. 'All through the bloody game nothing but stick and you're throwing *us* out!'

His small hooded head nodded to one side, as if there was somebody else next to him.

He was swept right past Beck. They locked glances.

A hot spark flashed through Beck's body.

That voice. Chemotherapy, Everton, no I'm not married. I'm an outpatient at Stonefield. St Helens.

He walked on.

The time had come, the time was now.

He was going to kill the little bastard.

A moment passed and he stopped outside the toilets. Waited. Dropped his cigarette, reached out with the heel of his shoe. Ground it out. Waited a couple more seconds. He turned and ran, the high brick walls of the corridors flashing past the sides of his vision.

The stewards were walking back towards him, alone, shaking their heads and cursing.

Beck pushed them apart and ran through them and along the darkened corridor. At that moment, the stadium rattled and thumped, a great uprush of joy bouncing around the boundaries. United must have scored, by the sound of it. Beck couldn't see Kinsella ahead.

He ran on, pulled out his radio, called, 'I've seen him.'

Around a corner, clattered down two flights of stairs. No exits on either side. There was a gate at the bottom of these stairs, he'd be making for that. E35.

The gateman was crossing to lock up, he must have let Kinsella through.

Beck screamed, 'Don't lock it!' and hurled himself through the gap in the doors and into the night.

The roads around the ground were picked out by the soft golden overspill of the floodlights. A movement in the darkness, a fleeing jerky-limbed shape. Kinsella.

It was easier to make him out in the long street beyond, which was lined by high, vandal-proof lamps. Kinsella, retreating into the night, scampering over the pavements, the slap of his trainers echoing back towards Beck. The route wasn't random, either, the little sod knew where he was going.

A stitch jabbed into Beck's side. This must have been how Bilborough felt, running from the supermarket.

He checked street signs as he ran. Some mistakes weren't going to be repeated. He knew this area well enough, every copper in the city knew Old Trafford. 'On Barnton Road,' he told the radio, ignoring Wise's confused cries for clarification. 'Heading towards Northridge Road.'

Kinsella ran out between cars, his rat's face caught for a second by their headlamps. Brakes screeched, the cars swerved, their drivers shouted insults.

Beck ran around the cars, turned into another street. He could still hear the noise from the ground, a near miss from Liverpool, a hiss of disapproval, you could tell just from the sounds, it was a universal language that united people. So Bilborough had believed.

'Banville Street.'

A couple of sirens started blaring behind him. Wise was on the way.

Bad move on Kinsella's part. The street was long, the end stretched away out of sight. A flashing blue light from the distance as a police car approached. Quicker than Beck had ever known.

And Kinsella started running back towards Beck. He was frightened, the bastard, scared for himself, Beck saw it in his face as it grew clearer. He took strength from it, savoured the terror.

They were getting closer, there was no way out.

Kinsella threw himself sideways, pushed past a woman who was putting milk bottles out and ran into her home. Slammed the door behind him. It shut in Beck's face.

'Here, what are you doing, then?' the woman screamed.

Beck raced back the way he had come. Saw more cars arriving, sirens wailing. Pulled himself around a corner. His side was bursting. Into the back alley, bins and bags of rubbish piled high. Counted off the houses at his side, counted down the yard doors until he reached the right one.

There were coppers coming down the far end of the alley. Beautiful, Kinsella had no way out.

Beck looked for a weapon. Kinsella would have his

bayonet out, no doubt. On top of one of the binbags was an empty Newcastle Brown bottle. Beck lifted it, smashed the top half off against the wall.

The little sod came hurtling out of the yard.

Beck brought the jagged edges of the bottle down on the bald head.

Kinsella went down, screaming.

Get him for me, Jimmy. Get the bastard.

Beck fell on Kinsella, grappled and held him down, pushed his bald bloodied head into the grime, heard the crunch of bones cracking, punched the little sod, beat him hard, his arm crooked at the elbow, jabbing back and forth against the solar plexus, cherished the sobs and cries.

He beat him hard.

He felt his own wrist break.

And up. Kinsella, face in the shit, weeping and shrieking. Legs drawn up to protect himself, a foetal curl. Crying out for his dad. Bastard.

Beck kicked him, kicked him in the stomach and kicked his head, kicked him in the face.

He got knocked over, pulled back, his legs lifted from the ground. He swore and lashed out, screaming something, he couldn't hear what it was, it surprised him, he was shouting one word, again and again.

Boss. Boss. Boss.

One of the blokes holding on to him was Skelton. Staring at him.

Other eyes were upon him. More cars had drawn up. Wise's big shaggy overcoated form was getting out of one, anxiety on his face.

Penhaligon and Fitz were standing together, eyes locked on him. Looking at him with disapproval, sympathy, a kind of pity. They were a natural pair. He wished both of them dead, why the boss, why not them?

Kinsella had stopped moving.

He could be dead.

Beck shook off the grip of the officers and walked into the wall, taking the full impact in his face.

United scored again.

NINE

They didn't take Albie to the hospital, just packed him in the back of a car, turned up the siren, raced off. He lay on the back seat, breathing heavily, croaking and gasping for theatrical effect, to let them know how much he was suffering. He was ignored.

The city lights flashed by outside the windows. Upside down he watched the view slide by. He'd made plans, sorted the details, and everything had worked out right. Even now, as he was led out of the car, a sack over his head, the sound of flashbulbs popping in the forecourt of the station, as he was taken down, deep down, the sack flicked off and in to the cell, one yellow bulb stinging his eyes, even now his plans were working.

He removed his clothing carefully, loving the bruises that were revealed. A line of swelling purple patches across his chest, beautiful. There was dried blood on his face, he wanted a mirror. Different types of pain all over him. He held out his hands, made them into claws.

'I want to see your boss,' he shouted through the door. 'I want to see your boss! I want to see your boss!'

Two minutes later Albie heard footsteps coming down the corridor. He curled up on the bed.

'You want me?' The new DCI. Older than David Bilborough, bearded, glasses. Thought he was tough as old boots. Surprise coming tomorrow.

'I want a photograph taken. I want people to know what he did to me.'

'Put your clothes on. You'll catch a chill.' Fellow was a Scouser, there's irony.

Albie shook his head. 'I'll put my clothes on when I've had a picture taken. I know my rights.'

The new DCI came closer. 'You've killed three people, son. One of them a DCI from this nick. Now put your clothes on before I chop your dick off. Right?'

He backed out of the cell.

'Four,' called Albie.

'Come again?'

'I've killed *four* people.'

Back in his office, Wise found Beck with his arm in a sling. There were a couple of superficial cuts and grazes on his cheek. He stank, large circles of sweat wetting his shirt under the arms.

Wise looked at him and only shook his head, shaking his heavy jowls.

'He resisted,' said Beck. 'Look closely and you might notice a few cuts and bruises.'

'You always were an ugly bastard though, weren't you?'

Beck smiled wearily.

'You want this man to get life?' Wise asked him.

'I want him hung.'

'If he shows up in court black and blue he wins their sympathy, it affects our chances. I shouldn't need to be telling you this, Jimmy.'

'Have you told Catriona?'

'Who?'

'The boss's wife. David Bilborough's widow.'

Wise reflected that he could have done with a less emotionally complicated entry to Anson Road. He barely knew this lot, and already he was an ogre stepping into a dead man's shoes. He was no part of their history. Still, with

Kinsella locked safely away he could concentrate on sorting the place out to suit him.

'I think it would be a good idea to tell Catriona that we've caught Kinsella,' Beck said.

'Phone her.'

Beck turned to leave.

'Not yet, Jimmy.' He flicked open a file on his desk and tapped the first page. Time to establish the new rules. 'There's a community relations course next week and you're going on it, right?'

'I've been a copper for fifteen years –'

'And when that course finishes, I'll find you another one. You're going on more courses than Lester bloody Piggot. And when this is all over and Kinsella's banged away you can come back to this nick.'

Beck nodded. He looked too tired to argue.

Wise pointed to the door. 'Now. Out.'

The phone rang. 'DCI Wise.'

'It's me.' A Scottish accent.

'He'll need a rest, Fitzgerald. But not much of a rest. First thing in the morning.'

'I'll be there.'

Wise put the phone down. There was excitement in Fitzgerald's voice. Their pet psychologist was really looking forward to his chat with Albert Kinsella.

For her own sake Jane was glad that Kinsella had been picked up so quickly. The muscular contractions that had tensed her body from the moment the boss's call had come in on Sunday morning started to lessen their grip and she managed a few hours' sleep. Tuesday morning began for her at six. She showered, got herself together. Wise had to know that she at least could be relied upon. As had been pointed out, her career was important. Driving to Anson Road it occurred to her how much Fitz's words of the night before had helped her. Actually helped her. She could feel herself weakening. Damn.

They met as they walked to the interview room.

'Fitz, there's sand in your eye and an eggstain on your collar.'

He attended to them. 'I was never suited to be a bachelor.'

A chant was coming down the corridor.

'Come on you Re–eds, Come on you Re–eds . . .'

Wise was waiting for them. He rubbed his temples and took off his glasses, making himself look much younger and friendlier. They went back up very quickly.

'We've had eight hours of this,' he told them. 'Eight bloody hours. I'll never go to a footie match again.'

Fitz pulled out a packet of cigarettes. 'Not much of a football sort, though, are you? Or you, Panhandle?'

'I've always thought it was a bit ridiculous,' she replied honestly.

Fitz lit up. 'Not the game. You understand that. It's being a fan that baffles you, right?' They listened to the chant for a short while. 'Given your backgrounds it's understandable.' He indicated Wise to open the door. 'I've got an advantage there.'

Jane followed him in, took her position at the desk with Wise. Kinsella, dressed in his own clothes, a dirty blue padded jacket, faded jeans and trainers, was standing in the middle of the room, staring right ahead, just chanting. She forced herself to look at him dispassionately. Looked like a Belsen survivor, with that bald head and the bruising. Five foot five, the rat face and the manic gargoyle eyes just like the photofit. And Beck hadn't seen it.

He was smiling. 'Come on you Re–eds, Come on you Re–eds . . .'

Fitz lowered his head like a bull preparing to charge and bellowed, 'Ce–y–el–ti–ic! Ce–y–el–ti–ic! Ce–y–e–ti–ic!'

Establishing his credentials, Jane realised. It worked.

226

Kinsella stopped.

He angled his head, produced a curious frown. 'Who are you?'

'My name's Fitz. I'm a psychologist.' He sat.

Albie took his place, giggling.

'You don't need a psychologist?'

'No.'

'I see. Killing people's normal, eh?'

'What's "normal"?'

Fitz huge and dark and slow, Kinsella wiry and white and crackling with anger.

'Well, putting yourself at risk. That's abnormal. You're Britain's most wanted, Albie. The last couple of days, you've been on the telly more often than Danny Baker. And you turn up to a football match, coppers everywhere. Why, I find myself wondering?'

Fitz, ahead of her again. Pushing for something, turning over facts Jane hadn't even considered.

'I went 'cause I had a ticket,' Kinsella said nonchalantly.

Fitz chuckled. 'Oh yes. "I went 'cause I had a ticket." That's way cool. It'll go down in folklore. In fifty years' time, I mean. Not now, of course, not while the widows and children', he spat the nouns, 'are still crying.'

And again Fitz was right, his technique worked, and hard little Albie Kinsella flinched. Emotional rape. In this case justifiable.

'Come on you Re–eds, come on you Re–eds . . .'

'Did he enjoy the match?'

'Come on you –'

'Your dad. Did he enjoy the match?'

The chant stopped again. Jane saw Fitz's angle. Kinsella used his football chant as an automatic escape route. A retreat. But he enjoyed talking about himself too much to ignore a question like that one.

'Thank you. This fourth body, Albie. Who is it?'

'Could you pass on my apologies to his wife?' Kinsella said suddenly.

'Whose wife.'

'The bizzie's wife.'

'His widow,' Jane said.

Kinsella nodded at her, his blood-encrusted lips twitching into a grin. 'His widow, yeah. I had to touch her up in the supermarket. To get him to follow me out. I didn't want to do it, I didn't get anything out of it. No buzz or anything like. I'd like her to know that.'

'I'm sure it'll cheer her up no end.'

Kinsella enjoyed revolting them. That was his kick, making people his enemies in order to define himself. As everything he was not.

'Peter Sutcliffe gets letters from women,' Fitz said. Kinsella didn't like it, the skin tightened over his imp's face. 'Lots of letters. Lots of women. He sends back signed photographs of himself, puts kisses on the bottom. He's a star, you see, he's a somebody.'

'Don't,' said Kinsella.

'Don't compare you with him?'

'Yeah.'

'Why not?'

No reply.

Fitz went on. 'You want to be a somebody, Albie. There are two ways of doing it. You can achieve something, but that takes hard work, stamina, and you haven't got –'

'You're talking crap –'

'– you haven't got it, Albie. You'll never achieve anything, so you take the other route, the easy route –'

'– you're talking crap –'

'– you kill, you destroy, you make yourself a name, a star, a somebody.'

Kinsella jumped out of his chair, backed away across the room.

'Would you sit down please, Albie,' Jane heard Wise say.

Kinsella nodded to Fitz. 'You've been watching too much telly. You think you can provoke me, wind me up, make me talk to you. No chance, so don't even try. Right?'

'Right.' Fitz shrugged. 'So, come on then, what is it you've done?'

It was like watching a dozing kid being picked on by a teacher. Kinsella assumed a cautious air. Most unlike him. A big giveaway. He said, 'I don't understand the question.' Falling into another of Fitz's traps.

'You knew you'd be caught. And your mission isn't finished. Only three down, there's ninety-three to go. So what have you done?'

'Four down. It's four.' He nodded to Wise. 'I told you.'

'I don't believe you,' Fitz said evenly. 'Prove it.'

'How?'

'Tell me where the body is.'

'I buried it.'

Wise leant forward. 'Where did you bury it?'

Kinsella shrugged as if it really didn't matter.

'I'm curious,' said Fitz. 'You didn't bury any of the others. Why this one?'

'Perhaps I felt like a change.'

Wise got to his feet and left the interview room. Probably to check up on missing persons. Jane remained seated.

A short silence, then Fitz said, 'Why now? Hillsborough was almost six years ago. Why wait six years?'

Silence from Kinsella.

'Shall I tell you?'

'You know nothing.'

Of course. Nobody was allowed to share in his grief. He isolated himself, and anything that increased that isolation increased his self-awareness similarly.

'Your father dies. Something snaps. You kill a Pakistani

229

shopkeeper. You need to rationalise it. You apply some kind of twisted logic and tie it up with Hillsborough. And now you've got to stick to that logic, you've got to keep on killing. Otherwise that first murder doesn't make any sense, it's just another racist killing.'

'I'm not racist.' Kinsella wasn't rattled. Jane wondered if he really had the measure of Fitz. If that was the case, he was smarter than her.

'Your cat had kittens?' Fitz asked Kinsella, trying another tack.

'Yeah.'

'Why didn't you drown them?'

He wouldn't be drawn on that either, dismissed Fitz with a look of contempt.

Fitz raised his voice. Genuine anger. 'I see. You can kill human beings, look them in the eye as you bury your bayonet, but you can't kill a few uffy-wuffy kittens?'

'They weren't doing me any harm.'

Fitz slammed a fist on the table. 'Neither was Shahid Ali.'

Jane recalled the immaculate body on the slab, the wound in the side.

'He was robbing me,' Kinsella said, smiling.

'Neither had Professor Nolan.'

'He assumed things.'

Fitz stood. 'Albie's law. The penalty for assuming things is death. Am I right, Albie?'

It reached him, he couldn't resist replying. 'It depends what you assume. People assuming things led to Hillsborough, so it depends what you assume. Right?'

'Explain.'

'I shouldn't need to explain. A smartarse like you ought to know.'

Fitz lit another cigarette. 'You couldn't drown the uffy-wuffy kittens. All together, aaah. What does that prove? That deep down Albie Kinsella is a good man?'

Kinsella sat, simmering with anger.

'Dig deep and we'll find sensitivity, eh? No. Dig deep and we'll find sentimentality. I've met a few killers now, Albie, and it's been there in all of them, the same sickening simple-minded sentimentality.'

Kinsella fixed Jane with his stare. 'Number four is buried on my father's allotment.'

She reached for the phone.

'Mind his runner beans when you're digging.'

'Of course nobody bloody well thought of this before,' Wise complained to Harriman as they got out of the car and ducked under the tape surrounding the allotments. 'It never occurred to anybody, did it?'

'We've been a bit shook up, boss,' said Harriman.

Wise wanted to grab his ear and twist. Sooner or later he was going to have to stand up in court and admit that one of his officers, a detective sergeant, had beaten up a suspect; that this particular division of the CID had neglected to search the suspect's own property; that they'd actually been watching the wrong end of Old Trafford and caught him by accident. What a jolly day that was going to be.

One of the local PCs was standing at the entrance to the allotment with a lit fag hanging from his mouth. Christ, what happened to standards?

'Put it out,' Wise growled.

'Right, sir.' The PC took out his notebook and pointed to a white Bedford van backed up to one of the allotment sheds. 'Belongs to a Mr Tony Joyce, quarry foreman missing since Sunday night. Didn't come home for his tea, missus got worried. Probably had reason, eh? There's bloodstains in the back and a box full of kittens.'

Wise pushed past him. A team were waiting for him to give the order, shovels at the ready, standing between neat rows of cabbages.

'Get digging.'

They set to work, the line of shovels flashing up and down, catching the glint of early morning spring sunshine.

Wise had a look over the way, to the rows of houses stretching away and up the hill and the rows of inquisitive faces peering from the windows. Kinsella had buried a body here, in full view, nobody had reported anything. Were people blind?

His gaze swept over the van. Quarry foreman. Hadn' Kinsella worked in a quarry?

'What time is it?' Kinsella asked.

'It's 9.30,' said Fitz.

Jane watched as he examined again the records that had been found on Kinsella.

'You reckon you're intelligent?' Fitz didn't look up. 'I ask because you look so thick, Albie. And you act thick. I mean killing a Pakistani shopkeeper, that's thick.'

Kinsella said nothing.

'Did you call him Paki?' asked Fitz.

'Yeah.'

'That's thick, Albie.'

'You know nothing.'

Fitz looked up. 'It's thick. And I don't even hate you for it, Albie. I pity you, in fact. Racism is born of poverty, lack of education. Ignorance. And I can't hate people for that, it's a bit like hating them because they've got bad teeth. They're unfortunate, they have to be pitied.'

'I'm not a racist.'

'You're to be pitied.'

Kinsella pointed a finger, jabbed it over the table. 'You've never lived on a Giro, walked into a Paki shop and been robbed. Try that and then come out with this kind of crap.'

Fitz leaned over. 'You're talking thick again, Albie. You like shouting and talking thick because it stops you from

232

thinking. And I know you can think.' He reached for a buff folder Jane had seen earlier. Kinsella's school report and exam certificates. 'Ten O levels, three A levels, and what's this here, yes, the Music prize. Didn't want to go to university, fair enough, but you always were a *Guardian* reader, Albie. And you've never lived off a Giro in your life. You've always worked. High street electrical shop, the quarry, Armitage & Dean's. A few other places too.' He waved the employment record. 'Dossers don't work in a nursing home for one pound sixty an hour, Albie.'

'You know nothing.'

Fitz's voice became softer. 'You're talking about your father, aren't you?' He searched for and showed one of the photos taken from the house. Kinsella senior, bald from his chemotherapy, but smiling through. A kindly smile that Jane saw in his son's manic grin.

He was off again. Seeking refuge.

'It's one-one at Anfield. Nothing's going right. Non-stop pressure, yeah, but nothing going right. A minute to go. And the ball's pumped into the middle and Hansen goes up and bumps it, and it's there –'

The kind of thing Bilborough used to say.

'You wanted it to be you, not him,' Fitz said gently. 'It isn't fair, is it, Albie? Years of struggle, poverty, none of the good things in life. In the name of God, if anyone's entitled to a peaceful death it's him. But it isn't peaceful. It's slow, lingering, painful.'

Kinsella stood.

'Please sit down, Albie,' she told him.

'Another victory. Another last-minute victory.' His body was shaking, sweat dripping down his brow, his hands tensed like claws. He fell against the far wall, looked up to the ceiling. 'And that's not down to eleven greedy footballers, it's down to forty thousand people praying. Praying, willing it to happen, believing it could happen. Making it happen.'

Fitz looked at his watch and said casually, 'It's 9.33, Albie.'

The cautious look again. 'I didn't ask you.'

'Just thought you'd like to know.'

Fitz crossed the room, joined Kinsella against the far wall.

'My father fought in the war. Yours too, Albie.' He leaned close to Kinsella, said emphatically and with apparent sincerity, 'I know what you've been through. Tell me about him.'

'Get away from me.'

'My father was a kind, decent man. Liked his football, liked a drink, liked a bet. Yours too, hmm?'

'Get away from me.'

Fitz looked up to the ceiling. 'I don't believe I'm ever going to see him again. But I believe he lives on, Albie. Somewhere, deep inside,' he placed his fleshy right hand over his heart, the nicotine-yellowed fingers spread, 'there's a thin seam of goodness, of decency, and that's him. He put it there.'

Kinsella shook his head in disgust and walked away. 'You'll use anything, won't you? Even the death of your own father. You'll use anything to prove how smart you are!'

'Don't lecture me on morality, you're a bloody killer.'

Jane flinched as Kinsella sneered at her, flung one of his bruised, twisted arms in her direction. 'Is it her, eh? Is it her you're trying to impress?' She looked down, forcing herself to keep calm. A couple of days ago she might have agreed with Albie. Now she had a different opinion of Fitz. Not a higher opinion, a different opinion. He was like an oddly shaped pill, difficult to swallow and left an acid aftertaste, but you felt better for it.

'You've never felt anything in your life,' Kinsella shouted at Fitz.

234

'Have you?' Fitz asked quietly.

'Your wife's parents, they're both alive ?'

'Yeah.'

'So she doesn't understand? All that anger and grief when your father died, she can't share it.'

'No. She can't.'

Fitz got closer again. 'And Hillsborough. She was out with the girls, she didn't even know about it. All those people dead and she didn't even know about it.'

'Yeah.'

'But you were there, Albie. I want you to tell me about it.'

Tears glistened in Kinsella's eyes. His face cracked. 'Liverpool at Old Trafford, seven, eight years ago. We play them off the bloody park, go round 'em like they're standing still –'

Jane watched him. His head was angled slightly, as if there was somebody else in the room. Of course. His dad. The only person that could share Albie's anger and grief, the only person that knew how it felt. The only person he'd never have dared to discuss it with.

'– we gave them a bloody football lesson.'

'My dad and I talked football,' said Fitz. 'It was safe. It never got deep.' He held his hand over his heart again. 'We could talk for hours about Celtic's chances, last week's game, how we were going to see off Rangers.'

Kinsella nodded.

'Your wife and daughter move out, your father moves in. He's dying. Slowly, painfully. That's too deep, can't talk about that. But after Hillsborough he won't go to the match. You can't talk football any more. What's left?'

'Nothing. We talked about nothing.'

Fitz put a hand up to his face, nodded. Jane decided. He was right. Better out than in. In had produced Albie, in created monsters.

235

'You want revenge, Albie?'

'Yeah.'

'For Hillsborough, for all the people that died?'

'Yeah.'

'Did you lose someone?'

Kinsella was weeping openly now. 'My father. I lost my father.'

'Your father died six years later.'

'No. It took him six years to die, that's how long it took. Right? It took six years, it started at Hillsborough.'

Fitz's technique was getting more familiar to Jane. He was after the truth, and to do that he needed to clear away the network of everyday half-truths, self-deceptions, drag out the motive. The true motive.

'OK. So it's all been on behalf of your father?'

'Yeah.'

There was a world of pity in Fitz's next words. 'Do you think he'd want it, Albie?' He held up the photo. The smile cutting through the pain, a teacup held in one gentle old hand. 'Do you think all the others would want it? They've been through it. The shock, the horror, the grief. That terrible day, the senseless waste of life, dealing with it for the rest of their lives as best they can. Do you honestly think they'd want other families to go through it?'

Kinsella drew a shaking hand over his face, wiped away his tears. The thin grey tee shirt under his jacket heaved up and down as his scrawny ribcage puffed in and out like a bellows.

'My father was a decent man. Right. He wouldn't want revenge. Right. The people who died at Hillsborough wouldn't want revenge. Right.'

He bypassed Fitz, looked straight at Jane. This is the man who killed the boss, she reminded herself. She couldn't feel sorry for him, she had to hate him, she couldn't live with the guilt of feeling sorry for little Albie Kinsella.

236

'But I want it,' he said loudly, savagely. '*I* want revenge. *I* want revenge.'

Fitz smiled, and Jane saw that the trap had been sprung.

'And you're going to get it, aren't you?'

Kinsella smiled his thick smile, bobbed his head up and down.

'It's a bomb, isn't it, Albie?' He turned to Jane. 'You see, Panhandle, you don't work for four years in a quarry without learning a thing or two about explosives.'

Her heart lurched. Why hadn't he told anyone about this? If there was a bomb, it could be anywhere. She thought of Albie's enquiries about the time, Fitz's suspicious reaction. Some sort of timer? Shit. He wanted to kill ninety-three people.

He was off on a sermon. The thick Albie had reasserted himself, it was time to justify it all again. 'People need to believe. People need to congregate. But there's nothing left to believe in, nothing left to congregate for. Only football. And they know that.'

'They?'

'The bizzies, the politicians. We're football supporters. We're working-class, and when the working class gets together, when it starts to get its act together, the bizzies get nervous.'

It was all such crap and her face must have shown it because he leant forward and screamed into her face, 'Are you listening to me, DS Penhaligon?'

'No,' she said.

He was really going for it, eyes rolling, nostrils twitching.

'They march us along, they slam us against walls, they treat us like scum. We look for help. We're working-class people, we're trade unionists, we're socialists, so we look to the Labour Party for help. But we're not queers, we're not lesbians, we're not black, we're not Paki, there's no brownie points in speaking up for us so the Labour frigging Party

237

turns its fucking back. We're the fucking underclass.'

Jane looked at Fitz. He was taking all of this in, sucking on another high-tar cigarette, thinking deeply. She knew what he was thinking, seeing through all of this. Kinsella covering up his true motive with his self-deceit.

'And we're not getting treated like scum any more, we're getting treated like wild bloody animals. Some bloody professor comes over from the States and says we shouldn't be allowed to breed, to bring up our own kiddies. And yeah one or two of us start acting like wild animals and up go the cages, and *ninety-six people die.*'

He whispered, 'The bizzies. The bourgeois lefties. They never lifted a finger. They assumed things. They caused Hillsborough. And they're going to pay.'

Fitz waved his cigarette airily. 'And old people, and children, and other', he smirked, 'white working-class heterosexual football supporters. Would you kill them, too? People like your father?'

'No.'

'But they'll die. That's the thing about a bomb, Albie. It's pretty indiscriminate.'

The thick smile. Very pleased with himself. 'This one isn't.'

'It's targeted?'

Fitz sat up suddenly. Turned to Jane. Really alarmed, and that was frightening. 'How do you target a bomb? You address it to somebody. And who's his number one target?'

'Us,' she said.

Charlie Wise believed in leading from the front. He threw his overcoat up to Harriman, who almost overbalanced as he caught it, and skittered down into the pit dug in the allotment. He brushed the soil from his shoes, poked about in the mud. Nothing about. As he'd expected.

238

'Well, if there's anyone down here, we can rule out suicide,' he called up.

They laughed. Well, that was something.

The local PC was walking over with the pet carrier. 'These need feeding. Shall I ask one of the people round here if they've any cat food?'

Wise waved him off. Looked again at the foreman's van backed up to the door of the shed.

The quarry foreman's van backed up to the door of the shed.

Bloody hell.

He jumped from the pit like a twenty-year-old. 'Forget the bloody kittens,' he shouted.

The station was evacuated in minutes. Jane watched from the window of the interview room as her colleagues assembled themselves into neat rows on the tarmac. Really she should be out there. She was alone with the officer on the door, and Kinsella, who was leaning back in his chair, looking very happy with himself.

'You're not singing any more,' he sang softly. 'You're not singing any more.'

Fitz returned. He was carrying a padded envelope at arm's length, holding the addressed side towards himself.

'Beck,' he told her. 'Sitting in his tray. Lucky he's at home.'

She let out a deep breath. Couldn't take her eyes off the package, the package in his hand. It would kill him. Kinsella would take him like he'd taken Bilborough. There was something deep inside, very deep, a true motive of hers that couldn't bear that to happen.

'I suggest you vacate the building, Panhandle.'

'What about you?'

He held the envelope a little higher. 'I'll be out in a jiffy.'

Without looking back, she left. The officer on the door

came with her. They left Fitz alone with Kinsella and his bomb.

'It's Skelton for you, boss, from the nick.'

Wise took the radio from Harriman. 'Yes, son?'

The words came out in a tumble. 'Boss, it's Doctor Fitzgerald. He says to tell you he reckons there could be a bomb planted with the fourth body and to watch yourself and to clear out of there, sir.'

Wise smiled. He clicked his fingers, signalling Harriman to help him back on with his coat. 'You can tell Doctor Fitzgerald that I'm not stupid.' He broke the connection.

It was ten o'clock.

From his position at the end of the road leading to the allotment, Wise watched the shed registered with the council as the property of Mr Albert Kinsella of number 37 Oundle Street, date of birth 20.1.26, transformed into a fireball. Kinsella must have packed a lot of stuff down there, it felt like the ground shook. Wise's ears popped but he remained standing absolutely still. There was an example to be set.

He waited a minute, waved the fire team forward.

The local residents, gathered behind the tape, oohed and aahed. There were a few seedy types mixed in with the crowd, some news cameras, the media were sniffing about. No sign of Clare Moody, thank God.

A journalist pressed forward, sidled up to Harriman. 'Can I have a few words with the DCI, mate?'

Harriman clamped a hand on his shoulder, pushed him away. 'No, you can't. No, you bloody can't.'

Fitz dangled the Jiffy bag in front of Albie.

'Shall I open it?'

Albie laughed in his face.

'I'm serious, Albie.' He sat down, brought the package

240

close to his chest. 'I reckon you're a coward, see. Big and brave with a bayonet in your hand but basically a coward.'

That did the trick.

'Open it,' said Albie.

'You think I'm bluffing?'

Albie sniffed. 'You drink a lot.'

Fitz offered him the Jiffy bag. 'You open it.'

He took it. Didn't take his eyes from Fitz.

'Wilson, Callaghan, Foot, Kinnock, Smith. Tony Blair. All those promises. All those lies. And war heroes are dying and getting buried on social security. Well, we're fighting back, right? Right?'

Fitz leaned back in his chair. 'Oh really? You and whose army? You talk a lot about "we", Albie. Where are your supporters?'

Albie's fingers tightened on the seal of the bag.

He told Fitz, 'You're looking at the future. You're looking at me and you're looking at the future.'

'Yeah?' Scepticism in Fitz's voice.

Tiny hands Albie had, slim sensitive fingers, a young girl's hands. Getting ready to open the envelope. Feeling for the edges, keeping his eyes on Fitz. Psyching himself up.

' 'Cause this country's going to blow. People like me are going to light the fuse. We've been robbed. The despised, the betrayed, the fucking underclass. We're going to light the fuse and this country's going to blow.'

His voice a whisper now. Important. Last words.

'This country's going to blow.'

He ripped the seal.

Nothing happened.

'We switched bags, Albie.'

Albie staggered up, did a spastic dance backwards into the wall, flung away the envelope, crammed a fist into his mouth, bit at the fingers until they bled. Mewed like a kitten.

Fitz sensed the presence of Panhandle. He caught her eye, smiled at her. Excellent, she was smiling back.

Cracked this one on all fronts.

'That smile's going to be wiped off your face, you arrogant bastard!'

The chant again.

'Come on, you Re – eds, Come on you Re – eds . . .'

Panhandle stepped forward. Hard as nails. In this moment, in this big emotional scene, all these outpourings, Fitz was certain he loved her. This time tomorrow, who could tell.

'The bomb at the allotment went off,' she told Albie. 'Nobody was hurt.'

Albie wailed, flung himself at Fitz. All that anger and grief, the frustration, in that tiny body. Fitz met it, used that strength, turned it back, pushed back, pushed Albie against the far wall. Held him like a father holds a child.

'Albie, Albie, *Albie*.'

The struggling stopped. Albie pushed him away. He looked like a broken doll.

'Come on you Re–eds, Come on you Re–eds, Come on you Re–eds, Come on you Re–eds . . .'

'I've got to get out,' Fitz told Jane half an hour later, tugging at his collar, draining a teacup in one gulp. 'I've got to get out. Back in an hour, I need time to think.'

She put a hand on his shoulder. 'I'll come with you.'

'Thanks, but,' as Garbo, 'I want to be alone.'

Wise, returning from the allotment, collided with him as he left the incident room. Harriman trailed him like a dog. 'I'm not stupid, Doctor Fitzgerald.'

White-faced, Fitz didn't react at all. Just shambled out, like a zombie.

Wise handed her a scrap of paper. A name and telephone number had been written on it in red biro. 'Mrs Joyce, wife of the quarry foreman. They've got a couple of kids, I think. Could you deal with that?'

He was into his office, Bilborough's office, beautiful Bilborough's empty office, before she could protest.

Albie was back in his cell. Shivering. It wasn't cold, the shiver was coming from inside. Not fear or disappointment. Anticipation. He was really going to get the message across.

'What's the time, mate?' he called.

'Just gone eleven,' the bizzie outside the door called back.

Somewhere, not far away, a pair of hands was reaching for an envelope. Albie didn't know how, he could just tell it was happening now, he could see it in his head. A pair of expensively manicured glossy-nailed hands. The hands of a monster, a pig in human form. Reaching for her in-tray, an envelope.

Even now it was working.

Five down.

Get the message across, give her the truth.

Fitz was heading for the melancholy pub, head full of Albie. Sympathy was too easy, and too difficult. Very confusing lad. Comes from St Helens, calls himself a Scouser. None of his own family claim a penny from the state, he rants on about the underclass. That voice, that unnaturally muddied accent, a *Guardian* reader whose mission was to kill bourgeois lefties. The politics of it corkscrewed around Fitz's mind. But what it came back to was that old chestnut, every loving wife's favourite bourgeois Western luxury, motive. Albie had a point, fair enough, but the motive was quite different.

And all across the Western world, Sarajevo to Los Angeles, there were lads growing up worse off than Albie with the same motive who didn't need to stop thinking because they'd never been taught to think. The same motive, and no bloody understanding or desire to make the point at all.

God, there were too many things pressing on him, Panhandle and all, he needed to get away, put things in some semblance of order, sort his life out. Keep himself sane and well, get things out in the open, everyone's motivation.

First things first. Judith. She didn't want to leave him, what she wanted was ritual humiliation. If he was honest, then. Yes, dear, I'm an emotional incompetent, I'm a physical wreck. Might work. Try the honest approach, work out how –

His head whipped up.

The noise. A deafening explosion. Coming from the city centre.

From the offices of the *Manchester Evening Post*.

The sound of the future.

The Cracker Writers

Jimmy McGovern

Jimmy McGovern's scriptwriting career began in the early 1980s with plays for Liverpool's Everyman and Playhouse theatres. His Merseyside association continued with scripts for over eighty episodes of Channel 4's soap opera *Brookside* between 1983 and 1989. During the 1990s he has written for over a dozen films and television series, including *El CID*, *Backbeat* and, of course, *Cracker*.

Gareth Roberts

Gareth Roberts was born in 1968 and was raised in Chesham, Buckinghamshire. He has worked as a clerk at the Court of Appeal, studied drama at university, and has written three novels for Virgin Publishing, as well as scripts for comic strips. He lives in Winchester.

The Cracker Stories

Based on the original scripts, Virgin's Cracker novels add depth and detail to the televised stories and provide a permanent record of Fitz's involvement with the police and of his relationships with his wife Judith and with Detective Sergeant Jane Penhaligon.

Series One

The first three Cracker stories, first broadcast on British television in 1993, were all written by Jimmy McGovern.

The Mad Woman In The Attic
Adapted by Jim Mortimore

Dr Edward Fitzgerald, who insists that everyone call him Fitz, is a psychologist with an apparently conventional life. He teaches and practises psychology; he has an attractive wife, two children, and a big house in a pleasant suburb of Manchester. But he's also addicted to gambling, booze, cigarettes, and pushing his considerable bulk into any situation he finds intriguing. His wife Judith has had enough. She leaves him. Fitz's life is beginning to fall apart.

When one of his students is murdered, Fitz can't resist becoming involved. The police have a suspect; they are sure he's the serial killer, but he's claiming complete amnesia. The police reluctantly hire Fitz to get a confession.

As Fitz investigates, he finds that the police theory doesn't fit the facts. He discovers, in solving murder cases, a new focus for his life. And he meets Detective Sergeant Jane Penhaligon.

To Say I Love You
Adapted by Molly Brown

People do strange things for love.

Tina's parents had nothing but loving intentions when they turned her into a talking guide dog for her blind sister. Sean, full of bitterness and fury, is prepared to kill for the love of Tina. And Fitz, psychologist and occasional catcher of murderers, would do anything to win back the love of his wife Judith – if only he didn't find himself working so closely with DS Jane Penhaligon.

In this, the second Cracker thriller, Fitz can find a murderer, prevent a catastrophe, and still find time to flirt with a pretty policewoman. But he also knows only too well the motivations that drive Judith into another man's bed and that push him to the edge of self-destruction.

Compared to the complications of Fitz's own life, tracking down a team of cop-killers is simple.

One Day A Lemming Will Fly
Adapted by Liz Holliday

Everything's going to be all right. Judith is back home, Penhaligon's falling in love, and Fitz has a new problem to solve from the police.

It's an open and shut case. A schoolboy – a young,

effeminate, scholarly and often bullied schoolboy – is found murdered. His English teacher – male, single, lives alone – tries to commit suicide. It's obvious: the teacher killed his pupil. The police think so. The boy's parents think so. Everyone in the family's neighbourhood thinks so. And Fitz thinks so. It's just a matter of obtaining a confession.

But the truth is as elusive as trust and honesty, and the case goes badly wrong.

In this, the third Cracker story, Fitz reaches the crisis in his personal drama. He has to choose between Judith and Jane. And that's the least of his problems.

Series Two

Cracker's second series was first broadcast in 1994. Two of the three stories were written by Jimmy McGovern.

To Be A Somebody
Adapted by Gareth Roberts

Having argued with DCI Bilborough and abandoned Jane at the airport, Fitz isn't welcome at Anson Road nick any more. He's back on the booze, his gambling is riskier than ever, and Judith's had as much as she can take. Fitz is at a new low.

When an Asian grocer is stabbed by a skinhead, the police assume a racist motive. Fitz knows better, and as usual he's right. But he can't convince Bilborough to let him help until the murderer has struck again.

Albie and his dad, Liverpool supporters, were at the Hillsborough disaster. Five years later, Albie's dad has died. And Albie wants revenge. He'll kill anyone who makes assumptions about white, working-class scousers. But he particularly wants to kill coppers.

The Big Crunch
Adapted by Liz Holliday

Kenneth Trant is a headmaster and the leader of an evangelical Christian group. He's above suspicion. When one of his pupils and church members – a teenaged girl – is found dying, her body covered with arcane symbols, suspicion falls on the disturbed young man who works for Trant's brother. It's an open and shut case.

Fitz doesn't think so, of course, but at first there's not much he can do. Anyway, he's distracted: Judith has moved out, the house is up for sale – and Jane Penhaligon is still very interesting. And interested.

Publication: April 1995

Men Should Weep
Adapted by Jim Mortimore

This story brings the second series to a shattering conclusion. The Anson Road detectives tear each other apart, and Fitz's life dissolves into chaos, as a serial rapist terrorises Manchester. This is the hardest-hitting Cracker story yet.

Publication: May 1995